Merry Christmas 2001

To Kathryn —

Love,
Lindsey

SKIRTS

Also by Mimi Albert

The Small Singer (poems and stories)

The Second Story Man (novel)

Skirts

A NOVEL

BY

MIMI ALBERT

BASKERVILLE
PUBLISHERS, INC.
DALLAS • NEW YORK • DUBLIN

BASKERVILLE Publishers, Inc.
7616 LBJ Freeway, Suite 220, Dallas TX 75251-1008

Library of Congress Cataloging-in-Publication Data

Albert, Mimi.
    Skirts : a novel / by Mimi Albert.
        p. cm.
      ISBN: 1-880909-13-8 (lib. bdg.) :
        1. City and town life--New York (N.Y.)--History--20th century--Fiction. 2. Beat generation--New York (N.Y.)--Fiction. 3. Young women--New York (N.Y.)--Fiction.
I. Title
PS3551.L263S55 1994   93-45929
813'.54--dc20   CIP

Manufactured in the United States of America
First Printing, 1994

To T.M.B.L.

ONE

"What we are witnessing is a delicate shift of total consciousness in America."
—Gregory Corso, 1959

"Skirt soup," says the very young woman, in a barely audible voice. The whiteness of her body glistens, naked, on the bed. In an enormous soup pot on the stove, her long red skirt steams and bubbles, a peculiar stew.

"Is it finished?" the very young woman whispers.

"Sure it is. Yeah. Finished." A tall, dark man leans over her, watching her closely with eyes so light and startling that they seem to belong in someone else's face; his own face is lean and sulky. He whispers back to her, patient and solicitous as a doctor.

"We'll eat it now, won't we? Red skirt soup for the people. Won't we?"

"Sure we will," he whispers. "Sleep," he says. "Sleep now."

He watches her.

She closes her eyes.

The rest of us sit in a circle around her. From a neon sign on the street outside, red light scores our faces. It flashes on and off, on and off, so we see each other for a moment and then, nothing. On and off.

In the shadows of the dark room, I touch my own hands.

"It's all right now," the very young woman says. She opens her eyes, but remains motionless on the bed. "I won't try to get out the window any more. Now that the skirt is gone." Her soft voice ripples through the room like water. "You can let me up now. You can let me go."

"No," says the dark man, still like a doctor. "We won't let you go."

"But I'm not afraid now," she murmurs. "Now that the skirt is gone. Now that the blood is gone."

"No," he says. "You're not afraid."

She lies back. The rest of us sit quietly. Some of the others close their eyes. In the silence, I can hear the skirt bubbling on the stove. They put it on to boil when she begged them to, weeping and tearing it off herself, early in the evening.

I want to leave. I want to be back out on the red-flashing neon street with this man, this almost-doctor with the sharp blue glance and the soft voice. Under my bare legs the carpet is scratchy and cold. A joint passes slowly. Inexperienced, I put my lips to it and pass it on, hoping no one will notice. I expect the man to scold me, to say, "Try it, Helene. Really *try* it." But he has eyes only for the girl, who's torn off all her clothing in fright because her skirt was red and she thought she was covered in blood.

Now, again like the sound of running water, her voice floats through the room.

"I thought I was there again," she says. "Always the same place. I was standing in the courtyard and my mother and my sister flew out of the house without their clothes on. Their arms and legs fell off and I said, 'There go my mother and my sister. What's the matter with them now?' But no one told me."

"What's she talking about?" I whisper to the boy next to me.

"She was in some concentration camp when she was a kid. Dachau, Auschwitz, someplace like that. Her whole family was killed. I guess she saw the bodies after they were stacked up in front of the ovens or something. I don't know. I guess it all came back when she did the mesc."

"I don't like red," the very young woman says. Her voice breaks and struggles, as if against sleep. "Why should I wear red if I don't like it?"

"Never do anything you don't like. Rest." The dark man puts his hand on her forehead and beneath it, her face settles and relaxes, and again she closes her eyes.

I have been watching the faces of the people around me and wondering, 'When I leave this room will any of them ever think of me again?' I try not to care, but these are the people I want to spend my life with, the people I want desperately to like me. Some of them are artists; the boy next to me is a dancer. There's a girl tall enough to be a model wearing a tight, black sweater and white lipstick, her black hair sleek around the gauntness of her face. Can she see me as anything but a pretty college girl from the Bronx, Zalman's friend? And Zalman himself? What does he see in me, besides a student, a kind of disciple? Someone to be spoken to as if he were a doctor or a teacher, as he speaks to the girl with the red skirt? Zalman is the tall dark man, and he has finished with the girl now, and looks up at me at last.

We go down into the street. It's almost December, the end of 1961, and wind blows newspapers along the sidewalks. The few trees set into the glass-sharded soil along the gutters are bare. I turn at the corner, to head back to the Seventh Avenue IRT, to my apartment on the Upper West Side.

"Why did you take me there?" I ask after we've walked

down the street together for a while.

"It was a scene," he nods, looking down into my face. "Wasn't it a scene, Helene? Wasn't it fantastic? Didn't you get turned on?" He stares at me for a minute. Then he shakes his head. "You didn't." In his voice I hear disappointment, and I struggle against my impulse to apologize.

"That poor girl," I begin.

"No. Listen," he interrupts me.

"But she was suffering," I interrupt him back. "Why couldn't anybody help her? Why—"

I choose my words a little too carefully, all traces of the Bronx erased on purpose. I've got the voice of someone who has fled her parents' home and neighborhood with the desperate agility of an escape artist. It's the voice of a young woman who believes she is a rebel. And it's the voice of a liar, because I belong to them still. I belong to my mother and my father and to the seedy terrible neighborhood in the Bronx, and to the steamy ugly streets and to the lives of my relations which are as intertwined and intricate as vines. I belong, really, to no one else.

The trouble is that I'm too bright not to know that I am lying.

And what am I doing there, with Zalman and his wild friends in the Village? I'm not quite sure, but the major desire of my life right now is to be taken seriously, to be thought of as both a serious student and a "hip chick," a woman on "the scene." I've managed to convince myself that Zalman thinks I'm pretty cool, because most of the time he talks to me as if I were.

Until tonight. Tonight is different. Solicitous and medical again, he takes my arm and steers me into a diner, where he props me up against one of those old zinc counters still so common in downtown New York. He orders coffee.

"It was the pills they were all taking," I contend, turning away from him. "The mescaline. That's what was the matter. Nobody could bring her down from it. She just went on and on in pain. I'm never going to get involved with drugs. Never."

"Not knowing what was inside her. That was pain." From out of his pocket he fishes a pair of glasses. He produces them, a conjurer, and puts them over my eyes. "Now she knows," he says. "Now she knows what lives inside."

And what about me? I wonder. Do I know what lives inside myself? And how am I going to find out?

I am just twenty-one years old. I study archaeology at one of the city colleges. I live alone in a dark little "pad" in the second-worst neighborhood in Manhattan. I've been supporting myself with a series of rotten jobs; now I type letters for a stationery company during the afternoons. I wear shabby black trousers and stuff my frizzy red curls into a thick secretarial bun to look as serious as possible, but my mother insists that I'm "gorgeous like a Fra Angelico madonna," although I don't think Fra Angelico even painted madonnas. My mother talks like that—she was a self-proclaimed Bohemian in the 30s, a professional whistler on a local radio station before she gave it all up and married my father—and I search the mirror desperately, trying to find out whether there's anything to it, or whether she's just blinded by parental prejudice. She speculates longingly about my moving back to the Bronx and being what she calls a "nice girl" once again, as if "niceness" can be restored the same way certain girls are rumored to have had their hymens replaced.

My father also wants me to live at home again, but his approach is a little different. "Get back here!" he screams when I call them on the phone, as if the sheer volume of his voice will intimidate me into compliance. "Live with your parents, meet maybe a nice boy, get married like somebody normal!" My father's favorite word is "normal." "Be normal!" he commands me.

How to tell him that what he thinks is normal seems to me like a life of unrelieved misery and failure? I can't even mutter,

"I'd rather be dead," because if he heard me say that, he'd put down the phone, drive straight to my tenement apartment on West 89th Street and Columbus Avenue, climb the six flights of stairs to my battered front door, force his way in, and hit me.

What I see when I look at myself is all too normal. Not quite ugly, but pale and colorless. Hazel eyes, flaccid skin against bright hair. A dead small face, a fetal face. I can't tell my mother that. "I'm still an embryo. I haven't been born yet. My body hasn't lived, except inside your body." There are things you can tell your mother. This isn't one.

The lenses of the glasses Zalman gives me are rose pink. In his own dark shades, the brilliant blue of his eyes suddenly quenched, he looks almost blind. But his mouth is smiling at me, and again we weave into the night, which now floats around me in pinkish smoke. I realize for the first time how stoned he is. He bangs against my side. "Am I weird?" he whispers. "Baby, am I being too weird for you?"

"No," I say. How can I tell him how much I love his weirdness, how much he means to me? I've known him for months but never before stood with him in a doorway, his lips pressed against mine, as hard and cool as I might have expected them to be. Since we met he's been a kind of teacher, eager to get me to see certain plays and movies, listen to certain music, read certain books. But until now, there's been nothing more between us. There are other women in his life; I'd long ago decided he didn't want me "that" way. What I myself want is a completely different matter. What I want is him.

In despair of being alive, I have settled for loneliness. I endure hard labor over my books in my dark little apartment; I appease myself with occasional nights out and frequent reveries, the distant dreams of someone whose goals are too far in the future even to taste. And now I appease myself with him—this dark man with brilliant eyes framed in black glasses. I know he's got other lovers, that he'll never live with me. But I know too that he can lead me to it. Because he knows it. The thing called "real life." The life of the body which I've never lived; the life that flows under everything. I can feel it in his vitality, in the way he moves and speaks. In his eyes.

His name is Zalman Finster. I am convinced that he's friends with every really interesting person in the city, that he's done and knows almost everything I want to learn.

I've been in love with him from the beginning.

After a while he lets me go. I escape to the subway station, shaking.

A month later he rings the downstairs doorbell of my building. It's the middle of the night and I haven't been expecting him. I almost don't let him in because in my neighborhood it's dangerous to answer the bell after midnight. But I do, and in a few minutes he appears at the top of the stairs, grasping a thick stack of LPs.

"You've got to hear some sounds," he says. He isn't even breathless; he doesn't miss a beat. He puts the stack carefully down on the floor and starts up my phonograph, which is rusty and old. The first record is Billie Holiday, who sings with a throbbing catch in her throat, as if she were crying all the time.

"That's her ruined voice," says Zalman Finster. "Billie had two voices, her good one and her ruined one. This is the one she had toward the end."

"But I like this voice," I say.

"I'm a fool to want you," sings Billie Holiday. Her voice breaks, husky and sweet.

"I wish you'd dance for me," Zalman says. "I've imagined you dancing for me. I've never seen you dance."

Although I've never danced alone in front of anyone else in my life, I find myself getting out of my chair. I begin to move into the texture of the music, balancing on it as if my threadbare carpet were a tightrope, inching my way through its notes and chords. I can feel him watching me intensely, the way he watched the young woman with the red skirt.

Then he comes to dance with me.

"I've thought about this," he says gently. "I've thought about being with you. But I wasn't sure it was what you wanted."

"Yes," I say. "It's what I want."

I lean into his chest, which is surprisingly deep and strong, and for the second time since we've met, I feel his lips against my own, sweet-tasting and almost cold, like a soft drink or candy.

"You need this. It's going to change you," he says, rolling an enormous joint and passing it over to me. And when I breathe the smoke all the way in as he shows me, to my surprise it does, indeed, taste like grass, like real grass, fresh and meadowy. "It's like going on a trip without taking the bus," he says. "People need to do that now and then," he says. My knees begin to sag and I stop dancing. One of his hands rests against the small of my back.

"A smoke bus," I exhale.

"A smoke bus." He runs his hand along my arm. I am astounded by my own great wit and perception. I am astounded by the lightness of his touch. Under my chin, along my arms. My breasts. His voice is casual.

"We're both free, Helene," he says. "No ties. No promises. That's the way I have to be, but it doesn't mean this isn't love."

"It's all right with me." Later I think, I would have said anything. He smiles into my eyes and I know I've said the right thing.

It doesn't mean this isn't love.

Then we ride the smoke bus together over the "sounds" on my low rolling cot. My apartment, in which I've studied and worked alone for a year, changes into a crucible, held still in time. Everything we do suddenly becomes secret, glowing, dimly illuminated. We speak in whispers although there's no one to wake, unless you count the actor living next door, young and clean, zealously trying to become a movie star. When Zalman parts my legs and pushes himself into me, I realize how little I have ever felt before. Nothing like this. Nothing, ever. I am penetrated so deeply that I have to scream, and he stops, terrified of my pain.

"You're a virgin," he whispers. "Helene, are you a virgin?"

"Go on, go on," I whisper back, and when we start again, it's like being drowned under his body. *The life of the body,* I'm thinking, as drops of moisture fall into my eyes. Drops of sweat, of sperm.

My body's life. At last.

And open to him again, exhausted by my willingness.

Having arrived at midnight, Zalman is barely ready to sleep by five. By four a.m. I've decided to quit my job. At eight I call in sick.

"You can't take any more sick leave this month," my supervisor says. "You're up to your limit."

But before she can even begin to lecture me about responsibility, I take action, immediate and swift. "Never mind, I'm not coming back," I shout, and slam the phone down. He looks up at me from the pillow and I imagine that his eyes are full of admiration.

"It's going to change you," he'd said to me. Now he just smiles. "Yes," he says.

At noon we rise. Smoke still wreathes the glasses and the lamps.

"These walls are too white," I protest, closing my eyes.

Again he becomes a doctor and gives me a pill, which glitters, a hot pink color, in my hand. As I swallow, it becomes a tracer, entering my system and leaving behind a visible trail, an incandescence like the silver left behind by snails.

"Trust me," goes his voice in my ear.

When I close my eyes, I find myself in an echo chamber, a resounding sunless space. All I can hear is my own voice saying, "I'm never going to get involved with drugs. Never," again and again, as I said it to him that night on the street. "Never," I hear again. "Never." What a laugh.

"How are you feeling? Is everything in place?"

Opening my eyes I find him smiling down at me benevolently. His eyes are amused.

"Did I really say never?" I ask him, forgetting that he isn't able to follow me into my mind. But he doesn't seem to care. He knows what's happening to me. He nods and goes on smiling.

"What are you finding out?" he asks.

What am I finding out?

Within an hour I'm in a delicately exploding world, leaves and skies of autumn invading me with color, a frenzy of movement in the park, where he has taken me.

"Come here," he whispers, pleading. "Come here and let me hold you."

On a rock high enough for us to see if anyone is coming, I lift my skirt for him. It seems to me that I have power over him; power, at least, over the heat of his mouth and the questioning desire in his eyes. And above us, all around, the park is a battleground of color, leaves shattering into particles of gold.

Dizzy, I stare up at the sky. "Ever since I can remember I've been trying to feel like this. I've never been able to feel anything before. Like nothing ever really happened, ever happened to me. Do you know what I mean, what I'm saying? Does it make any sense?"

"Yes," he says.

"It's real," I say. "The rest of it isn't real. My whole other life isn't real."

"Yes." He kisses me.

I think of my dark apartment and of my parents' place in the Bronx, on a bare street damp with city rain. I hear them shouting at each other and at my sister and at me. I think of the girls in my high school, especially the ones I didn't like, who called me "weirdo" and "oddball" because I wasn't good at doing what they did so well, going out with boys who had cowlicks and acne and shifty eyes, getting "pinned" and then engaged and then married, selling their lives away for a tiny diamond worth a couple of hundred dollars, ending up frazzled and wasted at the corner supermarket with a bunch of kids pulling on them, always worrying about meals and money and housework and how to keep their oxen of husbands interested, as if anybody cared. And it seems to me that the daily existence of human beings has always been a doomed and futile struggle, and that everyone I know except Zalman and his friends spend their lives locked in a dance with ugliness. Then I climb out of memory through Zalman's eyes, which follow me, filled with humor and the wonderful heat I've just discovered, and I return to the present again.

"Ordinary," he's saying. As if he really has followed me inside my mind. "Dead. The lights off."

"You've been there?"

"I've been there."

"And now," I say. I look at him.

"Have you been waiting for this, baby? Have you been waiting for me?"

"Yes."

"Trust me," he says again, parting my lips with his tongue. And then he whispers against my breath, "I've been waiting for you, too."

Our rock is on a cliff high over Central Park. We look out across its expanse and watch the sun glowing behind the terraced trees, the buildings blue as mountains in the distance. "We've come to the edge," he comments. "The edge of the known." He laughs.

This great edge. Beyond which is infinity, unexplored and yet not empty. What's special about Zalman is that he has filled it up in every way he can.

I know about you, I think, and feel an odd comfort in my

knowledge. At this edge is my own freedom as well as his. If only I can love him and want him and then just let him be.

After the park we go to a museum to look at the medieval enamels. They shudder and writhe inside their glass cases. I've forgotten the shimmering pill; it's Zalman himself who has made this happen. He has filled the air with visible molecules, with atoms, whose dance I watch where once I saw only empty space, the empty space of which I've always been afraid.

"Now I know what you were doing all that time." I sit facing him over coffee and muffins in an all-night restaurant on Broadway. Around us the transvestite clientele scream and elbow one another in their own version of real life. "You were preparing me."

He smiles. His smile is beautiful, softening his face as if it masks some sadness. I neglect to decide what he was preparing me for.

When it's morning again, we go to his apartment, in a place called Paradise Alley. When Zalman comes in, a few men get up to greet him.

"Zalman," one of them says. "We've been waiting for you all night."

The men remind me of ghosts. He alone looks alive among them. Although the shadow of his beard is growing in darkly under his cheeks, he's unrumpled, alert, even after our long day and nights together: his blue eyes shining, his mouth turned up in a smile. Sadly and shyly each of the men gets next to him; they nudge him against the wall, they whisper questions at him. Finally several small packages come out of his pockets, change hands, vanish.

Tea, I figure, looking at the packages. Or pills, because they're so small. There's something exciting to me about what he's doing. Something dangerous. I will myself not to care. He hands them over as if reluctant to let them go and in the same way, reluctantly, he accepts the rumpled, greying bills the sad men hand to him. Then they go away, appeased.

We're alone in the apartment. I wonder where all his friends have gone; I wonder about his other mistresses, at least one of whom lives with him, presumably in this very place, which I find strange, but also exciting. It's all exciting, to live this way. A step away from "normal." I curl up beside him on the stained sheets; after a while he says, "I have to go uptown." I notice that again the day is already more than half gone.

"Should I come with you?"

He shakes his head. "I'll call," he promises.

But my job is gone; all my classes have been cut. There's nowhere else for me to go. After he leaves the apartment I get up and open the curtains, hoping to spend the next night with him. Hoping his other girlfriend won't come home.

She doesn't. In daylight, the place is filthy. I sit for hours, quietly waiting for him, accompanied only by more sad ghost men who come in and go out, looking for Zalman. By nightfall he hasn't called or come back to the apartment, and to avoid the men, more nervous now, I return to my own apartment by myself, to wait.

He doesn't call for weeks.

"No ties," he said. *"No promises. It doesn't mean this isn't love."*

Still, he's left me his records. His "sounds," he called them. Left them there like trash scattered across the floor. Maybe he'll fill up my life with his things, I think, with his sounds and shades and film equipment, with his little vials of shimmering spansules, even with his friends.

Am I ready for him to fill me? And what about *my* freedom, even though it seems so dark and sad without him? To remind myself of him, I buy a pair of rose-colored glasses. I put his records on the phonograph; Coltrane and Miles Davis. Small groans strained through saxophone and horn. I listen without understanding. Only Billie Holiday has words for me.

I'm a fool to want you.

Eventually I return to school and find a new job, and in the evenings, having used up the last of his pills, I drink cheap scotch and cry.

TWO

"All women are wounded."
— *Gary Snyder, ca. 1959*

Three young women sit around a cafeteria table. Ashtrays filled with lipsticked butts and the paraphernalia of coffee. Spoons and saucers, cups pink at the rim.

One is tall, one is tiny and the third one is me.

"So?" the tall one is saying as smoke streams from her cigarette—a Camel, no filtertip, scarlet lipstick at the end—across the table toward the others. "Did you finally get to hear Zalman Finster's 'sounds,' or what?"

Thin honey-dyed hair falls over each of her cheeks. She's the daughter of a man who owns a furrier's establishment in a neighborhood spanning the broad lower flanks of the Grand Concourse, the most luxurious artery of the Bronx, but her own birth, twenty-one years before, was only whispered about and wept over. Until recently she has lived with her disgraced mother in a far more modest neighborhood; her only paternal legacies are her face and body, and maybe her disposition: the feminine versions of those of a brash, self-satisfied merchant, a seducer of women and a cutter of skins.

I've refrained from answering by staring into my cup, but I can easily imagine her behind the wheel of one of her father's fabled Caddies, slicing a path for herself down the center of the Concourse, protected (as in reality, she is not) by one thousand pounds of steel and the furrier's wealth.

"So? You're satisfied?" She answers her own question, putting out her cigarette and lighting another. "You got some stupid taste in men, I tellya. Zalman. What a reptile. Except he ain't bad *looking*, that guy, and he must have about a million friends. So you figure he's gotta have something. Not that I can see it myself. You go over his apartment and he gives you some tasty weed and then you get to sit. Just sit. What a bore. He's got all these records, big stacks of 'sounds.' So like the guy just pretends to close his eyes and he sits there nodding and saying 'fantastic, fantastic' over and over again like some old junky. And everybody goes, 'Ain't Zalman great?' Like I figure, who needs it? It's a crock."

Well, I think, looking at her, *you don't like anybody anyway*. But I'd never say it to her out loud, because I suspect that she doesn't like me any more than she likes anybody else, and I'm afraid of the sharpness of her tongue.

She bends over her cup of coffee. Her waist curves in with the help of a boned waist cincher, hard as steel. She lives the life of the body, all right. I've always envied her that body, a great big 50s Hollywood body, right for one of the movie stars of the decade just before our own, the 60s, which is permeated with the ladylike rustle of Audrey Hepburn and Grace Kelly. Under her tight tweed dress, I know, there's the waist cincher and a shiny black half-slip, a garter belt fringed with ribbons, and a pointy brassiere studded with lace. On one of her fingers flashes an enormous ring. She tells no one where she got it, or who gave it to her. She has no job, no visible means of support. But once, turning a streetcorner, I catch a quick glimpse of her standing outside a restaurant with a stocky man who wears a dark, rich overcoat; she turns away fast and doesn't mention it later. In high school, which we attended together, the other students had a name for her, a name that stuck. Her own name is Ruth, after our Russian great-grandmother, Rachele, who would probably have dropped dead at even the thought of her, but in high school she was called only one thing.

The Whore of the Bronx.

"You've seen a lot of him, haven't you?" I ask. Stirring coffee, pretending disinterest. We keep secrets from one another, Ruth and I. No one would ever guess we were cousins.

"So?" Ruth's voice is low and singsong, rich with the very Bronx accent I worked so hard to lose. "He's right next door, right in the next apartment. I could hear them whether I want or not through the goddamn wall. And like, don't come down on me for listening. Maybe it ain't cool, but so goddamn what? I don't give a shit."

"So maybe *you* want to start seeing him." Maintaining dignity, I set down my cup.

"You're so full of it." Ruth lights another cigarette. The Whore of the Bronx they called her, and now she wears this perpetually scornful smile, a defended sneer that goes with her thick face, her perfect body.

Cousins. Our mothers are sisters who look alike, but it's obvious that both of us take after our fathers, two distinctly different men who have never met and probably never will. Ruth is better looking, in my opinion, but the competition became mutual on the day when I, half a year younger, tottered out of my stroller into traffic in front of her mother's apartment house and got too much attention, and it's never stopped.

Now we are also friends. It's a way of keeping an eye on one another.

Ruth goes to the Cooper Union and is studying art, for which, along with fifty other things, she has always had a talent. Ruth was a child genius, an unlikely fact that went unrecognized until batteries of tests revealed it when she was twelve, just about the time her body developed too. Had she not chosen to study art she might have devoted herself to science or languages. Even now, as relief from the labor of painting she memorizes the hundred or so characters of Mandarin. Her chart of Chinese ideograms is almost the only decoration in her apartment, which, like Zalman's, is down on the Lower East Side, off the desolate courtyard known as Paradise Alley. It's a dark unheated apartment, in which Ruth lives alone, as I do on the Upper West Side.

We'd never think of living with one another, even though I moved out of my parents' house just a month after Ruth left her mother's. But there's that peculiar closeness between us and we often sit as we're about to sit now, in the near-dark of the basement cafeteria of my college or in the gloomy lunchroom of the Cooper Union, eating cheese sandwiches and rancid coffee black as poison.

"This place is a real bring-down," Ruth always says, descending into the gloom, "and the coffee's shit." Always ordering another cup.

Sitting down, sticking a fat Kool between my unpainted lips even though my mother says I look like the kind of young woman who shouldn't smoke, I always respond with something like, "Descent is a perpetual theme in all myth: descent and resurrection," so that the other two exchange long rolling glances and sneer at this embarrassing display of erudition.

The third person at the table is Victoria Andersen, a diminutive twenty-year-old with white-blonde hair and a big nose (although she isn't even Jewish). Victoria goes to NYU, where she now studies History of Theater. She always spurns black coffee for a dish of something sweet: a cake, ice cream, the glutinous white cafeteria rice pudding that trembles beneath her spoon like a naked breast. But to maintain the proper image of sophistication she manages to smoke while she eats, rejecting Ruth's unfiltered Camels and my Kools for a special brand of cigarettes called DuMaurier, that come in a scarlet tin box with gold letters—I suspect mainly for effect as she never inhales—and waves the smoke away with a tiny hand. She was Ruth's closest friend at the Cooper Union. In fact, she may even have been Ruth's *only* friend at the Cooper Union. What drew them together, I suspect, was a mutual fascination. Victoria was fascinated by Ruth's talent and poverty, and Ruth was fascinated by Victoria's lack of talent and abundant wealth. Now Ruth and I are both fascinated by Victoria, escapees as we are from the Bronx, where our parents still live, breathing air killed by exhaust fumes from the freeways, over which the more fortunate commuters escape to Westchester and Connecticut.

Victoria is an escapee from nowhere. She inhabits a six-room apartment on Central Park West with her mother, Elaine, who wears smart clothes and smells of Tanqueray gin and Joy perfume.

"My mother's got an interesting job," Victoria tells you when she first meets you. "She sits around all day thinking up reasons that my father should give her more money, and threatening that if he doesn't fork some over fast she's going to take him back to court and up the alimony payments. She's even got a team of lawyers on retainer. Some life, I tell you. But she says it beats working."

Victoria herself really wants to work, she says; the problem is, she doesn't know what kind of work she wants to do. Right now she's thinking about being an actress; a few years ago she was seriously studying art. What is she doing at NYU, surrounded by future schoolteachers and accountants, befriended only by two penniless geniuses from the Bronx?

"I was too dumb to get in anywhere else," she apologizes.

"But you have to be at least a little smart to get into NYU," we say.

"Never mind," Victoria answers sadly. "My mother says it doesn't really matter what a woman does because she's just going to end up married anyway, and then it will all be wasted."

"End up married? You mean like *her*?" we want to ask, but the resignation in Victoria's face restrains us.

"So?" Ruth continues to grill me now. "Is Zalman Finster instructing you in the theory of jazz?"

Victoria laughs; Ruth joins her, but I'm not even able to curl my lips into a smile.

"I've learned a little about it."

"So what did you learn?"

"About jazz? Only that it sounds like talking. The instruments, calling back and forth. Like people talking. Or even crying, maybe."

They sneer again.

"Well, what do you expect me to say? I don't know anything about music."

"You can say *that* again," says Ruth.

It was in Paradise Alley that Ruth met Zalman Finster and his horde of admirers, who live next door; Paradise Alley, an oblong of tenements grouped around a courtyard with a single tree on East Eleventh Street and Avenue A, far down on the Lower East Side. Too far down. But although she sleeps on a mattress on the floor and has no pots for cooking, Ruth wears alligator shoes and tight gabardine skirts pleated at the thigh with double arrows. The labels glow in their waistbands like jewels in a setting, bearing names like Saks or Jaeger or Best's.

She has cultivated other fancy tastes. All three of us love the Russian Tea Room on 57th Street, where we can sit for hours over wonderful coffee and cakes which will give us zits, and unless we make an actual spectacle of ourselves, no one will disturb us or make us leave. We can pretend to be fully adult; we can make believe we belong. Ruth always looks perfect, as if she spent her childhood being treated to fancy teas and sips of champagne offered by sophisticated parents; she looks that way even though she never has enough money to pay her share and usually waits for Victoria to pick up the check and then suddenly reaches into her bag and pulls out a solitary green-back, grey and faded, thrusting it almost angrily onto the waiter's tray.

Which is why we spend most of our time in my college cafeteria, or upstairs at the Cooper Union, or downtown in one of several bars.

Long ago, in our high school in the Bronx, where we both got straight A's but where little attention was paid to me—I had braces and babyfat until I was sixteen—the tall, flamboyant Ruth was fair game for everyone. Street-corner loungers snickered as she went by. The popular girls whispered, "Don't hang out with her; she's one of 'those' kinds of girls."

Even my best friend, Edie Scheinblatt—my only real friend in high school—kept saying, "My mother doesn't think I should spend so much time with you. Your cousin has such a bad reputation." So, although I tried not to hang out with Ruth too much, our relationship caused me constant anxiety.

Of course, despite the fact that I tried not to acknowledge her in public, I knew a lot about Ruth, even then. In fact I was the only one besides Ruth herself who could know if any of what they said about her was true. Not that she told me anything, but I watched her. I watched her carefully. To the others, even to Edie, whom I never told, it was all hearsay, myth. Ruth never even gave them a glance.

But I did know. And it was.

"Oh. Zalman *Finster*," Victoria says now. "Isn't that the man with the ridiculous cap? We met him one night in a bar. . . He was gorgeous, but he was with some woman with a funny name."

She pokes at a dish of cafeteria ice cream with a heavy spoon and repeats her question.

"Yeah. People call him 'Zalman the Cap' because he's always wearing this stupid hat," Ruth says. "But shut up. Helene likes him. She went out with him that night, remember?"

"I don't know," I say. My skin is so light that I blush wildly, despite all my efforts not to. "Sure. I like him. He's okay."

"So when did he let you hear his 'sounds'?"

"He came over with some records."

"Hah. I know what *that* means," Ruth says. Her smile is derisive.

"Oh no! You didn't!" Despite the nose, Victoria has a refined, angelic face. She stands just under five feet tall and weighs perhaps ninety pounds. Her fingers are covered with small gems, mainly sapphires, which her father sends her on her birthday to make up for the fact that he's too busy to come and see her. "You didn't actually let him *fuck* you, did you?"

In the greenish basement cafeteria a few otherwise tranquil heads swivel and stare with all the ruminative emotion of grazing cows, jaws still working over sandwiches. Most of the students at my college belong to a race which we scornfully call the Education Majors. The Ed. Majors can be found in all our schools but unfortunately, mostly in mine. Their tastes run to uniformly pleated plaid skirts and pastel sweater sets, adorned by "virgin pins," ugly coils of plain gold which have to be pinned directly over the left nipple if they're to be taken seriously, and which are meant to be replaced as soon as possible by fraternity pins worn in the same place and finally, if the Ed. Majors persist in being wise and lucky virgins, by huge hideous diamonds in platinum settings that look like stainless steel.

My high school friend Edie Scheinblatt has become an Education Major and is getting straight C's up at City College, as Ruth delights in reminding me. "Fat Edie," she calls her, humiliating me in front of Victoria: "You shoulda seen Helene here and Fat Edie hanging out in high school. The Chocolate

22

Babies. Two fine Ed. Majors in the making, if they hadn't been so hung up on ice cream sodas."

The recollection of which shames me so much that now I refuse even to say hello to anybody wearing a virgin pin, so I know almost no one in this basement cafeteria, and after a while the novelty of our weird conversation dies down and the Education Majors, ignoring us again, return to their gossip and card games.

I continue to blush and return to the topic of Zalman.

"Well. Why not? What if I did let him?"

Ruth averts narrowed eyes. Her eyes are black and snail-shaped, with arching, scornful brows.

"What if you *did*? Don't you remember?"

"I didn't say I did. I didn't say anything. It was *you* who said. . ."

"So." Ruth interrupts. "What did you think of them? I mean Zalman's 'sounds,' of course. How'd they do, anyway? Were they any good?"

The two of them laugh. Maybe no one else would find what Ruth says funny, but it's the kind of thing we always laugh at: double meanings, stupid puns. Anything to do with men, or sentiment. Or sex.

Only today I sit back and watch them, finding it impossible to make fun of this man who means so much to me. But then I see the derision in Ruth's eyes, and even though I don't really want to, I finally join in.

THREE

It was because of Ruth that I met Zalman in the first place. Not that she meant to introduce us, or even that she wanted us to meet. But there he was one night, Ruth's next-door neighbor, at one of the three night-time places to which we always go when we're together. And there was simply nothing else that she could do.

One of our bars is the Cedar Street Tavern on University Place. In an earlier incarnation the Cedar was a hangout for the first Abstract Expressionists, who sat here together in the evenings and got drunk and formulated a new ethic of art. The New York School.

"It's not the same any more," Ruth growls, when she thinks about having missed the Cedar's days of glory. "We were born too late."

Well, we all know that. We missed running into Willem de Kooning, who was a regular customer, and the dour, saddened Franz Kline, who came here often before he died so suddenly—right after becoming a success after twenty years of trying. We missed watching Jackson Pollock getting kicked out for being drunk and violent, and we missed flirting with Larry Rivers at the chipped oak bar. The old heroes are either dead or very famous and go to fancier bars or drink at home.

But this Cedar Tavern is good enough for us.

We come here when we can't afford the Russian Tea Room (which is almost always), and when we're fed up with the subterranean cafeterias of our schools.

Now, instead of Pollock, we have Gregory Corso being drunk at a back table, his head on his arms. Instead of Larry Rivers, his son Joe, who laughs instead of flirting and looks like Pan. We have dozens of artists and writers who want to say that they've been drinking in the Cedar Street Tavern.

The conversation is pretty good. It isn't really, as Ruth puts it, "an evil scene." Better than in the White Horse on Hudson Street about a mile west, where Dylan and Caitlin Thomas used to drink and fight and do what they had to do together and alone, but where there are now only packs of NYU boys who have remotely heard of Dylan Thomas but who don't really know who he was, and who shout and spill their Black'n'Tans on one another's shoes.

A block away from the Cedar Tavern on University Place is Dillon's, which isn't such a good bar, but to which we go if the Cedar gets too crowded. Occasionally, people fight in Dillon's; no one's sure why. It seems like the kind of place where people fight, while the Cedar isn't; there are too many people of all ages and sexes packed into the Cedar, talking and drinking against the long oak bar under very bright lights, and it wouldn't work.

We are often among them, the three of us. Wanting always to be exactly where events are most interesting, where the funniest things happen. I've been offered a part in one of Jonas Mekas's first movies (which I didn't take) just because of hanging out in the Cedar Tavern. The use of Grace Hartigan's old loft, which I didn't need. And, of course, invitations to innumerable parties, good parties where there's live music and lots of dancing, which I mostly watch from the sidelines. I love to stand on the sidelines in the Cedar, too, wearing a black coat over tight black trousers stretched across the thighs and listening to all the real and pretend writers and artists talking about literature and art; I wear as much black as an Italian widow because I firmly believe that the absence of color makes me look older. It's important for me to look older than I am because I actually look younger. Occasionally I have to convince the bartender—who is anonymous; the bartenders in the Cedar Street Tavern are all anonymous—that I'm old enough to drink.

The only other really good bar in the city for us is Stanley's, about a mile to the east on Twelfth Street and Avenue A, the worst neighborhood in the city. Worse even than where I live, on the Upper West Side. On Avenue A the fire escapes, blackly growing out of each front window, hang over the streets so desolately that the sun never reaches into the apartments or falls on the pavements below, and even the Spanish people of the city get a spent and anemic look after they've lived here for a while. This is the location of Paradise Alley, so I have the excuse of dropping into the bar on my way back from visiting Ruth, who's almost never home anyway. Sometimes she's in one of the bars, which is further reason for me to stop at Stanley's when I don't feel like being alone.

The bartender in Stanley's isn't anonymous. It's usually Stanley himself, a middle-aged, good-natured Polish man who bought the bar when it was just a small tavern for neighborhood clientele, and never expected it to be anything else. Stanley loves us. If we are young and wear black stockings and white lipstick and turtlenecks and corduroy pants, and if we come into his bar on a regular basis, he lets us use the phone, he cashes our checks, he occasionally gives us drinks on credit.

He knows us all by name; he grins and bellows, "Hi, Helene!" when I come through the door, making me welcome, making it easy for me to enter, which is probably the idea.

It was in Stanley's Bar, then still a dark little hole packed with people at the corner of 12th Street and Avenue A, that I met Zalman Finster for the first time.

And it was Ruth who turned around and saw him, lowering her dark lashes over a mug of beer.

"So like," she said, "there's this guy, his name is Zalman something. *Zalman*, for crying out loud. What kind of a name is that? And he's living with this girl, her name is even stupider. '*Flower*,' he calls her, but he's got this funny accent and it sounds like 'Flover.' Her real name is Flora, anyway. She changed it, or he changed it for her. They been living next door to me for a year now, and man, what a crew."

Victoria and I turned to catch a glimpse of his remarkable eyes, about which Ruth had said nothing, and of the cap, which crowned the usual pants and open shirt of the artist's costume of the period. Maybe it was to offset the effect of those eyes that we made so much of it, but we really found the cap ridiculous; it was an English driver's cap made of olive drab corduroy, neatly belted in back with a leather buckle and pulled down over his smooth mop of thick black hair.

"Dig the cap," sneered Ruth, hiding her mouth behind her hand. "He never takes it off."

"Never?" Victoria echoed in the soft shriek we used when something struck us as particularly funny, and the man turned slightly, to examine her over his upturned glass.

"Never," Ruth asserted, flicking a match across her thumbnail. To my amazement it lighted instantly; when I tried it myself I only burned my finger. "Maybe he's going bald or something, and trying to hide it. Who cares? But people call him 'Zalman the Cap,' and that's what they say about him behind his back, because, I mean, like the dude is really evil. He makes one evil scene."

So we all looked over at Zalman the Cap, the really evil dude. He didn't look really evil. Not to me. He looked dissolute and fascinating, the way I've always liked men to look. Next to him was a tall young woman, slender but solid. Thick neck, thick ankles. Thickly lashed black bright eyes, thick long hair as black as his. At a distance she looked like a Tahitian in one of Gauguin's paintings. A madonna of Papeete. She had the gleaming skin, strong body, absolute black cascade of hair, to which Gauguin would have added only the flourish of an orange flower but which was now stifled by a thick green sweater and a pair of shabby jeans and sturdy shoes, as if there were something wrong with her feet.

"'Flower,'" Ruth said, her mouth twisting. "She's only one of his 'old ladies.' There's at least two."

Next to Zalman, Flower beamed with goodwill and remained placidly silent. Watching her, I began to realize that her dark solidity wasn't really Tahitian at all. What it *was* was middle European, the same solidity which marked both myself and Ruth, despite all our efforts to disguise it. Like us, Flower was obviously an emigrant from one of the typical New York suburbs, neighborhoods from which troops of young girls come yearly, bearing their notions of romance like bouquets.

"She's high," Victoria whispered, and looking her over carefully I was forced to agree.

"Stoned," said Ruth in a nice loud voice. "Completely out of her mind."

Sitting to the right of her at the bar, Victoria nodded furiously as if defending something. She was drinking red wine. When in Stanley's, Victoria drank red wine, or occasionally ale. Elsewhere, or when men were paying, she drank scotch or vodka martinis or gimlets. But the truth was, the only reason she drank at all was that she thought it looked attractive. Left to her own devices she would have stuck to 7-Up.

"As a matter of fact," Ruth confided, "he also lives in another building with another woman. Whose name is Zelda.

Zalman and Zelda. Can you dig it?"

We began to laugh, more nervously now. Zalman had noticed us and had begun to observe us with attention. I felt a thrill of interest go through me when his eyes connected with mine.

This, I decided, could be embarrassing. But only for me. "You mean he lives with both of them? How can he live with both of them?" Victoria gulped her wine.

"He lives with one of them one night and with the other the next."

"You mean, he just goes back and forth between them? They know about each other?"

"And they don't mind?"

"Why not?" I wondered. "Why don't they mind?" But it occurred to me that I might not mind either, if it were the right man and I was busy enough. With my studies, for example.

After all, I thought. *The other side of loneliness is freedom.* (I had been reading Simone de Beauvoir's *The Second Sex,* which seemed an appropriate reference for this situation.) And I looked at the man.

"He must have a lot of toothbrushes."

"And a lot of bathrobes and pairs of pajamas and. . ."

Victoria and Ruth lapsed into a fit of hysterics, turning away from him in a futile attempt to be mature enough to be worthy of Stanley's Bar.

At our end of the bar, we could see ourselves in the mirror. Here was Victoria, tiny and dressed to the teeth, with golden hair and small, flashing rings. Next to her, balancing my towering bun that was about to collapse as usual and go cascading down my back in a rush of curls, I was decked out in my usual jeans, topped by a shabby black coat and turtleneck and purple scarf, all designed to make me look like a redheaded Juliette Greco, if maybe a little younger. And last of all was Ruth, elegant and out of place in one of her tight tweed skirts and an expensive sweater, with a velvet blazer draped over her arm, high-heeled pointy shoes and sheer nylons, her sallow, high-cheekboned face turned to all of us with an expression of permanent though unconscious disdain through the smoke of her ever-present cigarette.

It was too magnetic. Leaving Flower at her table—her expression remained exactly the same whether he was with her or not—Zalman came over to us.

The first thing I ever heard him say was, "Yeah?"

He walked over to Ruth and looked into her face and asked her, "Yeah?" as if making some profound statement.

Ruth smiled at him, and her smile wasn't quite as scornful as she might have wanted it to be.

"Too much," she greeted him, surprising me with her mildness.

"Really?" Zalman answered. He sat down uninvited, and smiled at all three of us. "Fantastic," he said. And looked us over.

He looked first at Victoria.

He studied her blond hair, fine as a baby's and windblown around her cheeks. She looked as if she had been running for an hour. Her tailored Thai silk blouse was pulled out of her skirt. There were filigree chains around both her wrists. Her fingers winked with gems. Her pocketbook had cost one hundred dollars, more than a week's salary for me at my most recent awful job. It was bought in a store so rich they gave away shopping bags of luscious glossy paper studded with violets, a store into which I had gone only once in my life, to accompany my mother, who now lived for sales and brand names and who never bought an article of clothing without making sure it was marked down at least twice. I had met her in this luxurious store during a sale so discreet that none of the women even pushed, only to make the startling discovery that the whole place smelled of violets.

As did Victoria, in fact; she had a friend who sent her ounces of perfume every birthday and Christmas, hundreds of dollars' worth of precious liquid in small crystal flagons and padded boxes.

So Zalman looked at her first, and then away, apparently not interested in violets and babyfine hair. Presumably he'd already seen Ruth in his building and had nothing very much to say to her that night, although, despite the fact that her thick profile was tilted away from him, she looked attentive to him, waiting to see what he would do.

He turned to me.

"Well," he said, looking down into his glass of beer. He eyed me with the hard glow that means attraction whenever I see it on a man's face.

But why had he chosen me? I wondered, watching Victoria and Ruth from behind my lashes. And what about the woman he had left at his own table, the woman named "Flower," one of the women who didn't mind? Ruth said he lived with her. Then what did he want with me?

"So what do you do," he asked me, "besides laughing too much in bars?"

Maybe nothing, I decided. Maybe he thought I looked intelligent. And so I muttered, "Archaeology," almost paralyzed by shyness and resentment in equal doses. After all, there was his girlfriend across the room, not even seeming to care that he was coming on to another woman. And there were Victoria and Ruth, nudging each other and giggling at us. *Like fucking high school sophomores,* I thought, annoyed, remembering my own existence as a high school sophomore, composed mostly of a string of miserable afternoons with Edie, cackling over nothing while we clogged our pores with chocolate and our minds with trashy gossip.

"What's that? What did you say?" He seemed a little startled by my resistance. His mouth turned up.

I said it louder, this time. "Archaeology." Forcing myself to look him squarely in the face.

"Oh yeah? Really?"

"You know what that is, don't you? Ur of the Chaldees and all that? Digging things up? Ashes to ashes, dust to Carbon 14? You've heard of it?"

His eyes hardened. "Where did you learn to be so rude, baby?" His voice had changed. Less soft. More steel. "Where did you learn to be rude to strangers in bars?"

"What do you care what I do?" I retorted. Ruth and Victoria were intent, and I sensed their approval, glistening at me across the counter.

"If you want to laugh at somebody," he said tightly, "why don't you laugh at yourself? You're pretty funny, you and your dust."

"We weren't laughing at you," I lied, but I knew it was too late. Already my cheeks were flushed, the brightness in my eyes was unshed tears, and what was worse, he knew it. We all knew it.

"Such defiance," he said softly, looking back down at his glass. "So what are you defying? What is there to defy?"

What was there? I echoed in wonder, and was immediately stunned by how many things there were. But none of them were him. And when I looked at him again, his eyes seemed as round and blue and full of promise as two tiny glowing models of the Earth, spinning configurations of continents and mountain ranges and oceans before my gaze.

Within an hour I'd gone with him, leaving the other two behind. This was in accordance with a code that we had made up long ago and always lived by. If a man beckons, went the code, cut out on your friends. But it wasn't entirely for romance that I abandoned them this time, because Flower came with Zalman, joining him in her slow, solid, sure-footed way, and we plunged west to find someplace where we could get coffee, preferably flavored with cinnamon, and sit up talking until dawn.

What did we talk about, that first night? Flower remained

silent until we parted in the early morning, but I found myself compelled to tell Zalman all I knew about the Hittites, to tell him about the Sumerians and their great goddess Inanna, the Queen of Heaven, who had resurrected the shepherd Dumusi as centuries later Jesus was resurrected, so that even now the peasant girls in the Tigris valley run through the fields in spring crying *"He is risen! He is risen!"* meaning, not Christ, but that one who came before him.

I told him about the spirit of creativity that had awakened the Australian aborigines out of the Dream Time, and about the Harappa civilization in the Indus Valley, to which, I was certain, I was someday going to find my way and there on the railway lines of the Indian National Railway touch for myself what remained of the pottery shards left by the great civilization of Mohenjo Daro, which had traded with the Sumerians thousands of years ago and thousands of miles away, and invented plumbing and great highways when the kingdom of Minos was just an island village.

"So do you mean," he asked me once during that night, "that you only read about civilizations three to six thousand years old? Cylinder seals and King Lists? The contents of tombs? Dig it, baby, that's great, but what about what's going on around you in the world right now? Haven't you read any of the great books of the twentieth century? Of the nineteenth? Don't you know anything about music, about theatre? Even about the movies?"

"Not very much, I'm afraid," I had to admit carefully, admiring him more with every word. I knew this about myself: I could only fall in love with a man who had something to teach me. "I *did* read Simone de Beauvoir's *The Second Sex*. But almost nothing else."

No boy I had ever dated had cared about my studies or my mind. They had all been intent on only two things: getting me in bed, and discussing their own exploits and endeavors. That first night, Zalman seemed interested in neither. He had listened to me. He had watched me. His watchfulness seemed overwhelmingly careful, attentive. He was handsome and soft-spoken and knew about almost everything, but as far as I was concerned, the most important thing about him was that he took me seriously. And once, as he was beginning to tell me about the artifacts of the present and about who was enriching the kitchen middens of our own civilization, our own times—the writers Dostoevsky and Kafka and Beckett and Burroughs and Ionesco and Kerouac—he lifted his hand toward the window of the place in which we sat, beyond which I could see the western skyline of the city, just being lit by a single crack of dawn.

And suddenly I could see the city of New York, wholly and precisely, revealed in the same way in which the great excavations had exposed the cities of the past, caught in the glare of what's called history. I could see it as an island civilization standing precariously at its very peak and ready to succumb, ready to transform into a corridor of fine dust, milled by time, from which someone would someday pluck artifacts that held half-life, and breathing in their smell and air, say, "Here, lives passed. Life went over. See it. Here. Here."

It was plain to all of us after that night that Zalman Finster had decided to take me on.

What I wasn't sure of was why.

He never touched me or tried to make a pass. And as he was encumbered both by Flower and by Zelda, a heavy, raucous-voiced blonde whom I later met and disliked intensely despite a cautious respect, I couldn't believe that he was ever going to, no matter how much I might have liked the idea.

Although the other women made me nervous, I was happier when I was with him than at any other time, and he seemed to enjoy instructing me. We started with a book by Faulkner. *Pylon*. It wasn't Faulkner's best book, and later they turned it into a movie, which wasn't such a good movie either. But even in this thin book I found a wealth of images, of people painstakingly captured in their strangest, most revealing moments: a woman ballooning across the sky in a parachute like a stray Zeppelin, her skirts wound around her waist and nothing at all below because she was afraid of soiling her underwear. . . a man, carefully cleaning a scratch in a newly-bought pair of leather boots so he could return them, which he had to do because he had lost his job and was starving.

Next we went to *Sanctuary*. To *Requiem*. To *The Hamlet*. To *Absalom*. Eventually I stopped caring what Faulkner wrote about. The words by themselves dazzled me. They seemed to capture light with as much magic as a good painting. Which I had already, through Ruth, learned to appreciate.

We proceeded to Dostoevsky.

"Haven't you read *Notes from Underground?*" Zalman demanded. "What about *White Nights?* *The Idiot?* *The Possessed?* *The Brothers Karamazov?*"

"No," I said, and he couldn't believe it. He led me into the Eighth Street Bookstore and I came out carrying an armful of reading matter. He had paid.

"Pay me back by reading them," he said when I protested. So I read, the books coming alive in the shadow of his huge, light eyes, the threat of dark beard constantly sprouting under his skin, as if his ancestors were taking revenge on him for having shaved it off in the first place, the softness of his mouth and voice.

I read. What I'd always loved about archaeology was the discovery of distant civilizations, ways of life which I could never otherwise imagine. But here too, I found, were civilizations, fixed, spread out before my eyes like giant excavations, digs. Words were the pick and shovel. I stayed awake and read until my eyes burned, then dragged myself out to school and work with dreary reluctance.

Soon Zalman started taking me to movies and to the cheap off-Broadway theaters where the most interesting plays were being put on. Flower or Zelda often came with us, but he always bought my tickets, knowing without comment that I was too poor to buy them for myself. As his guest I saw Ionesco's "Jack." "The Bald Soprano." Karl Dreyer's film, "The Passion of Joan of Arc," which starred an actress named Madame Falconetti and the young Artaud, his face as chiselled as an angel's on a Gothic frieze. There were the early films of Fellini and Ingmar Bergman, and the first plays of Genet: "The Balcony," "The Maids." The Living Theatre doing Brecht and Pirandello.

"Soon," said Zalman, meeting me after the theatre one night, "I'm going to come by and lay some sounds on you."

Meanwhile I went with him and Zelda to some little box of a nightclub down on the Bowery where a man named Ornette Coleman played the sax and another man named Don Cherry played a silver cornet, tiny as a child's toy horn. The 5 Spot, the place was called, and it filled with smoke and concentration and the intense voices of the cornet and sax as if with light, and afterwards the audience went reeling out onto Third Avenue almost drunk with appreciation.

"Why," I asked him later, "why haven't I ever heard anything like this before? Why haven't I ever seen any of these things in my own city? Why hasn't it ever been so beautiful? Where have I been until now?"

FOUR

I wanted something, someone
I could not have, until I began
to sound like him, imitate him.
                    — John Wieners, 1969

A month passes after our day and night together. A month since we became lovers. A month since I gave away my life only to have to take it all back again.

I've listened to each of his records at least three times. I've gone for walks through the park and the museums wearing my rose-tinted glasses and sat through all the best movies, imagining him at my side. I've tried to laugh at him with Victoria and Ruth, but it hasn't helped. I long for him. I long to smoke with him; to watch the way the light slows down, glimmers, becomes iridescent as we get stoned and then more stoned. To take one of the shimmering red pills and stay awake for days. It doesn't seem possible to do any of this alone. Getting high is part of being with Zalman; I can hear his droning, lightly-accented voice in my ears, commenting on everything.

"Look at the way the sun sets over the river," he is saying. *"Look at the stone gargoyle carved into that building. Look closely now, stand still, stop time, quiet yourself down. Pay attention. Look. Did you ever realize so much beauty was right here, in this city? Did you ever wonder why nobody even bothers to notice?"*

Waking, I think I see him hanging over me like a ghost; his big eyes open, as they had remained all the time we were making love, as if the most interesting thing he could do were to watch me, to register my cries and movements on some inner graph of his own.

"Nobody notices you much either," he said to me later that night. *"But you also have your brilliance. I saw it right away, and someday, maybe everyone will see it. Even you."*

He's giving me life, I thought as I lay there.

But then he went away, and I live, during the next four weeks, as though he's watching me still, from somewhere in my apartment: I move more gracefully than usual, I speak softly to myself, I put my hands over my body when I step into the tub. Finally, made nervous and ravenous by so much self-awareness, I decide that I have to forget him in order to survive. I devour an enormous dinner for the first time since he's left, study a little, forget to turn on his "sounds," read a paperback book he wouldn't have dreamed of recommending. At ten p.m. I climb into bed and fall into the deepest sleep I've had for weeks.

At two a.m., my doorbell rings.

It's him. I know it must be, and yet it's hard to be certain. In fact, it could be anyone ringing the downstairs doorbell. So at first I'm afraid to answer. The buzzer in my apartment opens the street door, and if I press it some unknown person may enter the building. But now it rings again, and then after a silence, yet again, and holding my flimsy robe around myself I press the buzzer, which feels like a great act of faith. And, in fact, within a few minutes I peer through my peephole and there's Zalman, coming up the stairs. One of his eyes looks blackened and there's blood on his face, but when I open the door he smiles and puts his arms around me as if he saw me just yesterday and nothing much has happened since.

"So why didn't you open for me, baby?" He holds me, acting totally delighted to see me. "You knew it was me. Why didn't you open the door?"

"But I did," I whisper, returning his embrace. "I did." And this is how it's done, I think. Not to mention that I've waited for him for weeks. Not to say, "Where were you?" Simple and uncluttered, letting him come and go as if it's the easiest thing in the world. On the other side of loneliness is freedom. Two o'clock in the morning, I haven't seen him for a month, and he doesn't even say hello.

But then he amazes me by saying, "I missed you so much, baby. I know I was gone too long, but it was such a really heavy month. So many things came down. Did you miss me?"

"Yes," I whisper. "I missed you."

"Why are we whispering?" he whispers.

"Because of the neighbors. It's very late."

Should I mention that the walls are paper and that I live in morbid fear of neighbors, human and otherwise? Should I mention the incident with the rats?

I'd always known there were rats in my apartment. When I first moved in, I would hear them gnawing through the plaster with a sound like gentle drilling, leaping and scampering over the rooftop in the middle of the night, scattering pebbles, congregating in drainpipes. Until one of them succumbed to some rat-killing force—maybe a disease, maybe a stronger rat—and died inside the plasterboard, eaten into its own grave, no way of anybody knowing it was there until it began to smell.

"It was a smell so awful," I whisper to him now, pulling covers up to my chin like a child warding off nightmares, "a smell so bad that even the thought of calling up the super and asking him to clean out the walls was better. So I did it."

The super, a metropolitan toughguy with the air of a samurai gone wrong, has his eye on me. I can hear him late on Saturday nights getting bombed on Thunderbird and beating up his wife, a woman shaped like a tiny runestone, short and widest in the middle, but on whose face is written nothing, not even the grief and outrage that make her scream wildly during the beatings, despite the fact that she endures them week after week without further protest. Not even resentment for me, whom her husband follows so obviously with his eyes, turning his stubby cigar around and around in his wet mouth as I pass him in the hall. The idea of inviting this man into my apartment for any reason repels me so thoroughly that I endure the smell of dead rat for more than a day before calling him. When he comes, he acts as if the situation were somehow my own fault. Whether he blames me for the presence of the rat itself or for its death I never figure out, but I find him on the staircase more and more often as I climb to my apartment, turning his cigar and staring.

"He's dangerous, too," I whisper to Zalman now, nervously watching him fiddle with the radio dials. "I think he's the leader of a protection-and-vice ring; this building has the only mailboxes on the block that aren't regularly ripped open and pillaged, and it must have something to do with him.

"And speaking of danger," I add after a while, "what happened to your face?"

"My connection got mugged."

"No. What?"

"My connection got mugged," he says again. He has this strange accent; he makes it sound liked *mogged*; "If you weren't in love with him," Ruth has sniggered on more than one occasion, "you wouldn't be able to keep a straight face around the guy."

To which I retort predictably, "I'm not," and nonetheless can't bring myself to find him funny, which I know is the scariest of clues.

"That's terrible," I say now.

"Yeh. In Harlem. I sent this chick up to Harlem, I was supposed to meet her on your corner. I waited for hours. The corner with the newsstand."

Five blocks away there's a corner with a newsstand. It's famous for junkies and teaheads who stand around, waiting for connections.

"So finally she calls me on the corner telephone and tells me to come up there, and when I do we both get mogged, I almost lost a tooth and I'm wiped out, wiped out," says Zalman. But he doesn't seem particularly wiped out.

He refuses my sympathy, my offer of mercurochrome and aspirin against infection and pain.

"I don't believe in infection, baby," he says, rolling me a joint, a serene look of wonder on his face and his eyes lit, as usual, with notions of what could possibly be interesting about this experience. "And I don't believe in pain."

"Put on some sounds instead," he says, leaning back happily. In anticipation of Coltrane. In anticipation of Ornette Coleman. And in appreciation of the fact that he has just been "mogged," and even that means that something is happening, and something happening—anything—is always better than nothing happening at all.

That night he begins to give me glimpses of himself. Quick blinks of time, moments excavated from his personal archive.

Zalman's personal diggings, dusted off to please me.

He wants me to know that he didn't start out to be the man I see now, peddling weed on streetcorners, zooming through the city, living in at least three apartments and therefore really living nowhere.

He wants me to know that somewhere he has a mother and

a father, a wife and a child.

"My parents still live in Bensonhurst," he tells me. "The section of Brooklyn famous for its old-fashioned Jews who wear black coats with long skirts down to their ankles and beaver hats. They're called the Chasidim. You've seen them, haven't you?"

I nod. In that neighborhood and in exactly such a costume lives Zalman's father, who is a great rabbi, a holy man. And of Zalman too, the most gifted scholar, the favorite of all the people in the community, it was once said as well: that he would be a great rabbi and a leader of his people. A prince of the Jews. A holy man. Perhaps even the One—but this last part is never spoken, for fear of God. Whose name they cannot even write, much less pronounce.

"What has to be understood about these people," he tells me gently, "is that they have a patience for which gentiles no longer have a need; a patience most Christians have forgotten. Because they're always waiting; they've been waiting for thousands of years. They've spent whole lifetimes, waiting."

"Waiting for what?" Born Jewish myself, what do I know about *his* Jews? Those medieval people, foreign and resplendent, who never go without cumbersome, striped prayer shawls under their shirts and pants and dark, long-skirted coats, or without their beaver hats—because they must never go bareheaded before God. Which explains Zalman's little cap. He has managed to shave off his *payiss* and his dark, luxuriant beard but can't quite bring himself to abandon his headgear.

"For the Messiah. They're waiting for the Messiah." He looks so warm with pride when he tells me about his people that I'm tempted to ask him why he left them. But I hesitate, and he goes on.

"In anticipation of the Messiah's arrival, every aspect of their lives is measured, which lends them an innocence and eagerness no Christian can know, who has already been saved or who has tasted the failure of salvation. To the Talmudist,"

Zalman says that night, "there's neither salvation nor failure—
only expectation.

"Any son could be the One. It tends to make men arrogant
and women smug. Any woman could be the Mother.

"The Messiah himself has to be either completely redeemed
or completely fallen—has to have the energy for either great
good or great evil. The good is self-evident. From the evil he's
supposed to develop the strength to become the Messiah by
overcoming his own impulses." He looks at me slyly as he says
this, daring me to draw any conclusions I want to draw. His
own conclusions are obvious; in the tilt of his head as he
speaks, in the way he draws on his elegantly tapered joint.

Saintliness, with all its rituals, its feast-days and fast-days,
its prescribed rituals for every moment of one's life, has
already disappointed him.

Now he is trying the other.

He rarely speaks to me again about this past, but it seems to
me that he carries it around like a small, dark suitcase. He's
tried to lose it; it isn't easily lost. Tall and blue-eyed, with a
goyish, delicate nose, he studies himself in the mirror and asks
me, "Do I look like a Jew? What do you think, Helene? I don't
really look Jewish, do I?"

For some reason, then, I think of Ruth's lips curling with
scorn when I say his name.

But later he tells me about the Nazis. "We got out of Poland,
you know, just before they invaded. It was fantastic. I was
eleven years old. I liked my first girl.

"She was a Polish girl. A girl in the country. I was staying
with my cousins in the country; they didn't escape and later
they were all killed. And there was one cousin about my age,
a boy, and both of us liked her, and we both wanted to get her
alone. That's what we wanted. If I was eleven, he was—maybe,
thirteen."

A long pause. He's awkward with his story. He holds his
childhood in Poland before me like an unwieldy package.

"So," he goes on, "we figured out a way to get her to meet us behind a barn. She was older than both of us. Fifteen or sixteen. With a beautiful face. Breasts. . . " He waves his hands, sketching a curvaceous body in the air.

"We schemed and schemed, and finally we went to where she lived with her family in the village, and we hid behind a fence and talked to her. And we convinced her to meet us."

His eyes are certainly the eyes of a man who has been looking at women from the age of eleven, and possibly even the eyes of a great rabbi, a prince of the Jews. I can see him as a child very clearly. I can imagine him standing, small and lost, in a sea of Polish green. The meadows. Visiting his country uncles, all of whom were killed by the Germans, later.

He must have been loved for his beauty even then, I think.

"You have to understand, in that part of the world, a Jew was an expendable being—mess with the local virgins, you could find out what it meant to be castrated," he continues.

"Like a black in the South."

"Like a . . . maybe." He gives me a look. "But we managed to talk her into meeting us anyway. And she agreed. She said she'd show up at this barn. We went home and planned what to do with her. But I looked at my cousin's face and it occurred to me that what he wanted to do made me nervous. It made me hurt to think of it. And I stayed up all night waiting and worrying and thinking, how to get her away from my cousin. He was talking about how he was going to throw her skirt up around her head to smother her and hold her down. I knew he wanted to rape her. I didn't know the word for it at that time, but I knew what it was. I thought I knew what it was. In the morning, when I had decided to sneak back to the girl's village and warn her not to come and meet us, suddenly there was my father in his long black coat, come to bring me back to the city. I knew that something was strange about this; my father almost never traveled anywhere. 'But I have come to get you, Zalminki,' he said, and so I packed my bag and we left. And that was the end."

The end, he says. With his parents he escaped across the long, green stretches of Poland. Across Russia on a slow train. At each hamlet in which they stopped, there were the Jews of the region, waiting to greet them. And even the others, the gentiles; the lean Poles, the Russians who would as soon have killed them as looked at them—even they were there to see them. The word had gone out in the little towns. "A prince of the Jews is traveling here. A holy man, a high priest. . . a Prince of the Jews with his family and entourage."

They were a mile ahead of the Nazis. A town, a night ahead.

They swung through Russia by rail, into the long Siberian wilderness. No Nazis there. Only a slow train, wood burning in the forests as it crawled through new-fallen snow, through the long nights, Zalman's father the great rabbi, his mother whose hand no one ever touched except her children and her husband, as no one else may touch the hand of the rabbi's wife. And beside his father and mother, curled up on the train's hard benches as if to protect themselves from cold, Zalman himself, the rest of the rabbi's children (his brothers and his sisters, whom he mentions only once and only briefly), and the rabbi's closest disciples. In their fur hats, in their fur-collared coats, with their prayer shawls, their skull caps, their phylacteries, the huge, dusty volumes of Talmud from which they read when the motion of the train allowed them to read. In the bags stuffed under the seats, warm woolen clothing for the children, the brass or silver candlesticks inherited from relatives. In the hems and linings and intimate clothing, a few jewels, family remembrances, maybe a negotiable diamond or two. These were people accustomed to running, a people whose history had taught them the methods and techniques of flight.

Now their flight took them through Archangelsk, to Vladivostok, where a ship would take them west.

Europe was cut off from them by the ovens, by the cattle cars.

They left it all behind. They arrived, at last, at the end of their journey, where friends and relatives awaited them. In New York City. Brooklyn. Bensonhurst. Neighborhood of low brick buildings, small trees, stunted light, impoverished *shuls* huddled together in basements. City of freedom. In which Zalman found himself imprisoned as effectively as he had been back in their *shtetl*, their ghetto village in Poland, which all Jews were forbidden to leave after sundown, like prisoners. Here they could leave if they had the courage, but in the other, rougher neighborhoods of the city they ran the risk of getting attacked and beaten, not necessarily (as in Poland) because they were Jews, but because of their long forelocks and rough beards, and because, as was natural in the villages they had left behind, even the men wore skirts.

"The end." He flashes me a quick, bright smile. He rarely speaks again of that childhood, its roots unknown to me. He rarely speaks of his parents, or of his personal knowledge of the great Chassidim of Bialystok, some of whom I've seen in the streets and subways of New York, but of whom I know almost nothing—the adherents of a faith by comparison to which the Reformed Judaism of my Bronx family is almost *trayfe*, a vile diluted substance. But he does tell me about the great Jewish saints and teachers like the Bal Shem T'ov, who lived in as great a state of austerity as any Christian saint or Buddhist Boddhisattva. And he teaches me, too, about the brilliant sixteenth century rabbis who covered their fingers with gems and their tables with the best cuts of meat because they honestly believed that God expected this life to be the ultimate feast, a celebration of His existence.

So that I come to see him as their true son, their descendant.

"So how did you get out of Bensonhurst, after all? What made you go away?"

Restless later in the night, we decide to walk. We descend the staircase on tiptoe, avoiding its dangers; we cross through the dank night air to Broadway, where the lights have dimmed before morning, and down seventeen blocks to hunch over coffee in the all-night cafe near 72nd. Now, sitting at the littered table, he suddenly looks tired.

"I didn't 'get out' of Bensonhurst. I still go back," he says finally.

"You do?"

He crumbles greasy Danish between his fingers. There's a strange expression on his face and it occurs to me that sometimes he might even miss Bensonhurst and the people he left behind, might even wonder why he went away. But the thought is brief, and his expression changes into a pleasing smile. "Sometimes. Did you 'get out' of the Bronx?"

"Yes."

"You feel like you escaped from there like from a prison?"

"Yes."

He shakes his head. "Well, I suppose anyplace can be a prison, for that matter. Even this city can be a kind of prison for us, if we let it be." He stares suddenly through the window into the still dark street. "Haven't you ever wondered why you felt that way? How come you just had to get your own pad in a tenement so you could go running around the Village with your inseparable girlfriends, instead of just hanging out on the Grand Concourse with your mother and your father like you were probably brought up to do?"

"And my grandmother and my sister Ellen," I mutter softly. Conjuring, for myself, the memory of what it was like to live with my family. To share a cramped room with my younger sister, only one closet between us, nowhere to put my things or to be alone, the noise from the television or the street outside invading all through the busy evenings, only the relative silence of the very late nights allowing me any time to study. To think.

Or of what it was like in the mornings, everybody trying to get ready for work or school at the same time. One bathroom.

My father taking precedence, seeming to cram the whole apartment with the sound of his wash ritual, as if he were pouring water all over himself, particularly into his nostrils, for half an hour. I'd go into the bathroom afterwards and everything would be wet. How to say any of this to Zalman, who might find it all embarrassingly trivial, certainly not worthy of any kind of discourse? How to explain to him that on the night before I finally packed my things and walked out of the house, my father had caught me all alone in the living room, sitting up with a book and a chicken leg at four o'clock in the morning? And that he'd raised such hell you'd have thought he'd caught me in the act with a boy?

"Leaving the goddamn lights on all over the apartment! Not sleeping! It's abnormal!" he'd screamed.

"I just couldn't stand the lack of privacy," I summarize. Then we're silent for a while.

Zalman says finally, breaking the silence, "For me it was a woman."

"What?"

"It was a woman who got me out of Bensonhurst. It's always a woman."

Our eyes lock. He laughs and reaches for my hand.

"I was a young boy," he says, playing with my fingers. "All right. Maybe not so young. Fifteen. Tops of all the boys in the yeshivah, the seminary. A good student. They were letting me teach some of the classes. I was a rabbi. I had already been ordained.

"There was this woman in the neighborhood. Not a bad-looking woman. She saw me in the street. She began to speak to me for a while every day. She could have been just an ordinary neighborhood woman, a typical woman in Bensonhurst. That's what she looked like when I first saw her. I didn't really notice her very much. I was fifteen years old, and she was about forty. Maybe she was married, maybe she was a widow, I can't remember. But it doesn't matter. Because when I got to know her I began to see something special about her. A kind of brightness, an intelligence, the kind of thing that leads to loneliness for a good-looking woman in neighborhoods like that, that are almost little villages. And she was very lonely. I could feel that, even at fifteen. I could feel her loneliness.

"So she took an interest in me. One day she said to me, 'Why don't you go to school?' I said I did. I said that the yeshivah was school. Studying Talmud was school. I said it was enough. Of course, I was lying. By then I had learned some English, I had begun to watch and listen to what was going on in this new place, and I knew that what I was doing was not enough.

"But it was hard for me to say it. No, impossible. How to tell a man like my father that what he was doing in his life did not mean enough for me to follow? To him it had been everything. Teaching. Worship. Everything. You couldn't understand."

"Yes I could," I protest. But at that moment he's right. I couldn't.

"So she went to my father and talked to him. I don't know what she said. But she convinced him—I don't know how she did it—that I had to go to regular school in Brooklyn. That I should go to college, because I was smart. That it was cheating and depriving me not to let me go to college. And that many boys of our community had gone to college in New York, and they had come back, become leaders of the community, were learned men in both the old ways and the new.

"So he let me go. I went to high school, and when I finished there, he let me go to college. I went to Brooklyn College and within a year I'd read the modern authors, names I had never even heard of in my life before, names that were unknown in the seminary or in my father's house. Names that meant nothing to any of the people I knew. Dostoevsky, Chekhov, Joyce, Beckett. I was afraid to bring these new books home. I left them in a locker at school. And after a while I met another woman, a woman my own age, and I forgot about the first one, the one who had helped me go.

"I would see her sometimes in the street, on the avenue carrying the groceries or laundry, and she looked much older to me all the time, and she looked very lonely. But of course, I was going to school and working and there was this other woman so I had no time for her, and after a while I forgot her. I don't know what happened to her, now. But it's always a woman.

"And this next one was a very smart woman," he goes on, reminiscing. "Of course she was. I married her."

He watches my face as he tells me these stories and he reaches over once to stroke my hair, to let me know that I too am important to him, that I may even reckon in future stories about the wonderful women who've changed his life.

"Yes. Well, she's a successful businesswoman now, and very different, but when I met her she was still a student and she wore tight little vests and big full skirts. It made her look like a peasant. A Polish peasant."

There's a quick movement of his eyes, a lowering of heavy lashes; he's just given me a new way to see him, to stitch together my memories of him like patchwork. His first love was a Polish peasant and his wife reminded him of a Polish peasant; a theme of attraction and longing for the forbidden weaves throughout his life, the hunger of the Jew for the non-Jew, even for the anti-Semite: a familiar theme. "I don't look Jewish, do I?" he asked, combing his thick black hair before my mirror. And in fact, he really doesn't; his coloring and features could belong to a man from anywhere in Northern Europe, which makes me wonder about the journeys of his people: how many times had they crisscrossed that continent, from Spain to the Caucasus and back again? And for how many reasons?

So Zalman married and they had a child. Sonya, his wife, was Jewish but not of his community. Not of his people. He was forced to leave his father's house in Bensonhurst and his position in the seminary and his future as a great teacher and leader. He was forced to leave his community altogether, and to take his wife and new daughter to live in Red Hook, an even more desolate Brooklyn neighborhood in which the rents were even cheaper.

"My father didn't come to my wedding," he tells me. "I wasn't quite excommunicated from his congregation, but I was ostracized. No one would speak to me except my mother, and all she did for a while was look at me and sigh."

Jobless, he had to take whatever work he found. He was still a rabbi and he found occasional employment chanting at funerals, officiating at weddings, praying over the animals before their throats were cut, to make them kosher. Even plucking chickens. His father was shamed and then more shamed. His wife, still dressed like a Polish peasant in a tight vest and full skirt, still smart, started a small neighborhood employment agency while he plucked the chickens. She had been the president of the chess club, active in the mathematics society, was still a woman with a good brain, a fine curve, a sense of how to make two and two add up to five. She began to make more money than he did, but insisted that he work as well — "For pride," she said. "A man has to work."

He was miserable. He had neither the tight network of belief that had held him through his boyhood nor the brilliant life of literature and art that had beckoned to him thereafter.

"I wanted to write," he says. "I wrote in the evenings at the kitchen table when I got home from work. But it wasn't enough. It was never enough to make up for the drudgery and toil and loneliness. I had no friends that I could talk to. I accomplished nothing that made me proud. It couldn't last."

I can see him there if I close my eyes as we sit together in the coffeeshop over a muddle of empty plates and glasses. I can see him in a pool of light falling over his kitchen table in the Brooklyn apartment. He looks very young as he bends over his work, and there's a splendor in him; he knows that he can conquer all obstacles—his poverty, his father's shame—if only he decides what he wants to write about, what there really is to say. What he really wants to do within that one, ultimately elusive fine curve, that of the undiscovered world, the world outside the cage created first by his father's cheder and his mother's house and by the great Chasidim of Poland who are so holy that they dance with one another holding handkerchiefs so that their hands won't touch, and then by Sonya and the child. He dreams of the great world beyond the giant, misted trees of the Siberian wilderness through which he had travelled many nights ago, still a child in love with a Polish virgin whom he would never touch, and all the hands that he would never touch, and all the many things that he might never live to do.

I see him there and it seems to me that he feels everything I've felt inside the prison of my parents' apartment, inside the cage of my own career as a high school and then college student, trapped by the thousand mediocrities and misunderstandings of a life I never liked. Trapped. Him too.

"Until," he tells me reluctantly, "the little girl I met in a Village coffeeshop released me. She set me free. Like I say, it's always a woman." He means Flora, I realize, trying to suppress a pang of jealousy. Soon called Flower. Who broke, as completely as he himself broke the hymen that marked her own respectability, the spell which his wife, his family, his community, still worked on him. As all spells can be broken—by another spell.

We walk back from the all-night cafe, twenty blocks or so to my apartment, through battalions of bums and roving muggers and the scent of impending rain. One of the worst neighborhoods of the city, and nothing touches us. It's four o'clock in the morning; four-thirty, five. He has enchanted the night out of its danger; he has enchanted me out of my need for sleep.

We return to my place so he can take a bath, and he sits in the bathtub washing his black eye and the smear of blood still on his face. His smart little cap perched on his head, he lathers his body with soap.

"Why don't you write any more?" I look down at him, scrubbing his shoulders and back. "I'll bet you could write something wonderful."

"Writing isn't enough in the moment." He smiles at my homage, taking the washcloth out of my hand. "I discovered the camera, you see. I discovered paint, collage. I need the power of immediacy, the moment just as I see it. Besides, Beckett has written everything worth reading in the twentieth century. So I bought a used Bell and Howell and I shoot everyone and everything I see, and I splice the shots together in interesting ways so that nothing follows with the usual sense of continuity. I call it upsetting expectations; I call it working the alchemy of art. To watch anything with care is to work a change on it." His face has turned splendid and brilliant again. "By its very watching, the movie camera has changed our lives. Do you understand that, Helene? How much our experience and our concepts of ourselves have changed because of film?"

"Yes."

"Yes, you probably do. It's always so easy to talk to you; I feel like I can say anything and you'll understand. Do you know how special that is for me? Do you have any idea?"

Conversation stops as we stare at one another in appreciative wonder. Later, I learn that he also works the alchemy of art by forging wild collages out of discarded milk cartons, old newspapers, gallons of acrylic and a sea of glue. And observing them, I try to imagine what experience of life they might have changed for anyone.

Now he clambers briskly out of the bathtub, leaving tidepools of dark water on my bathroom floor. At six o'clock in the morning, he hasn't slept for days, and he knows that I won't let him sleep either.

"I met a man who knows Burroughs." He turns restlessly in my bed as the sun comes up and slants at the windows. I lie against his shoulder, his hand curling into my hair; I'm happy to be sharing the adventure of his life.

What are we going to do today? I wonder. Hide from the sun at a movie, a museum? Pursue it in the streets?

"He's going to introduce us," Zalman confides. "I wrote Burroughs a note."

He shows me the note, which is delicately worded, almost too carefully; the possibility of a friendship with the famous writer looms majestically over his life like a gigantic ocean liner looming over a smaller, but equally fascinating vessel, freighted with the promise of new experiences, new horizons. Greater, more powerful magic. I can imagine him standing in the loft of the mutual friend, smiling his noncommittal smile at Burroughs. And his smile at that moment will be sweeter than it has ever been, and his eyes brighter, more compelling.

But why does he need it all so badly? The question pokes through my happiness as delicately as the sun pokes through my dusty Venetian blinds. I mop the bathroom floor so his bathwater won't soak through and destroy the ceiling of the man downstairs. What is there about all this adulation and influence and friendship that he needs so much that he has to give up his sleep for it, give up all his time and most of his energy?

He ends by taking me to the zoo, where we stand for what seems like hours outside the iron bars, staring in at the eyes of the animals, eyes yellow or black or amber, the pupils slanting lines or pinpoints. Unhappy animal eyes, always restless, untamed, misunderstood.

"Will we change them if we watch them long enough?" I ask.

"We've already changed them." He smiles up at the spires of the city. "We've brought them here, you see. Into this prison."

And as if to show me exactly how he himself has managed to survive the prison we are in, he gives me another pill.

FIVE

"Come on, baby. Take off your clothes."
— Bob Kaufman, 1967

When Ruth, Victoria and I get together, everything has to be a joke. We laugh at everything around us; our parents and our classmates, the idiocies of our professors and the friends who don't happen to be with us at the moment. The Education Majors, our special targets, regard us with stern suspicion; to them, education is just something to be acquired while waiting for the right boy to cough up the right-sized diamond, and since we don't know anything about either "rightness" or diamonds, and wear neither virgin pins nor frat pins, they know we must be strange. And we are.

We insist on laughing at things that no one else would laugh at; we balk and skitter at the faintest scent of understanding or compassion. Our humor doesn't thrive on understanding or compassion, and our rules are inexorable. Either we spend our time together laughing, or we separate.

But what we really have in common, we three, is men.

We collect men. It's our only hobby. We hold them out and compare them to one another like rare samples, like stamps or antique coins.

I've always been the most timid collector of the three. Maybe because of my sad past in high school, I have no real confidence in myself.

"Ahhh, you're okay now," slurs Ruth, charitable over coffee. "A little too thinskinned, I guess, but cute enough. I don't know if you'd make it with the really far-out guys, but the other kind could probably dig you."

What other kind is there, I wonder? Balanced on the taut and fraying rope of New York's dark streets and crowded nightspots, I feel like a badly trained acrobat, moving through the air without a net. My contributions to our witch's brew have so far been few, and none of them are really prizes. There is one slightly cynical bartender. One bumbling Pakistani business-man. A smattering of undergraduates, well-brought up, young and inarticulate, who spend whole evenings buying me too many drinks in the hope of getting laid—a hope I invariably dash, simply and without afterthought, by slamming my apart-ment door in their faces with a series of moves I've worked out beforehand—an intricately choreographed ballet.

Of course, now I've got Zalman. But I want to keep him to myself.

The bartender, incidentally, I also met in Stanley's. In Stanley's there's one other bartender besides Stanley himself, a man in his thirties named Wallace Wigmore. Somehow Wallace Wigmore has acquired my telephone number, prob-ably from a check which I gave Stanley to cash, and every morning, early, before I leave for school and work, for one entire year, he calls.

"Hello? Helene? Is this Helene?"

Sometimes on weekends I'm still sleeping when the phone rings and I let it ring. Sometimes, after the first few times he calls, I simply take it off the hook and drop it on the table next to the bed. But usually I lift it, if I'm home and free to lift it.

"Hello? Helene? Is this Helene?"

"Yes. Who's this?"

"This is Wallace Wigmore. Wallace, the bartender at Stanley's?"

"Oh. Sure. Hi," I always say.

"So are you free today, Helene? I wondered if I could take you out to lunch today."

Victoria and Ruth often ask me why I never go out for lunch with Wallace Wigmore. He's intelligent, he's interested, and he isn't bad looking. But I always say no. There are two real problems about going to lunch with him. The first is that I'm never really free for lunch. Either I have to work or go to school, or else I have to stay home and study, or else I'm so exhausted from all the rest of it that I can't get up to eat lunch anyway, and will probably not eat anything till dinner.

But I neglect to say any of this to Wallace, probably because of the second reason, which is that there's a sarcastic, closed, matter-of-fact quality about him. There would be nothing much to learn from Wallace Wigmore, I think, and even less to laugh about with Victoria and Ruth. He's just naturally not funny. In fact, I suspect that he might have some odd male counterparts of Victoria and Ruth himself, with whom he might sit in private, laughing about *me*.

So I always say no, no matter how many times he calls. And Wallace never asks me out for the next day or for that evening or for Sunday afternoon, when I might be free. He seems to expect me to refuse him. Sometimes he even says it before I get a chance to: "No," in a mincing voice. "I can't go out for lunch with you, Wallace. I'm busy."

It never occurs to me to ask him why he keeps on calling, and it never seems to occur to him to ask me why I don't tell him to quit. We just go on like this, and when we see one another at the bar we smile at one another briefly, and do not mention it.

The Pakistani businessman is another story. I met him at a student party and I've managed to keep him as a kind of courtier, one of those genuine suitors of the time, a "date." In his presence, I'm able to forget the grind of my daily routine, the rats in the walls of my apartment, the fact that Zalman calls seldom and visits briefly, and that there's no way for me to participate more fully in his life without stepping on his freedom. Or my own.

But do I really want my own?

The Pakistani businessman has never even been inside my apartment. He takes me swimming and admires my figure in a grey jersey bathing suit. He takes me to a dark French restaurant in a basement in which I order, for the first and only time in my life, cervelles in black butter, which it turns out I detest.

And once he tells me that I'm beautiful, which is no small thing when that's what you need to know.

One night, after six months of dating, he takes me to the movies. He lets me pick the film and then sits grimly beside me in the dark, patiently observing the brooding atmosphere of Bergman's black-and-white cinematic Scandinavia without a moment's pleasure or comprehension.

At the end of the evening, still not having even touched my hand, he walks me home. He stops before the door of my shabby, peeling apartment building, looks down into my face, and announces rather grandly in his singsong accent, "I should like very much, my very dear Helene Elphrick, to go to bed with you."

"What? Tonight?" I want to shout at him, bursting into laughter at the thought of how funny this is going to sound to Victoria and Ruth. But for the sake of survival, any young woman who dates in New York City must have some sort of line down pat, without which life can be very difficult, something like swimming naked in a shark-infested sea.

"Oh, Motilal, I'm so sorry," I murmur with deep insincerity. I have just spent the last night with Zalman, and besides, chock full of "Wild Strawberries," I want only to be left alone to digest them.

"Oh, Motilal," I continue, "I really can't sleep with you. Of course not. There's nothing wrong with you at all, but I need much more time before I could ever do such a thing. I'm just not *ready*, Motilal."

"Ah, that is very good," Motilal responds. "I shall, of course, give you as much time as you might need."

But before I can blush and simper and make the next date for dinner, he goes on.

"I shall go to the corner of your street now," he says, "and stand and wait to give you as much time as you require. Shall fifteen minutes be sufficient, or shall I give you twenty?"

The whole incident makes for so much amusement between the three of us that I use the same line a few months later, with another "date," a Nepalese prince who has come to New York to study law at Columbia. But this time it doesn't work—Nepal must be a fiercer state than Pakistan—because Amrit simply bites me on the mouth and strides away in a rage.

As Victoria has more leisure time and money, she's actually the most resourceful collector of the three of us; her men are the wildest, the most way out. After all, she has the least to lose. She knows that, if necessary, she can always marry somebody even richer than herself and everything will be taken care of. Or she can skip marriage altogether and devote herself to a career. She'll become an actress and make commercials on television or she'll write soap operas or teach third grade. She's already made her position on divorce clear: "I'm never, ever going to be like my mother," she declares. "It's just the worst, waiting for your ex to come through with the support check. I hate it. When I get married, it's for sure going to be permanent."

In the meantime, Victoria is very good at collecting men.

One of the prizes of her collection is a Korean import/export magnate she met at International House on Riverside Drive, who threw himself at her feet and proposed marriage to her two dates later, although she was only seventeen.

"But Mr. Wo, you already have a wife," she reminded him demurely. "You told me about your wife and your two excellent sons, don't you remember? You told me they had left Seoul and were living on Taiwan."

"Taiwan is very unstable," speculated Mr. Wo, with a gleam in his eye. "The Communists are coming. The Communists enter Taiwan, wife and sons all die."

Mr. Wo was fascinated by death. He invited Victoria, who by now had almost convinced him that his wife and sons deserved a chance to survive even a Communist invasion of Taiwan, to commit suicide with him. When he made this proposal they were, in fact, in his small car, one of the first Volkswagens in America, racing up the West Side Highway on their way home from an elaborate Chinese meal.

"I think we are going to die now," Mr. Wo announced, heading the Volks toward a supporting wall. "I want to commit suicide with you. For love, you see. Many couples do so, in my country."

"Please stop the car," Victoria had bawled, beginning (she tells us) to take him seriously. Mr. Wo accelerated. She put one small hand against his arm, and he smiled down at her.

"This is a good way to die," he said, beaming with tranquility. "Clean and fast. No trouble. Good."

"I'm going to be sick," Victoria sobbed, pitching her tiny body against the door, frantically sucking air as her stomach heaved.

"You don't wish to die with me?" he asked. "You don't love me at all?"

At the last minute, he guided the car to safety and his

passenger leapt out and fled. But when she tells it to Ruth and me, the story has already undergone its metamorphosis. We smoke some of the grass Zalman laid on me during his last visit (ransoming his "sounds," which he took away with him), and go to eat blintzes with roe at the Russian Tea Room, Victoria's treat because her father has just sent her some money, and under the Tea Room's perennial Christmas lights we stuff napkins into our mouths and gasp with laughter. It's not just Mr. Wo at whom we're laughing so uncontrollably. It's at Victoria's flight across the wilderness of the West Side Highway, an accomplishment which in the undertaking was so scary that she almost wet her pants. It's at the concept of a couple committing suicide for love, something so remote and foreign to the three of us that we can't even imagine it. And it's even at the idea of death itself, an idea which is still funny because we're only twenty-one years old and we don't want to know anything about it for a long time to come.

Eventually, having collected all she can without actually having done so, Victoria decides that it's necessary to lose her virginity

"I'm so tired of it all," she confides, just after her twenty-first birthday. "Being a virgin is such a drag."

In 1961, you're *supposed* to be a virgin at twenty-one (think of Edie and all the other Ed. Majors with their virgin pins), but of course, Ruth and I aren't.

"How did you manage it, Helene?" Victoria wants to know, spooning ice cream.

"I fell in love, I guess."

"That sounds like an awful lot of trouble, if you ask me."

"It was," I agree. "But he was the first man who ever paid much attention to me." I flash Ruth a look. "The first *interesting* man." (Does she mutter, "And the last," flashing me a look in return? It doesn't matter; as long as she doesn't know it was Zalman, I don't care what she thinks.)

"What *I* did, I made it with one of the male models in the

Life Class at the Art Students League," Ruth volunteers. "I was in the scholarship class and I knew he could dig me. So I waited for everybody else to go home and then I got him to screw me on the dais. The smell of turpentine still makes me hot."

Victoria despairs of ever topping this much bravado or willpower, until one night she meets a merchant seaman whose tattoos are so extraordinary that once he did a stint as a professional tattooed man in a freak show at Coney Island. She falls in love with the tattoos. The man she barely notices.

The night she meets him, she happens to be alone in a Village coffeeshop after one of her classes at NYU. Ruth and I are nowhere to be found; the college cafeteria is closed and the Russian Tea Room is serving up Chicken Kiev, too expensive even for her.

His name, he tells her, is Patrick Parker. He lets her know almost at once that he frequently comes to the Village to pick up girls. This is very honest of him, but otherwise not unusual. She even yawns a little, delicately, into a dark suede glove and considers going home alone. Until she notices that his hand, emerging from the sleeve of his shirt, is covered by an intricate webbing of color.

"What's that?" she inquires, staring rudely but charmingly at the design, which intrigues her by disappearing up his sleeve.

"Tattoos," he says, shooting his cuffs modestly, his eyes down. The tattoos, she is to learn, are vestiges of an early flamboyance, born on the high seas and regretted too late. Patrick Parker has had the misfortune of outliving a taste for his own skin, and now spends his time in search of a quiet, undecorated life and the perfect relationship, which, upon meeting Victoria, he believes he may have found.

"Tattoos? What for?"

He shakes his head.

"Have you got women's names and that kind of thing?"

"Better than that," he beckons, remembering his quest.

"Wanna see?"

"Let's go." Victoria elegantly snaps the clasp of her expensive handbag and gets to her feet.

"Go?" he stammers. "Where?"

The tattooed man looks her in the eye; even without the round gold pin hanging off her sweater above the left nipple, it's obvious to him that she's a virgin. Could he be wrong? Still whetting his appetite over his first espresso, he hasn't expected to be successful so easily or so soon.

"To a hotel," Victoria says steadily. "Your room. Anywhere. I *do* want to see."

Dumbfounded, he takes her to the Hotel Earle on University Place, which is the nearest half-decent place he can afford. Then he proceeds to undress for her. She finds that what he said is right; he is "better than that," better than names and hearts with pictures in them and dancing Hula maidens. He has been designed by Japanese craftsmen, whorled and incised like Asian pottery. There are dragons and plummeting ships circumnavigating his chest and back, ribbons unfurling from arrows in his armpits, clutched in the curled claws, over his shoulder blades, of sharp American eagles. There are scrolls unfolding names and dates and deeds in colors more luminous and exquisite than those of the Flemish enamel triptychs in the study of which, under the tutelage of her favorite art history professor, Victoria once specialized. He is precious scrimshaw; he's a magic lantern, a Ming among men. When he turns around to drop his pants for more effect, he finds her under the covers of the broad double bed in the room, all her clothing scattered over the armchairs and the floor.

Patrick Parker has never experienced such tenderness.

He comes to her very gently in the creaky bed. This man who thought he had tasted everything—mamasans on the Ginza, dusky beauties in Rio, once, even, very strictly (he tells her) out of curiosity, a good-looking Argentinian sailor—has never before experienced a high-class New York college girl.

While she runs her eyes over his body, he's very tentatively running his fingers over hers. Already impressed by the silk of her blouse and her brassiere, the suede of her gloves and boots and handbag, he finds the velvet of her hair and breasts more compelling than any texture he's ever known.

Most tellingly of all, she bleeds. And Patrick Parker, realizing after the fact what damage he has done, cries in her arms.

"Did I hurt you?" he whispers, muffling his harsh voice in her hair.

"Nope," she answers cheerfully, hardly noticing the pain. Wondering, in fact, what he's so upset about.

What she really wants, having finished with the necessary physical stuff ("Out of the way at last," she tells us later), and having let him light her a cigarette, is to leap out of bed and cry, "Wow, I did it!" Thinking of what our faces will show when she reveals him to us, safe in the seagreen depths of the Russian Tea Room over petits fours and coffee. The wonder in my eyes; the envy in Ruth's. Only modesty silences her. Modesty and the awe brought on by seeing him naked for the first time.

With the triumph of the collector who has acquired the great prize of her collection, she even considers introducing him to us.

Meanwhile he lapses into a turbulent state, full of self recrimination and regret. "You *are* a virgin," he whispers to her reverently as they get up, preparing to leave the room.

"Not any more," Victoria responds, practical to the last.

"I'm in love with you," Mr. Parker says.

"Uh-oh," says Ruth, when Victoria tells her this. "Now you can't go on seeing him."

"There's so much of him to see," answers Victoria. "Why not, anyway?"

None of us can think of any good reason why not. So she does.

But she never introduces either Ruth or me to the tattooed man, although she begins to see him almost nightly in the bar across the street, going with him first to the Hotel Earle and then to his new apartment, which he rents, for her convenience, near the hotel.

"Maybe she's afraid we'll steal him from her," Ruth says one night, stretching and preening as she cruises the night crowd at Stanley's.

"Maybe." I agree reluctantly, knowing that I couldn't possibly do such a thing to a friend, even if I wanted to. But Ruth's reflection in the mirror above the bar tells me something else.

In fact, Victoria hides Mr. Parker from us because she's afraid we'll laugh at him. He's dumb, she says. And yet she goes on with him, week after week.

"What are you so attracted by? The tattoos?"

"Yes," she tells me, one day as we sit together in Washington Square. But her eyes are troubled and sad.

"Not just the tattoos," she confesses, after a few minutes. "Don't tell Ruth."

"I guess I wouldn't want to." I feel shy, suddenly. Victoria seems to be opening some new chapter between us, some page on which Ruth may not have a place.

"I really like him." She looks into my eyes. "I mean, I *really* like him. He. He's nice to me."

Her face, stripped of make-up and paler than usual, seems different, almost serious. Her eyes are grey and huge, and it's even more obvious than usual that her nose is too large for her other features. Someday, I think, Victoria may turn into a rather plain woman. I imagine her middle-aged, short and thin with lovely silvery hair, wearing a twenty thousand dollar mink coat, standing at the entrance of an auction gallery, bidding on a vase.

"I guess that's pretty important." I think about Zalman. "Being nice."

She lowers her eyes. "Sometimes I think that it's all I need." She tries to laugh. "You know, to walk into the sunset with somebody. Even get married, like." She giggles a little, forcing it. "I mean, you kind of fall in love with somebody *that* nice. Don't tell Ruth."

But one day, after she has been sleeping with Patrick Parker for six months, Victoria answers the bell and finds him at the door of the apartment she shares with her mother, Elaine. He looks very sober and solemn, dressed in a blue suit with a knit tie and his hair combed straight with water, and holding, perched upright between his fingers, a small blue velvet box.

"Patrick!" she squeaks, opening the door a crack. "What are you doing here?"

"Come for a visit."

"Well, you'll have to leave soon. My mother'll be home any minute and you don't want to run into her, do you?"

And yet this is precisely what he does want—to ask for Victoria's hand in marriage. Just then, in walks Elaine—a good-looking woman in her forties. Under different circumstances he would probably have liked her, too. So Victoria is forced to introduce them.

"Mother, this is Mr. Parker. Mr. Parker, my mother."

Elaine is a tall woman, about as different from her daughter as two women can possibly be, except that she has Victoria's wide excitable eyes and easy laughter, and in the middle of her olive-skinned, rather impressive face, looking barely large enough, the very same nose which on Victoria will someday look enormous. She has thick honey-blonde hair—almost the same color as Ruth's in fact; it's a popular color that year—although she, too, was obviously born brunette. And her clothes always represent the absolute summit of fashion. Today her height and slenderness are adorned by a green silk shirtwaist, high-heeled black suede pumps, and—yes, a mink coat, suitably dark and lustrous.

Patrick Parker, seeing this presence standing behind him in the hall, beginning already to remove the small veiled pillbox hat which crowns her outfit, is taken aback. She isn't very much older than he is, as a matter of fact, and here he is, nervously playing with his velvet ring box, about to ask for the privilege of becoming her son-in-law. That this is such an overwhelming privilege has never occurred to him until now, for after all, hasn't Victoria shared herself with him with abundant, almost shocking generosity? And isn't this a time in which women accept offers of marriage from their lovers with eagerness, even with gratitude? Especially once they've "given away the milk," as he's heard it put. (The logical inference is that if you can get the milk for free, why buy the cow?) But here's his very own cow in her very own home, and behind her is her mother, and her mother is Elaine, a masterful portrait of a certain kind of woman—a rich woman, a divorced woman, a woman who knows her way around the world. And her presence changes everything.

For Victoria, it's a moment of intense, uncomfortable truth. She's ashamed of Patrick Parker. She's ashamed of the nights she has spent with him, boldly kicking aside the sheets so she can watch the blue serpents on his buttocks wiggling as he lurches above her. She wants to forget the serpents; she wants to forget his buttocks; at that moment, neglecting even her responsibility to make fun of it all with us, she wants to forget everything.

She introduces them anyway, pulling her company manners out of that bag of tricks which she carries around within herself like a racial memory. So Elaine Andersen and Patrick Parker meet, and smile politely, and look one another in the eye.

My God, Elaine is thinking. *What does Vicky think she's doing? If she gives the milk away to just anybody, who's going to buy the cow?*

But she extends her hand anyway. There are graces and understandings which certain mothers possess—frequently divorced ones—which more conventional parents usually lack. Mr. Parker, grateful, takes it, and with great solemnity the two hands hold one another, shaking.

During which deeply formal procedure Victoria stares at the floor and Elaine stares at the vision of a tattooed scarlet ribbon which encircles Patrick's wrist. If she squints she can just make out the lettering on the ribbon; she thinks it reads, "Excelsior," but it might even be a woman's name. "Elizabeth," perhaps; the script's so tiny she's never going to be sure, but she realizes even as she stares at it with an expression of unmixed horror that the workmanship is special; all the details of the ribbon, even the tiny loops that run along its edges, even the slight gloss of its satin, all, are imprinted with loving detail on Patrick Parker's hand.

"You will come in?" she flutters, retracting her own hand as though she has touched something very cold.

"Uh. Well."

Poor Patrick has finally begun to realize the hopelessness of his quest. He slips the box into his pocket. He follows Elaine into the room. Which is wide, and painted white, and filled with stark black couches and those weird chairs that seem about to swallow you when you sit down, like man-eating plants.

"Will you have tea?" Elaine gasps, dying to get out of there. Except she's stalled by her daughter, who beats her to the kitchen door saying, "I'll make it, mom," and retreats like a fox into a hole.

"Well." And throwing her mink into a closet, Elaine smooths down her skirt. "May I take your coat?"

"No'm," Parker mumbles. "Don't think I'll stay."

Nothing on the wide seas has prepared him for this. What he thought would be so easy—the way he paved for himself with the tiny diamond—crumbles before he can even speak. It might be difficult to make up something funny about this moment, but sitting with us in a coffeeshop, Victoria tries.

"He wanted to marry me," she burbles, holding the ring up to the light. For yes, he gave it to her anyway. As a good-bye present. There's no possibility of their continuing as they have—not now, since he realized that he isn't using her—that actually, it's the other way around.

But there is, also, another possibility, which Victoria mentions to me only later. The possibility that he really loves her. That he can't go on with her without a deeper commitment. Even that the whole incident will leave him shattered and sad, as if broken by too rapid an immersion, too sudden a move from burn to freeze. He has been made small and cold by the differences between them. Even his ring is dwarfed by the battalions of her father's sapphires; she wears it on her pinkie, one more trophy in a battle none of us have named.

"He was going to ask my mother!"

"And he didn't?" Ruth yawns. Her face has changed, though. There seems to be compassion shining through the usual boredom. Because if ours is a game of the have-nots against the haves, isn't Victoria really one of the haves? Can she make fun of this hapless seaman, covered in the wild cloth of his own imaginings, his seamed and beribboned skin, and get away with it?

"What'd your mother do? Put him down?"

"Oh, she wouldn't do anything like that," Victoria defends, retreating slightly. "I think, when he saw the house—when he actually met her—he realized it was impossible. I'm too young, for one thing."

"Too young to get married?" Ruth pursues, relentless. "You're twenty-one, aren't you? People get married at twenty-one all the time."

"Well, *I'm* not getting married at twenty-one."

Ruth looks her in the eye and sneers. I know those sneers; I fear Ruth for them, but I admire her for them too.

And this sneer says, "Not unless Patrick were some phony out of Harvard, you're not. Just because he's Patrick, you're not getting married at twenty-one. Just because he's only good enough to screw."

It's Zalman who labels Ruth for me, just as she labeled him.

69

"Zalman the Cap," she called him, her voice ringing with contempt despite his brilliance, his good looks. But of her, he says only, "She's demonic, that one. A daredevil. There's nothing she wouldn't do, if you told her not to do it. But you're a little afraid of her, aren't you?"

I look at him, wondering how he read my mind.

"You shouldn't be," he comforts. "You're softer than she is, but you're just as smart in your own way. You ought to know that."

What I do know, though, is that Ruth is our real leader, the one who goads us by going too far, by taking too many chances herself. Danger is one of the few things in life she knows she can't control.

"There ain't no hope for the male-female relationship anyhow," she concedes to Victoria that night, after finally agreeing to admire the small diamond. "Us chicks are in really deep shit, if you ask me; we're the ones who take all the flak for everything while the guys get to have most of the fun. The only way out of the whole mess is for us to treat them as much like they treat us as we can get away with. Right?"

Virginity, circumspection, the things that make men "respect" you in 1961—these have no meaning at all to Ruth. She was fourteen when she seduced her male model on the dais of the empty figure-painting studio at the Art Students League, to which she had won one of her first scholarships. He was a slender black man whom she'd been admiring for weeks for his total unconcern while posing in a scrap of jockstrap; she was already probably aware of (1) his bisexuality, (2) his availability, and (3), his elusiveness, and none of it bothered her. She stripped. Piece by piece she removed her outfit, the proper trappings of a New York virgin in the 1950s; a white angora sweater over a white bra that sharpened her breasts into arrowheads, and a black velvet skirt so tight it was hard to walk. She was excited by the scent of turpentine, sharp and rarefied; by the dusty model's podium on which they writhed, surrounded by the fossils of still-lifes; by the reflected glitter of her own black vinyl eyes.

"You got such eyes," he breathed into her ear. Later he took her to Rienzi's, the Village coffee shop, and then let her go home alone. Where she was met by her stepfather, Louie, the man who finally had the goodness of heart, as everybody said, to marry her mother—and was soundly strapped by him twice, the first time for getting home so late, and the second time when he learned that she was with (not how with, just 'with') a boy he'd never met.

She never saw the artist's model again.

Ruth acts as if she has never heard of high school love in the 50s, never listened to Johnny Mathis or Joni James or Teresa Brewer singing about smoke getting in the eyes or ricochet romances, never removed a date's exploratory paw from her chest with a sharp demeaning grin and the standard, "Please, Harry. I'm just *not* that kind of girl."

Never gone to a prom or even cared about going to a prom. Which is true. She never has.

And despite my embarrassing high school connection with the highly conventional Edie Scheinblatt, and the fact that the real reason I didn't get to either my Junior or Senior proms is that nobody asked me, the truth is that in my heart of hearts, I too have never listened, never cared.

We are members of that anomalous group of the 50s, the oddballs. The misfits. We have never identified ourselves with Sandra Dee. We look lousy in pastels, especially in the kind of pastel prom dresses they made for girls in the 50s out of cheap tulle and satin that stood up all by themselves and were scratchy against the legs.

When we have grown up a little bit—when it is the 60s—we put on black turtleneck sweaters and talk about banning the bomb and view foreign movies, which we call 'films.' Some of us begin to paint or act or write Beat poetry.

We have been scarred by the perilous 40s, the war years,

during which we managed to get born, and even by the long-ago penurious 30s, of which our parents speak often, as oracle and warning. The next generation will either ignore us or hail us as precursors, because unlike any other members of our own generation we know for certain that the children's crusades of the 60s are coming, and we want to be ready for them.

At which time, like all human bridges, we also know that we will be too old.

Ruth has never needed a mentor like Zalman Finster to inspire her, to guide her to the right museums and books and theatres. She started going to museums alone when she was barely old enough to reach the subway turnstiles at the Sheridan Avenue Station. She's seen every new play and movie that's opened in New York in the past two years; she's read every book about art she could ever get her hands on. Great artists, she has read, have never been particularly given to self-restraint. Self-restraint is bad for art. Self-restraint is against art.

Already, Ruth's hand produces a line so deft and forthright that she has been able to enter school after school of art without needing to ask for a single penny of her mother's hard-earned income (which she realizes she wouldn't have gotten anyway). She has that sense of line, and she understands color, and there is something else in her art as well; a virulence, the same brilliant determination that makes her eyes bright—"Such wonderful eyes," gasped Cecil Loomis, the male model—and her jawbone very hard as she sets her mouth. It doesn't matter to her that the painters she has decided to idolize—Rembrandt, Masaccio, Matisse, and later, Kline, Pollock, Motherwell— are all men.

Modigliani and Burne-Jones were also men, but this didn't necessarily prevent them from being mediocre painters, in her opinion. And "mediocrity" is the most scathing epithet she knows. At twelve, she read *Lust for Life*; she isn't certain about Van Gogh (carefully and accurately pronounced "fon khokh"), but she knows for sure that he was never mediocre. About anything else on earth she doesn't give a shit. She states this fact abruptly.

"I do not give a shit."

She and Zalman contemplate one another across rooms, distanced by scorn and recognition. I'm fascinated by them both because in some essential way, they've both achieved something I want desperately—freedom—but they've managed to skip out on the loneliness.

True to her own philosophy, Ruth treats most of her lovers like call boys. She picks them up because of their looks, she uses their bodies, and she asks them to keep their mouths shut in public. Of course, I know there are others as well, men whom we've never met or heard about; men with bulging wallets who are the providers of her huge bright rings and tight skirts (for where else would she get them?), who probably help her pay the rent for her place in Paradise Alley. But there's nothing funny about the kind of need which sends her to them, and therefore it's against our rules to talk about them.

One afternoon, meeting Victoria and me for coffee at the college cafeteria, Ruth tells us that she's found a new friend, a gypsy clarinetist named Fred. She's obviously pleased with this conquest, and she watches us smugly for reactions.

"What do you mean, 'gypsy?'" Victoria scoffs. "You mean he's a real gypsy? I don't believe it."

You can tell she's jealous.

"Eff you," Ruth says casually. "He's real, all right. His band plays all that Middle Eastern kind of music in a nightclub, some real seedy little place in a basement, and you two can come and make the scene. You'll dig it. They even got a belly dancer."

For some reason we find this statement funny, and begin to laugh, as usual.

"It's a gas," Ruth says. "You gotta come."

Yes, we will, we say. We look forward to coming, we say. Especially to seeing the belly dancer. Ruth gives each of us

Fred's address and we step together out of the college cafeteria into the twilight, into the glittering city, in the heart of which we're all still young enough for hope and everything's a joke.

SIX

My electrical meat
chatters for
a wink of eternity
between dark cunt
and the grave.

     —Ed Sanders, 1961

"Jeez," says the voice. "It's a skoit."

Victoria and I stand patiently at the door, covering our mouths so our peals of laughter won't be heard inside the apartment. Where we might, God knows, maybe even embarrass Ruth, who's supposed to be waiting there for us with Fred the Gypsy and the members of his band.

Although Ruth is a hard one to embarrass, as a matter of fact.

But the constraint's too much for us, especially because we're both wasted on some first class weed I scored from Zalman. Looking at one another, we crumple slowly against the door, trying to avoid the floor of the hallway, which is filthy.

Victoria's stocking suddenly runs. She fusses over it, dabbing little bits of spit on it with her index finger to make it look darker and hopefully less obvious. I feel one of the huge, inadequate stitches in my too-long hem give way.

"God, I hate wearing skirts," I whisper. "What a mess we're going to be. I would have been so much happier in jeans." And thinking how funny it would have been if we'd shown up in jeans, we begin to laugh again. Mascara dribbles down our cheeks. We realize in our shared hysteria that we're disqualifying ourselves as objects of desire—objects of desire may laugh, but they do not fall to pieces outside the doors of potential lovers, proving themselves unfit to share in the adult world of tragedy, dilemma and fright.

From the other side of the door, the voice comes again.

"But I tink der's somebuddy *der*," it whines, an explanation so plaintive that we almost roll backwards down the stairs.

At last we compose ourselves sufficiently to knock again. But before she can raise a kid-gloved hand, Victoria is stopped by the harshness of another voice, raised in anger or annoyance.

"Oh shit, I know who it is," this voice exclaims from within, and the door swings wide. There we stand, smoothing our coats over our hips. Framed by the doorway, Ruth purses her lips and looks out at us with scorn.

"Hel-lo," she beckons. Obviously for someone else's benefit.

We do not really want to, but we enter.

The room is full of men. Young men, all of them dark-haired, but of different heights and sizes. Most of the men have olive skin, the kind of hair that seems to accumulate a sheen of grease all by itself, and large slanting noses. Which one of them is Fred, the gypsy clarinetist? Not one of the men in the room strikes me as being "cute," and Ruth disdains to introduce us to any of them, herding us with suspicious haste into a corner of the room.

"We're going out dancing," she declares, "as soon as your dates arrive."

"Our dates?" I wonder. "I didn't know we were even going to *have* dates."

"Some guys kind of asked to meet you. I thought you wouldn't mind." As ever, she is wearing a stunning tweed dress which is so tight around her large firm hips that she can hardly bend. After a few new men come in, she hands Victoria and me over to our "dates;" mine is a small, cream-skinned youth who at first sight makes absolutely no impression on me.

"Dancing?" I wonder.

The word "dancing"—except when I'm with Zalman—conjures only two pictures for me. One is of teenagers leaping around somebody's finished basement twirling one another to the strains of "Blue Suede Shoes;" the other is of supercool adults dressed in evening suits and cocktail dresses dispassionately doing the chacha in some glitzy night spot. Right now, neither of these fits.

"Dancing?" I say aloud.

We're taken to a Greek Orthodox church on 23rd Street, where about two hundred Armenians have come to dance. Probably because she was so impressed by Fred's nationality, Victoria's paired off with another real gypsy—this one, unfortunately, a short balding man with a large wen in the center of his head which he wipes a lot with a greying handkerchief.

"From Hungaria," he responds, when she politely asks him what kind of gypsy he is. After that, they don't exchange a word.

"But he's a *real* gypsy," Ruth whispers to me, across our table. "I thought that was what she *wanted*."

My date is an Armenian and so, it turns out, are most of the other men there.

Although Ruth keeps him away from us, I get a pretty good look at her Fred. He's tall and hulking with a big nose, not "cute" at all but nonetheless good-looking in an odd, skinny, swarthy kind of way, and he plays the clarinet pretty well. It's peculiar to see him with Ruth. She obviously thinks he's very handsome, but he's the one who said, *"Jeez, a skoit"* in answer to our knock, and I can't stop wondering how she can spend so much time with a man with whom she can't possibly have a conversation about anything important.

What do they do, for instance, when and if they ever get out of bed? When she takes him home to her studio in Paradise Alley, where she worked for two weeks scraping and polishing the floors until they gleamed like picked bone, does she show him her latest work, which she has impaled on the plain brick walls so she can decide what she really thinks of it, making up her mind whether she's going to destroy it or let it survive, be seen, even be framed? One of the paintings that she hasn't destroyed is very small, as small as a sheet of typing paper, its surface completely covered in graduated shades of buff, blending to tan and cream. Just at one edge up at the top of the canvas, which has been elaborately stretched and primed, is a slash of luminous, untampered-with blue. The name of the picture, printed deftly on the back of the canvas, is just that. "Blue." She built a tiny frame for it; she varnished it until it glowed like an enamel or a butterfly's wing. She painted it when she was only eighteen years old. And here she is at twenty-one, bedding a hulking troglodyte who calls women "skoits" and barely remembers her name when she isn't there.

"Ah, Fred's not so bad," she chuckles later, when I ask her about him. "The only hangup is, I've always got to be the one to phone him. I think he forgets who I am."

"Who's dis?" he always shouts into the phone when she calls.

"Ruth!" she always answers, never at all offended. "It's me, remember? Ruth!" Having to cover the receiver with her hand so he won't hear her laughing, as if being forgotten by him is a kind of joke.

"Oh, yair?" she hears him shouting at the other end. "Yair? Rute! Howahyuh?"

She wants to keep the matters of her life in separate compartments. Her work is her work, her friends her friends, her sex her sex. Why mix them up? Why suffer?

Fred goes to sit with the rest of the musicians, and the rest of us are left at a table where we sip bad drinks of ginger ale and Seagrams, and wait for the music to begin. My date is excruciatingly polite, maybe to make up for Fred's boorish behavior; maybe, I think, because he too wants to get Ruth into bed. The reputations of women fly through the gossip of these guys like brushfire, I can tell. I hear them whispering to each other and catch the smirks on their faces when they look at us. Before the evening has even begun, Victoria and I have obviously been judged guilty by association and are known as fair game. And I think suddenly how lucky I am to be with Zalman, for whom such judgments don't exist.

In this world of "good girls" and "bad girls," there's absolutely no hope of passing ourselves off as "good." I can see that by the sarcastic gleam in the Armenian's eyes as he hovers over us, taking our every order, bringing us drinks and ashtrays. Obviously, from the way he smiles and pretends to defer to me, he's sure that I, like Ruth, am "*that* kind of girl," and can all too easily be "had." And maybe he's right. I gave away my maidenhead without a struggle, for love I said but maybe, too, for revenge on my straitlaced father, on my own nondescript high school image and on my girlfriend Edie, so smug in her intactness. On all the Education Majors with their virgin pins. But even if I went to bed with this Armenian, who would be "having" whom, I wonder? Wouldn't Zalman even approve of my independence? "*We're free, Helene,*" he'd said that first night. And is it possible to "have" a human being who doesn't hold anything back, who doesn't even care?

As for Victoria, I can see her looking around, wrinkling her nose, wondering whether there's anyone here to add to her collection. She's wearing a high-waisted blue wool dress, her mother's rope of antique glass beads, her hair in a chignon. Since her experience with Patrick Parker, she's become a little more reserved, and now, despite her apparent availability, her date sits morosely over his drink and nobody else approaches. Her clothes are too expensive and too smart, her hair too elegantly "done." And in her eyes is too much caution, too little interest; it's obvious that she'd rather be taking a vacation from us right now, maybe off with her rich friends on Madison Avenue.

"I'm going to get a cab," she says after a while, clenching lips etched in pale rose lipstick. The Hungarian gypsy half rises drunkenly and then collapses back into his seat, ignoring her. I know that she wants me to go with her, but by then I've fallen in love with the music and cannot leave.

At dawn we're still dancing. We've left the drafty church and the lines of undulating Armenians, hundreds of them, all putting their feet into the circle at the same time, all turning together, joined at the waist or the shoulder by a single stem of arms, like a vast, rootless vine twining around the floors and windows of the church, curling around the music like an overgrowth of green. We've left the church and are dancing somewhere else only because the Armenians, most of them, finally staggered home around two a.m., and the church ball-room finally emptied and closed.

The rest of us, the musicians and their women and one or two stragglers like me who have been captured and ultimately hooked by the insinuating, plangent sounds, the drone of bazoukia and clarinet and flute, have flocked in a noisy drove to an after-hours nightclub in the West Village which is so tiny we can barely squeeze in to sit down at the tables. And yet we actually manage to jam ourselves into the aisles between the chairs and go on dancing. As far as I'm concerned, movement has become a necessity; like the girl in the story of the Red Shoes, having danced all Saturday night, I would dance all day over Sunday's pavements if I were able, except if I left this club I wouldn't be able to hear the music.

And in fact it's already Sunday; I can hear the bells of the Italian churches in the Village, ringing for matins through the sleeping city air.

The suave Armenian is still beside me, still patient and attentive. He has never raised his voice, even to be heard above the music; he barely speaks to me. I doubt that he even knows my name, and yet here he is beside me. If there's anything I can possibly want, anything to drink or eat, another pack of cigarettes with which to cut my wind and bring on cancer, anything, he's at my elbow with it in a minute. His devotion is utterly unselfish, utterly passive, utterly dedicated. He seems to want nothing for himself except what is going to please me, make me happy.

He reminds me of a snake.

Finally he says, "Aren't you beginning to get tired?"

"Oh, no," I say. "I'm used to this. I love to stay up all night. I always stay up all night, either studying or playing. It doesn't matter if I get any sleep at all."

He smiles, a remote and unself-conscious smile, especially when I say "studying or playing." He doesn't move. I go on dancing. But fifteen minutes later we're standing out on Seventh Avenue looking at the sky, because the music has finally come to an end. The bazoukia player needed a cigarette; Fred the clarinetist suddenly remembered Ruth.

"Pay up!" the waitress is shouting; a tough, stringy, American blonde wearing a tiny shell top with spaghetti straps, the veins and hollows of her shoulders flex as she scoops up empty glasses and reaches out for cash. What's left of the crowd has spilled out onto the sidewalk as if panicked, everyone rushing to the corner for a cab like people running from a fire.

Only I walk slowly, looking at the trees above the club, and the low, old-fashioned buildings that line King Street, bright pink brick under white facades.

The sky has turned that delicate blue which comes in New York just before nightfall and then, in perfect symmetry, just when night is ending. It's the precise color of the streak at the top of Ruth's painting, a blue so intense that it seems to be painted over silver paper. And there are the trees on the avenue, leaves lit by the streetlamps which turn them an unearthly green against this sky, the illuminated green of the trees in a stage set. And there's my favorite New York smell, that faint odor of the ocean and the boats, that faint premonition of the sea, and there's the sound of foghorns in case you've forgotten that this is a riverside city, a great port city, tied through time to all the great cities whose names and smells I think I know.

I can imagine Zalman's voice ringing gently in my ears. "Isn't it fantastic?" he'd be saying of this street, this early dawn, this scene. But he isn't here, and my Armenian "date" insinuates himself into position beside me once again, because he's wasted the entire night waiting around for me and he's probably made up his mind that he's not going home alone.

His name is Alex.

He doesn't even ask if I want to come with him. He simply gets into a cab with me and assumes I will, giving the cabdriver his own address, somewhere on Central Park West, only a few blocks from Victoria's. Speeding beside him up the lamplit emptiness of Sixth Avenue in the greying dawn I'm forced to forget the music and begin my usual end-of-the-evening routine. *Sorry, I'm just not ready,* I think, remembering Motilal.

"Sorry. I want to go home." I feel around in my bag for a final cigarette.

"Sure." Alex lights it for me.

"West Eighty-Ninth," I direct the cabbie. "Between Columbus and Amsterdam." My voice sounds calm and strong in my own ears. As I so often have before, I rehearse the movements of my goodnight choreography, effective for getting rid of even the most persistent courtier. *One:* insist on being taken back to my own apartment; *Two:* allow him to climb optimistically behind me up the stairs; *Three:* insert the key in the lock; *Four:* wheel around while mouthing the formula "thank you goodnight I had a lovely time;" *Five:* step inside swiftly; *Six:* slam the door.

But something happens to me as I settle down beside Alex in the cab, creaking up the avenue. I remember how Ruth finally took off with Fred, giving me a dense, superior glance as they left together. I remember Victoria and her funny conquests: Patrick Parker, abject in Elaine's fancy living room, even Mr. Wo behind the wheel of his car. And suddenly I wonder if I'm being challenged in some way; if Ruth and Victoria aren't daring me to have as good a time as they've managed to have, to have an affair without involvement, complication, anguish. To become aggressor instead of victim. Predator instead of prey.

Tonight there's something about the music and the night that allows me to believe that I'm invulnerable. That I can sleep with this man without caring, or wanting him for more than one night. That I can be like Ruth. That I can even be like Zalman and love more than one person at a time. Freedom without loneliness.

"I need cigarettes," I announce, suddenly pleased with myself. I like my own smell of stale tobacco and worn-out perfume; I like the sound of my nylons swooshing against one another as I cross my legs. I'm excited by being desired, if only for a moment, by someone new.

"Sure. Stop the cab. I know this corner." Alex hasn't budged from his side of the passenger seat, even to take my hand, but now he jumps out and buys me a pack of cigarettes at the cigar store at 49th and Broadway, which I had passed with Zalman only a few weeks before, at the same hour of the morning.

"I've changed my mind." I stare at him when he returns.

"Yes?" he asks, without surprise.

"Your place."

I lean back against the seat.

His apartment turns out to be in a surprisingly fancy building, across the street from the park, like Victoria's. We say
nothing to one another in the elevator. We barely touch.

The apartment is large and well-furnished and he has
equipment for every different kind of sport—tennis, racquet-
ball, weight-lifting—just lying around.

"What do you do?" I look at it all as he pours me a drink.

"Nothing much." The drink is Haig & Haig scotch from out
of a clear pinch bottle, the color of amber and as odorous and
sweet as perfume. "I enjoy myself, mostly." He clinks ice
cubes into a cut crystal glass and looks at me over the rim. He
hadn't seemed very impressive when I first met him at Fred's
apartment or in the church and cafe, but now I realize suddenly
that Alex, in his unassuming way, is a playboy.

"My father owns a chain of stores. You know. Bargain
stores, they're called. He sells a little bit of everything. I
manage one over on Upper Broadway. It's a living, I suppose,
and I don't have to be there that often."

I nod briefly, staring into his refrigerator as he hunts for an
opened bottle of club soda. If the contents of its shelves are any
indication of character, his intense need to keep fit is the result
of a passion for Greek pastries, feta cheese and a variety of
olives.

"You do want to go to bed with me, don't you?" Alex the
Playboy says.

We've been in his apartment long enough for me to get used
to this new idea of him. He doesn't say it pleadingly, or even
like a man asking a question. He says it with a smile, with
certainty, as another man might bestow a first kiss. As openers.
As a maneuver.

"Sure. Okay."

"You don't still want me to take you home?" (Not that he means this).

"Of course not."

"I'll give you a good time," he promises.

"I'm sure you will."

He pushes me gently toward the bedroom and removes his clothes. So far he has barely touched me. When I undress he looks me over. I expect him to be disappointed, but he reaches for me eagerly, obviously making the best of what he's got.

As for me, I've been trying to find something funny about this situation to share with the others later, but coming up empty. The only part of it that's even mildly amusing is the way I manage to get all my clothes off with my eyes closed. It's hard to unbuckle my shoes and my garter belt without looking at them, and almost impossible to reach my back zipper, but it makes it easier for me not to have to look at Alex.

"You don't even really like me, do you?" I demand suddenly, from under his sheets, which are remarkably peach colored and made of satin. Showgirls have lain between them. "Models," trying to make it either in the fashion world or in the marriage market. I can feel the ghosts of their pink-and-gold perfection like the smell of old smoke.

"Do you want me to like you?" he asks, putting his arms around me finally, in his bedroom decorated with fencing epees and tennis racquets. With satin sheets.

"How should I know? I don't even know if I like you very much myself."

"Then what are you doing here?" His eyelids have grown heavy. I wonder if I'm boring him to death.

"Because it's my right to do what I want to do. Isn't it my right? What do you think?"

"Of course. You should do everything you really want. We should all do everything we really want." His eyes are a little less sleepy as he searches my face. "I mean, if it's not hurting anybody. It's not hurting anybody, is it?"

"Maybe," I mutter, between my teeth. He pretends not to hear.

"The rest of it is just old-fashioned morality. You don't want to be old fashioned, do you? To live like some nun?"

"I'm not," I grit my teeth, "living like a nun."

"I know. Your cousin told me all about you," he murmurs, smiling. "She said you were cool, you knew the score. That's why I wanted to meet you."

"Ruth said that?"

"Your name is Helene, right?"

"Are you sure that's what she said?"

Instead of going on with this conversation, Alex starts sucking my neck. "She didn't tell me how good you look," he whispers in my ear.

I kiss him back, trying to feel appropriately flattered. His skin is very thick and very soft, as if he's rubbed himself all over with lanolin, and he handles me with expertise, putting his head between my legs and going at it as if I were an especially tasty piece of feta. It might be pleasant, except that, once I'm beside him in his playboy bed, I know too late that I'm not going to find what I want; not there—and that this is the way it's always going to be for me, no matter how much I want to be like Zalman or like Ruth.

No matter how much I thought I wanted freedom without loneliness, love without complication.

The life of the body, untrammeled and pure. *It doesn't mean this isn't love.*

Now, pinned under an efficiently churning Alex, I burn for Zalman. I long for his huge blue eyes and for his soft voice, instructing or praising me, for his mouth so open to mine that I feel melted in his heat. For the nights we spend together, first riding across my bedroom on my rolling cot, then walking miles through the city, a city which no one else has been able to give me so perfectly. An illuminated city where I have never been before, and which I know that no one will ever give me again, no matter how long I live.

I burrow as if for shelter against Alex's thick, cream-colored skin. But Alex won't put out this fire for me, or give me any shelter from it. There's nowhere to go with him. I orgasm and feel rested and soft, but after we finish sex, there's nothing to talk about. There's nothing to do but sleep.

Exhausted, I slink out of his too-soft bed with its luscious, silky sheets, with his lanolined skin bumping against mine in sleepy trust, as if we were really lovers and were going to wake up in the morning and look into one another's eyes and be happy.

"Mm," he responds vaguely. "Shut out the light, for God's sake."

I go into the other room and hunt through his refrigerator until I find some more ice and another bottle of Schweppes. I add the amber scotch, and drinking, figure it's really not worth staying, trying to sleep in the unfamiliar bed, looking forward to waking up together in the middle of the day, with a stiff, difficult breakfast to be gotten down. Which is the way it happens, as a matter of fact. Lots of feta and olives chewed through sticky smiles.

Only the threat of the empty, dangerous city has kept me in the apartment.

Is this what Ruth goes through all the time? I wonder, getting myself home the following afternoon. Sleeping with men who don't really know her, who don't really care to know her? Yawning and snoring and bumping her side against strangers?

The Broadway bus belches and lurches on the way up from his neighborhood to mine, and I feel unwashed, smelly, a rank taste in my mouth.

"Cab fare, darling?" he offered me as I left, making me think once again of showgirls, tall blondes with perfect breasts who expect no less than whatever he can give them. What was he doing with me, who shook my head of tangled curls and muttered, "Never mind, man, I'll grab a bus," clutching my shabby pocketbook in unmanicured hands?

And now I sigh at my own recklessness, whether with envy for the likes of my cousin and Zalman, or with fear—for Ruth, for Victoria, for all three of us—I myself, at that moment, find it impossible to tell.

SEVEN

I sit in Lees. At 11:40 pm with
Jimmy the pusher. He teaches me
JuJu.
                    —*John Wieners, 1958*

Zalman's voice at the door.

"Hey, Helene, I've got something special for you! Let us in, hurry!"

Us? I think. And in fact, there he is with another person, someone leaning against his shoulder as I stare at them through the distortion of my fisheye peephole. Two funhouse-mirror figures, marooned in the filthy tunnel of my apartment build-ing hall. There's a young man leaning heavily on Zalman's shoulder, clothes disordered, hair falling in his eyes. It would be a scene of disaster if both men weren't smiling.

So, I think. My apartment has become one of his homes. One of the places at which he stops when he wanders around the city. One of the places to which he brings his friends. Part of his life.

I let them in, feeling both joyful and afraid.

"This is Darryl," he says, introducing the thin young man beside him, casually offhand as they stagger into the room. "And this," he lifts my hand in his, just briefly but with an expression of pride, "is Helene."

Their eyes meet. Am I imagining that their expression is of conspiracy? They grin at one another. I know I'm being shown off as the new "old lady," to be approved and admired. But is there anything more? Some rite of possession which I'm supposed to undergo? Some other reason that Zalman brought this young man here, and is holding me out before him so he can look me over?

He *is* looking me over, and it seems to me that there's a peculiar hunger in his eyes. Suddenly I'm teased by grim scenarios, the products of my own imagination. What's Zalman cooking up? I wonder. Into what schemes, what combinations, is he manipulating me? Or am I just getting paranoid because of the weed?

"There are certain things I just won't do. . ." I can hear my own sad voice squeaking as I sink between them, between Zalman and the friend he has brought with him. Darryl. *"No, I won't . . ."*

But once we finish a few joints, all Zalman does is to scrounge and forage in my kitchen.

"I'm starving," he complains. As usual, there's nothing to eat in my apartment. I think of the contrasting opulence of Alex's refrigerator; too bad I can't take Zalman there.

"Why don't you ever have any food?" He tries to appease his appetite by gnawing half a piece of stale sour rye bread and gulping the last of my grapefruit juice.

"I don't believe in food."

He stares at me skeptically.

"No, listen, it's true. I've escaped from food. All my mother ever does since she married my father is shop and cook and fuss over food, and my father practically kills himself so he can afford all fresh fruits and vegetables and porterhouse steaks once a week and lox and whitefish every Sunday. Between the two of them and their food they drive me crazy."

"But you're never going to be like them. Why do you worry so much?" He hugs me, and I curve into his side as into a familiar safety. Suddenly I feel guilty that in my house there is no feta, there are no olives, there are no flasks of amber whiskey. I wish I could offer Zalman and Darryl more than some dead white wine, an onion . . . But in the few years I've been in school and living on my own, I've survived on hamburgers and Twinkies from the school cafeteria, so why should I have any food?

The "something special" Zalman's got for me is a brand new pill called Dexamil, a kind of breakthrough, he says, because it stimulates like Dexedrine and calms like Miltown at the same time. The little granules in the spansules are pale green and white, making me feel calm and energized just by looking at them.

"These should keep you awake without making you jumpy," he assures me. "Think of it. You can stay up all night and still go to work in the morning feeling fantastic."

I swallow one immediately to try it out, daring myself not to feel jumpy. He puts a little plastic container of them in my medicine cabinet.

"A present," he says. We smile at one another.

Meanwhile Darryl has carefully laid himself down on the floor beside my bed. His face is white as tile. His eyes are closed, and I think I can see the pupils moving, blue under the translucent blush of the lids.

"What's the matter with him? Is he sick?"

Darryl is as pale and sweetfaced as a cherub or a male nymph. He has unusually long hair, which floats around his head as if he were drowning. He raises one round arm as if to salute me.

"I nod out a lot," he explains simply, and lets his arm flop back to the floor with a thump. "Don't let it bother you."

"The neighbors," I think. My nights with Zalman, infrequent as they are, are always a difficulty because I'm aware that as Zalman and I come and go and do what we have to do, around us in the building my neighbors are all having their deep sweet sleep disturbed by our thunderous footsteps or by the "sounds" we like to play. What a penance, to be awakened by John Coltrane's "Mating Call," or by Betty Carter telling the world how much she likes her favorite things. Or, worse still, by the rolling of my cot across the floor as we make love, which has compelled me to put little ruglike cushions under all four wheels, which do not help a bit.

Now here is this boy who drops his arm with the kind of thump a basketball makes when it hits the ground.

"Can you please be a little more quiet?" I remonstrate, looking at him sharply. "People are sleeping."

"Don't worry about it," Darryl says again, his eyes barely open. "I just nod out a lot." And he flops into noisy sleep.

"Now, Darryl, what are you doing? Do you want to just fall out like this? You're letting it control you." Zalman bends over the boy and his voice is soft. Fleetingly I remember the very young woman in the dark room, making a soup out of her red skirt.

"You can fight it, you know. You can sit up now, you can come out of it now," Zalman murmurs, and the boy stirs, rises a little, wipes his eyes, falls back. Into Zalman's arms.

The boy is probably younger than I am. His chestnut hair falls over his face. The veins in his arms curl, blue, seeming to strain against the skin.

Zalman kneels beside him. "Darryl?" he calls, leaning against his ear. "Darryl?"

"But I *always* nod out," the boy repeats, out of his stupor. He opens his eyes and grins at us, self-abasing. "I just always do."

"You don't have to." Zalman raises Darryl on a bundle of pillows I fix behind his head, and the boy's eyes close almost at once. "You can come out of it. Listen to me. Do you want to be a slave to this thing? Do you want to be at its mercy? Come out of it. You can just come out of it."

I watch in confusion. Now Darryl's eyes have opened again. Staring upwards, the violet of each iris is profound. The pupils have almost vanished. *Something's the matter with him*, I think. *Something's really wrong.*

"You're going to be all right," Zalman whispers.

And as if a door has opened, I understand. I know why Zalman's brought this boy here, in the middle of the night. He is sick; there is something wrong with him, and Zalman wants to fix it. Like a doctor, I realize, remembering. Like a doctor of the soul.

Now the bursting of color in the park seems very clear to me. Our careful tiptoeing through museums, his lists of magical books, offered and discussed. His expressions of love and admiration; his wisdom about films and "sounds." The heat of his body. Even the brand new bottle of pills in my medicine cabinet. He gives me what I want, in return for—what? For his whispered instructions in my bed at dawn? For my eyes turned on him with the wonder of a disciple's? Or will there be something else, later, when I'll be even less able to refuse?

And what did he get from the young woman with the red skirt? And what will he get from Darryl?

"I can't breathe," says the boy.

I open a window.

"Darryl," Zalman whispers. "Listen to me. You can. You can do anything. Lie still. You can."

They clutch one another, oblivious to me. The boy's face is white and stark with tears.

"Helene will make us coffee," Zalman says. "Helene, make coffee."

I don't move.

"I can't breathe," the boy gasps again, struggling.

"But you have to know it's nothing," Zalman whispers. "You have to know that it's all nothing. You're in control of everything, your breathing, your pulse. Close your eyes. Now breathe. . ."

He holds Darryl upright against the wall. Some dynamic is taking place around me. I whiff the sulphur smell of life. I'm very frightened, but I feel oddly exhilarated at the same time.

"I don't have any coffee."

They don't hear me.

Darryl struggles and nods. His skin, pale at first, seems in the crude light of my bedroom study-lamp to turn almost blue.

"I've got tea," I say. I go into the kitchen and come back with some at last, sweet and steaming in a broken cup.

With a great effort of will Darryl pulls himself into a sitting position and, leaning against the wall beside my bed, takes a tentative sip.

"Helene, come to bed," says Zalman.

Trembling with paranoia, do I really see or do I only imagine that the two men make a sign between them, that they nod and smile in my direction? I refuse to take off my clothes, even though Darryl's hands are shaking so violently he can barely hold the cup, even though within a few minutes he has gotten to his feet and begins to wobble toward the other room. Still sick and shaken, he walks with a plummeting roll which I imagine must sound like not-so-distant thunder to the man downstairs, a delicately-built transvestite who works as a plasterer during the daytime, but who sprouts up wildly in the evenings, floating down the tenement stairs decked in satin ballgowns and elaborate wigs and surrounded by a retinue of gorgeous boyfriends, all dressed to the nines.

"What do you *do* up there all the time to make so much noise at night?" he asks me every time we meet in front of the building mailbox, or in the supermarket. "I mean, I'd come up the stairs to find out, but I'm too *embarrassed*. After all, how do I know what you're *doing*?"

"Probably a whole lot less than *you*," I finally snap, goaded, after which he never speaks to me again, but follows me with a silent, resentful stare. And I wonder briefly what he would have to be embarrassed about, when it's I who have to keep from howling at the sight of his buddies tripping over their four-inch stiletto heels, with nylons stretched and running over their burly calves.

Still, it's too late for me to ask Darryl to at least take off his shoes. I content myself with making sure that he doesn't crash into the wall, but continues down the corridor into the other room.

"Nice pad," he mumbles, trying to sound offhand, like a relative come for a visit, inspecting my place for the first time. I'm glad to learn that he likes my decor, however, which is a desperate attempt at order executed in dark brown and olive green, colors I thought might look suitably sophisticated and not show dirt at the same time. On one wall, an artist friend of mine has rendered a copy of the cave paintings of the Kalahari desert, willowy stick figures leaping across the plaster and brandishing assegais at fleeing animals, a masterpiece I deemed suitable for the home of a budding archaeologist. I pray that all the shields and spears don't terrify Darryl, but when I follow him into the room I find that he's simply keeled over onto my lumpy brown sofa, and, safe from the needling eyes of Zalman, gone back to sleep.

"What are you doing?" calls Zalman, from my bedroom. "Come to bed!"

We go to bed. Nothing happens. He presses against me, but even now, with Darryl out of the room, I can't respond. When he touches me I stop him. However, he doesn't seem to mind. He stops easily—too easily, I think. Smiling, he too falls asleep at once, maybe even grateful for the respite. Fully dressed, I lie very still with the covers pulled up to my chin.

Later, I think I hear the boy moving around the other room. I can imagine him going through my meager possessions, helping himself to my treasure horde of broken ashtrays, scratched records, kicked furniture. Something about him— his beautiful face, his mysterious ailment, his closeness to Zalman—makes his presence sinister.

Zalman sleeps. I stay awake beside him. In the middle of the morning, numbed by lack of sleep and the Dexamil, I get up. Rising from bed very quietly, not waking Zalman, I go into the front room to check on the boy.

Who lies where I left him, on the brown-covered cot, my "sofa."

His eyes are wide open. His body is completely still. I can feel its chill coming at me across the room.

"Zalman!" I scream. "He's dead!"

Nobody answers. Zalman goes on sleeping. The boy blinks and turns over.

"Hi," I say.

He looks up. His expression is not friendly.

"Hand me my pants," he commands, after a moment. "Don't get uptight, lady. Ain't you never seen a cat naked before? I don't want to mess with you. I just gotta turn on."

Shaky, I hand him his pants.

"You don't care if I do it here, right?" He barely looks at me, rummaging through his pants pockets. His hair spilling over his rounded white shoulders, he looks like an angel who has fallen upon hard times. Despite myself, I stare.

"Why should I?"

He shrugs. "It's your house."

"Actually," I say, "You could turn me on too, if you wanted. I could use a few drags. I never got to sleep."

Instantly his eyes harden. "There ain't enough," he snarls.

We stare at each other.

"My God," I say. "How much can one person smoke, anyway?"

Naive me. He doesn't smoke. As if in answer to my question, he fishes out of his pocket an old eye-dropper, a needle and a spoon. He wraps his arm with a catheter tube till the veins stand out and then he squeezes the boiled up powder into the eyedropper and does all the rest of the unsightly ritual. It seems not to matter at all to him that I'm standing there, watching him. When the needle hits his vein the blood churns up into the dropper like the evidence of some great internal life. It's almost blue. When it subsides, a residue of maroon bubbles remains in the dropper. He sits for a while, holding his arm straight out before himself like a piece of statuary. He looks solemn, almost penitent, with his long hair hanging against his cheeks. In one hand he holds the other hand. His arm is braced across his knees.

Shaky, I go back in to Zalman and try to rest.

"But it can kill you," I say.

My argument sounds thin, unconvincing, even to myself.

Zalman and I are alone; we've gone together to the White Horse Tavern, where, emulating Dylan Thomas and trying to ignore all the NYU boys who have turned it into their special hangout since the 50s, we order huge beakers of Black'n'Tan and face one another across a small table.

I keep remembering the residue of blood in the eyedropper. I keep seeing the way it surged over the edge of the dropper and onto Darryl's arm, like a sign of the life which surged within him, ready to spill over at a moment's notice.

"He could have *died*. Right there in my apartment. I think you have to be crazy to risk that. And it has to *hurt*. It has to. There were sores on his skin, and you should have seen the blood . . ."

But I know that the blood isn't what disturbs me. What really disturbs me is that I have failed even to convince myself. What really disturbs me is that I have been fascinated, even attracted, by what I saw. And I know it. My argument, my

shock, my conventional primness—none of them are true.
They do not go deep.

"I'm never going to get involved with drugs," I said, and
now I've begun to smoke almost every night, just a single joint
to relax with when I get home, I tell myself. I get wasted with
my friends, am careful to replenish my little stash of weed,
think suddenly with a thrill of joy about the bottle of green-and-
white spansules Zalman deposited in my bathroom. What
would prevent me from going further? What if he offered
heroin one night, what if he said again, *"You need this, Helene.
It will change you."*

But he hasn't, I tell myself. He hasn't. And I realize
suddenly just how much control I've given up to him.

"Didn't you know what was happening?" He looks at me
now with his huge eyes, half amused and half defiant over his
Black'n'Tan. "Even before I brought Darryl? You knew. You
must have known." He smiles.

I remember the packages he passed the ghostly men the first
day we spent together, the time he got beaten in the junky's
park. And I think, looking back at him across the table, 'Yes.
He's right. I did know.'

I splash my drink and some of the bubbles go up my nose.
Acrid. What superior highs have I been missing?

"It's an act," he says, "all this being shocked."

I consider leaving. He puts out his hand and takes mine.

"I'm afraid," I say.

"Why?"

"Because it's dangerous." But not because of the blood, I
think. Not because of the fear of death or pain. *Control,* I
realize, queasy suddenly. He's the one in control here. Not me.

What will he want from me later? I'd wondered the night
before. *When I'm even less able to refuse him? Less in control?*

He smiles at me and changes the subject. "Do you know
what Burroughs said about death?"

I shake my head.

"That it's the greatest high of all."

"How could he possibly know that?"

He looks at me. "He shot his wife. Burroughs did. Shot her in the head. He said it was an accident. They were playing William Tell and he was shooting an apple off her head. He was tried for shooting her and acquitted."

"But *he* didn't die. *He* was alive. So how could he know what death is?"

"Certain kinds of living," Zalman says after a while. "Certain kinds of living are worse than death. There are plenty of people who don't have a clue that dying would be better than the way they live. There are people like that; people who don't know, and who just don't give a shit."

I hear a voice say, "I do not give a shit," and remember my cousin Ruth. But it can't be true, can it, that Ruth doesn't care about her life? If it were, how could she make such remarkable paintings, be so smart, even arm and guard herself so carefully against attack? And would she, I wonder, relinquish control of her life as easily as I have done?

I do not give a shit.

I narrow my eyes at the college boys, rowdy and stupid even this early in the evening. What are they doing here, anyway, all these sons of contractors and dentists from Long Island and New Jersey? It's summer; there isn't any school semester to escape from, and yet the bar is full of them, all jostling one another and shouting and swilling beer, testing their voices and their ability to argue and their sexual attractiveness, all obviously wanting to live lives spiced with a little trouble just at the beginning.

And then I look at Zalman, sitting across from me at the table, and feel a thrill of pride that I'm with him. He's so different from them all, so obviously cut from another cloth. With his chiselled features and his beautiful eyes, he's clearly someone special, someone whose life is meaningful, serious. Small wonder that I've trusted him with so much. And after all, is it really so much? Haven't my parents always tried to control me, too, to make my choices for me? If they were here, it would be these college boys they'd be pushing at me. I can almost hear their voices: *Why not go out with someone nice, someone your own age, what's the problem? You say his father's a dentist, so what's wrong? It's a nice profession.* They would hate Zalman on sight; they'd hate the dog-eared copies of Joyce's *Pomes Penyeach* and Beckett's *Malone Dies* laid out before him on the tabletop; they'd hate his little cap and his chiselled face, his turtleneck and his eloquence.

And what he says. I can imagine how they'd feel about his sermons on drugs and freedom, on human potential and beauty.

"There's only one thing that kills," he goes on now. His eyes are unusually cold and still. He doesn't look at me. "Only one thing. The rest are all excuses. The rest are what we do to pretend that the real killer isn't there."

"What real killer? What are you talking about?"

"Ordinary life." Grimacing, he turns to me and puts his beaker between us on the table. It's still almost full: I can tell that he doesn't really like Black'n'Tans. "That's what smothers everything. Creativity. Joy. Aliveness. That's the only thing that kills."

"Ordinary life? I don't know what you're talking about."

"Yes," he says. "You do."

And of course, I do. I know exactly what he's talking about.

"Even my father," he says suddenly. "I would look into his eyes and see emptiness. I used to stay up nights sweating over that. Emptiness? But he was the one man in the world who knew everything, I thought. The greatest scholar of Talmud. The greatest judge and teacher. His students came from all over Europe to be with him, but the only real thing I ever knew about him was that he loved my mother. Even now, as a very old man, he loves her. For the rest of it—by the time I was fifteen years old I began to suspect he was lying about himself. That he, too, had been killed by ordinary life, and when he pretended he wasn't, he was lying." He looks down at the two books before him on the table. Joyce and Beckett. He had told me once that Joyce's daughter had become schizophrenic, and Beckett had been in love with her. Did they know about aliveness, or were they, too, lying?

"Think about your own life," he's saying now. "Think about long hours at a job you hate, nights spent cramming for exams, misunderstandings with your friends, trouble with your family. Is that what you told me you called 'real life?' Is that what makes you go on?"

"But there's always the hope that it can be different." I feel as if I'm pleading. "There's always the possibility that even ordinary life can be splendid, isn't there?"

"Maybe." He's very quiet now in the boiling, noisy bar. Coiled but smiling, like an animal about to spring. "Maybe. But think of how it feels when we're together. When we get high. Like a light coming on. And isn't that more real than what you go through, all day, every day? All the boredom, all the greed, the fear, the panicky littleness? Sure, maybe it can be different. But I have made it different, Helene. I have made it different *this way*. And who knows if there is any other way, Helene? Who knows? How can anybody tell?"

I look at him. *So let me try some,* desire makes me want to say. *Give me heroin to try, next time.* And I will give up all control, I think, and be free of my life at last.

Only I say nothing. Fear keeps me silent. And he must know, because he, too, says nothing more about it. But the question lies between us, like the bright coins and crumpled bills he has thrown down on the table, paying for the untouched Black'n'Tans.

Where we go next is to a party in someone's huge Upper West Side apartment. Eight p.m. on a summer night. Music playing. The sun still out. "I'm meeting Flower there," he says softly in the cab on the way uptown. His eyes are on me, and he probably notices the way my face falls when he mentions Flower, because he adds, his voice as gentle as some other man's touch might be, "She'll be glad to see you, Helene. She's been wondering where you were."

And Flower's eyes do light up when we come into the room. "Oh Helene!" she exclaims, smiling. "It's been so long since you've been around!" She speaks without a trace of jealousy or malice, offering me her own lit joint. She has come directly from the uptown restaurant where she drudges every day as a full-time waitress; maybe it's from her he gets his money—I've never asked.

There's a Peruvian band at the party, led by a tall, hook-nosed fellow with a reed flute. People dancing. I stare at them, awkward and envious.

"So?" Zalman takes me by the hand. "Why aren't you dancing, Helene?"

I'm about to say, "Because nobody's asked me yet," when Flower, in response to him, begins to dance alone, riding sensuously into the music.

"I love to dance," she says lightly, meeting my envious eyes. Her voice is soft, with just the slightest hint of the suburbs in the way she slurs her words. "I never danced before I met Zalman, but he got me to do it. Crazy."

She's both awkward and graceful, in her rough jeans and her thick-soled waitress shoes. Her dark hair ripples down her back. Her movements are sometimes heavy and solid, and then, as if in some way her body is slowly learning to transcend its own boundaries, she leaps into a position of sinuous grace and ease.

But more than anything, I feel her need to please him.

Is this the stuff they call true love? I wonder. Or just self-denial, a kind of destructive force which will end up killing her? Whatever it is, it must be stronger than what I feel for him, I think, watching her. She lives with him; she has no other life. And she knows about Zelda and about me, and doesn't mind, as I am minding her, now. Why not, I wonder?

My questions root me to the spot.

"Come on, Helene," Zalman says seductively. The sound of my name on his lips makes my knees go soft. "Why don't you dance like Flower? Isn't she fantastic?"

"She really is," I say, feeling confusion. Feeling envy, desire, even disgust. "She really is."

"So? What's the problem?" He begins to move. Slowly, I begin to follow.

His hips waggle back and forth. He raises his hands just to shoulder height. A Chassidic Talmudist doing the boogaloo, his mouth a little open, a smoking roach between his fingers, his eyes are wide, blue, and filled with secret laughter, as his body sways back and forth like that of a charmed cobra. Back and forth.

After a while he and I encircle Flower. She lets us do it; she draws herself between us, watching us both and smiling. Her face, as usual, is bright and placid, despite the wildness of the music. I shiver a little, approaching her. Her willingness to go on dancing without him, or with me, or to let me join them, to dance with the two of us, together, tells me something about her that I don't really want to know.

That there are great lengths to which some women will go in order to be permitted to love whom they choose. And that Flora will go them all.

Soon he foists me off on some fellow who looks like a goat, and he dances her out of the room.

EIGHT

With the first cool days of autumn, my heart lifts.

The school semester begins and I start out, as always, with a sense of renewed faith in my studies. I take long frenzied nights to research my papers, cataloguing bones for a course in osteology, dissecting rats for one of my professors, a mad-eyed Swiss who's been conducting hundreds of unnecessary experiments in genetics. I stay awake for days on nothing but the Dexamil Zalman gave me and lots of black coffee. I don't eat at all for a week and eat too much the week after that, so that finally, bloated, pale and sickly as I've been every semester since I started college, I drag myself down to the Cedar Tavern to find him and score some more Dex.

This time, apologetic but firm, he makes me pay.

It isn't cheap to keep my energies expanded, I realize as I hand over the last of my grocery money, but what other sources of relief are available to me? What have I got besides making love with Zalman or getting high with Victoria and Ruth, bright punctuations in a cold twilight existence, most of which is spent poring over books or working? Nothing much, I decide, and measure out my energy in spansules.

Green and white, calm and alert. Stop and go.

As for archaeology, it's never occurred to me to study anything else, not since I was ten years old and read my first books about Crete and the Minoans to discover that the cities of the past were still alive. It was my father who had brought me those first books, who came home with them from the Bronx Public Library, which my mother also visited, emerging with armloads of novels. My mother was addicted to modern novels, maybe to relive her interesting youth—she often said she knew the authors from her days in Greenwich Village as a young woman, and made a point of telling me their particular weaknesses or neuroses.

But it was my father who was in love with archaeology.

"The people of yesterday," he'd nod his thick-jawed head over one of the broad, glossy picture-books he'd borrowed, presumably for his daughters' sake but just as much for his own. "They got the lessons to teach us. Think about the ancient Jews, Helly. Even the Greeks, and them Egyptians. Think about the things they did—the Dead Sea Scrolls, for God sakes. The pyramids! The rise and fall of their societies. Then it all looks pretty insignificant, what's been happening to you and me. It all looks like so much dust."

A working man who'd never had the opportunity to get an education of his own, he instilled in me a passion for learning that nothing else has ever quenched.

"You could get a Ph.D.," he told me once, when I was only ten years old. "You got the brains for it, kiddo. Believe me. You could be *Doctor* Elphrick. The first one in the family."

He beamed with pride, as if the piece of sheepskin were already in my hand. I didn't even know what a Ph.D. was, then, but now that I'm actually involved in the scholarship to which he himself has drawn me, it seems to have lost all value for him.

"Don't be stupid, Helly!" he harangues, no more than half an hour after my arrival from my detested downtown apartment. I still reek of the subway and the street when he begins; it has taken me at least twenty minutes to remove my coat and go to the bathroom.

"Money and security! Money and security is what matters! What's wrong with you, you shouldn't understand that?" He circles his arms in a broad expansive gesture, as if bullying an audience into agreeing with him. "I met the father of your friend from high school, Goldblatt or Scheinblatt or something, and he tells me she's finishing college a year earlier than she was even supposed to and getting married right after graduation. An engineering student she got, from a nice Jewish family in the Midwest. He even gave her the ring already. So how come your friends know what's good for them and you don't?" he bellows. "What's the matter with this dumb kid she's got to be different from everybody else?"

Nor am I above shouting back, despite my shock over Edie's engagement and my idealistic desire to turn this into the first tranquil family dinner of my life, with the help of a few milligrams of Miltown prescribed by a friendly doctor on 86th Street. (Zalman tells me that it's wise to have as much legitimate 'scrip' as possible, but I can't convince the doctor to give me Dex—he thinks I'm too skinny to begin with.)

"Who's the one who made me different, anyway?" I retort to my father, my cheeks flushed, my eyes beginning to overflow. "Who's the one who brought me books, who said how important it was to study the past? Who always told me I was smart?"

"Smart yes, normal no," is the rejoinder. My father— heavier, tougher, with more years of experience—has always won, has been accustomed to winning since I was five and he gave me my first spanking.

"You're the one who made me special! You and mother!" I go on, nervously gauging my distance to the door. The

Miltown has the odd effect—just the opposite of what I wanted—of making me feel more vulnerable, and I know that my father's still capable of socking me when even mildly enraged; he tosses whatever lies in his path, like a lava flow. "And now that it looks like maybe I'm going to be different from Edie—and admit it, you couldn't stand her, *ever*—and not turn into some boring housewife who finishes college in hurry so she can settle down and teach grade school until she has a baby, all you want to do is keep me down!"

"Stupid! Teaching school is the best job for a woman, every moron knows that." Like a lava flow he can also subside, freeze or unexpectedly change direction, settling back in his special chair to listen to the news on the radio.

"Feh!" he dismisses me with distaste, rattling the paper. His eyes are a lost, light gray in his olive-skinned face; beneath the vanishing crown of his still-black hair which rings his scalp like a monk's tonsure, he might be the citizen of some old Greek city, sitting respectably among his daughters. A Hellene.

Sometimes I wonder, *Is that what he named me for?*

He himself has settled for menial, strenuous but well-paid labor. He works for a butcher, a purveyor of meats for various chain stores. He smells of the vaguely shitty odor of his own cigar smoke—even today, on the holiest of the Jewish Holy Days—and because he spends his life lifting huge sides of meat back and forth into supermarkets, his back always aches and his hands never feel quite clean.

So it's with a certain wistfulness that he advises me; he would rather I do anything than end up filing papers in a musty office like my mother's sister, or standing behind a cash register jingling other people's change.

"It's the best job for a woman, Helly," he mutters now, mouthing an imaginary cigar. He's prohibited from smoking on this fast day, but nothing can stop him from reading his paper, even though that too is prohibited. "Teach, for crying out loud. If I had it to do over again, that's what I'd do myself.

I'd pick kindergarten, say, to start. Them kids are little enough to listen to you and it's not hard work. Then, when your own kids are old enough to go to school themselves, you get home at three, summers and vacations off, and there you are with a job that don't interfere with your housework. And your husband would appreciate the extra dough, let me tell you."

"But I don't even *have* a husband, for heaven's sake," I retort. "What are you talking about?"

"Well, you're *gonna* have one someday. Someday soon, I hope. What, that friend of yours should get a good man and you shouldn't? She ain't got half your looks. And I'm going to have a daughter who's not even going to live a normal life and give me grandchildren? God forbid. You listen to me, Helly. Take my word for it. No matter how successful a woman is, if she don't have a husband and kids she feels like a nothing. Everybody knows that. It's the way of the world."

"Well, I don't like it."

"Nothing you can do about it, kid." He's almost cheerful, turning his New York *Post* to the editorial page. "Next time don't get born female."

Thus disposing of both the theory of reincarnation and Freud's "Anatomy is destiny," he begins to read.

As this discussion comes on the occasion of Yom Kippur, the Day of Atonement, his easy capitulation is understandable: fasting has left him weak. The Jewish High Holidays arrive at the end of every September, just in time to interfere with the beginning of the college semester and its flurry of early assignments. There is Rosh Hashonah, New Year's Day, the day of celebration when they blow the ram's horn to herald another year—it's the sixth millenium for the Jews, which I imagine ought to prove their superiority, at least in managing to stay alive—and then Yom Kippur a week later, when Ruth and I are always summoned to fast and suffer with our family, probably so we can try to atone for our considerable sins of the previous year.

Which is impossible, I realize. And yet I always go, and sit in the synagogue with my grandmother who soothes her fast-wearied nose by sniffing a lemon stuck all over with cloves, and then I always walk home slowly to help my mother greet a mob of relatives who spend the rest of the evening stuffing themselves with an enormous post-fast meal, most of which isn't even Kosher, because my mother has always hated Kosher food and refuses to cook it.

"Hey, listen, Ruth," I shout at my cousin during the long subway ride uptown, during which we're condemned to sit together in the rank subway car, out of place in our stiff holiday finery in the dimly lit filth and bored by staring out of crusted windows into darkness, unable to exchange more than a few words.

"What?" screams Ruth, shouting above the clamor of the train.

"Isn't this the pits?" I moan, smoothing my nylons and trying to elicit my cousin's confidence. "What a pain to have to come visit all the time."

"So don't," Ruth retorts, snapping the conversation shut with a crack of gum. "They wouldn't die."

"It's okay to see them as long as they don't interfere in my life too much," I try to confide above the roar of the train. "But when you stay away from one family holiday they greet you on the next one as though you were Jack the Ripper, and it's not worth going through the grief."

What I don't say to Ruth is that despite the hard time I get from both my parents these days, I really am fond of Sylvia, my mother. She may have crushed herself into the housewife mode when she married my father and developed weird notions about food, shopping, and even proper attire for me, but her ideas about other, more meaningful things aren't too bad. She's tried to raise my sister and me with an appreciation of life's finer values: to be tolerant and open to all people (except

immediate members of my father's family who have frequently and invariably hurt her feelings during her married
life), to marry a rich man instead of a poor one, and never to use
evil and ugly words like "nigger" or "fag."

Jews, she feels, should be particularly sensitive to such
labels and their implications. So when one of my father's
nephews informs us over a juicy drumstick that he no longer
likes the beach at Coney Island because too many "colored"
people go there, she fixes him with a stare and says, "Ronnie,
do you know that on private beaches in Connecticut, there are
signs that say, 'No dogs or Jews allowed?' And do you know
about Hitler and what he said about the Jews? Well, since you,
as a Jew, have been slandered that way yourself, how can you
talk that way about any other human being?"

The fact that Ronnie is only eight years old makes no
difference. She lectures him as earnestly as she might lecture
a fully grown adult. My father, for example, or her own sister
Mildred.

Which is exactly as she has always spoken to me.

Mildred, Ruth's mother, isn't like her at all. In fact, observing them now, seated at opposite sides of the holiday table, I
find it hard to believe that my mother and Mildred are really
sisters, although they don't look that different. Ruth's mother
is stouter, but both are short, bird-eyed, black-haired women
who might have been pretty in their youth, but probably
weren't. However it's my mother, Sylvia, who was always
interested in art and music, and still is. Whereas the only thing
besides a low metabolism that Ruth ever inherited from her
mother is her ability, like Mildred's, to do exactly as she
pleases, no matter what anybody thinks.

It's because of this ability that Ruth was born in the first
place, and raised by her natural mother, rather than ending up
aborted or given away, like almost all other babies born out of
wedlock in the Bronx in 1939. When Mildred conceived Ruth

she made up her mind to have her, despite the fact that Ruth's father the furrier refused not only marriage but any contact at all.

"How do you know it's mine?" he sneered, as would any honest cad of the era. (Mildred's only regret, she said later, was that he was too old to go into the army when the war came to America in 1941.) And Mildred's parents, my grandparents, threatened not only to disown her, but to drop dead from the disgrace as only aging Jewish parents can threaten to drop dead, leaving her to bear the burden of both her blighted seed and guilt for having caused the destruction of her entire family.

So what could she have possibly done to make them accept her and take in her illegitimate baby? I often wondered, but nobody wanted to tell me anything. I learned the facts by persistently bombarding my mother with so many unwelcome questions that she finally broke down and succumbed to her natural inclination to gossip.

"The fact is," she confided, pursing her red-lipsticked lips in a cozy way that indicated delicious secrets, "Mildred just plain *had* her. Just went off to Florida, you know? After *promising* to leave Ruth for adoption in some orphanage. And just came home, carrying the baby in a basket. Of course we didn't think of the baby as *Ruth* then, just as 'it' or 'the baby.' But there she was, you know what I mean? There she *was*. Everybody said, 'Thank God it isn't a boy. We didn't have to have a *bris*.'"

Mildred had ignored the whining of her parents, whom she was expected to support in their dotage, had ignored everything but the fact that she was already thirty years old, an old maid by the standards of the time, and that this was probably her only chance to have a child.

"All she had going for her was her sexiness, which men, I guess, or at least Gutterman the furrier, could smell on her like perfume. You wouldn't think Mildred was sexy, would you? But she was."

I wouldn't, but she was, and she also had the intense persistence that kept her going after Ruth was born. No one had suspected it of her, but they certainly should have. I can understand it now, watching Mildred eat. She swims through enormous plates of food, going after one piece of meat and then another—doggedly, tirelessly, sucking the marrow out of every bone, picking over every piece of gristle, until the entire plate shines in its emptiness. She has turned out to be the same way about her life. She has swum through every obstacle, turned a deaf ear to every complaint. Slowly and persistently she went about finding a new job where nobody knew she hadn't been married; said to her mother, "Ma, if I can't leave the baby with you then we're going to starve;" thereafter *did* leave the baby with her, and went out to work, every day for years and years in the same, musty office. Came home with bags of groceries and clothing for the baby, cared for her with an expressionless devotion—lived, thrived, flourished, and always, always refused to listen to anything that other people said.

When Ruth was ten years old Mildred married for the first time, although by then she had invented a sort of first husband and divorce or widowhood for herself—she was always vague— and kept saying she was "marrying again."

She married Louie, an indigent lawyer who spent his life in the dingy room he called his "office," waiting for the phone to ring and clients to come, which they hardly ever did. But that's another story.

Now Louie is dead and Mildred is alone again, a fixture at our family dinner table, to which Ruth and I are summoned as many times as possible during the year. Ruth, less sensitive to disapproval, manages to bow out most of the time, but I feel absolutely obligated to be there on the Passover, at Thanksgiving, and on the first night of Chanukah, when I'm expected to play with dreidels like a child even though I'm just about a grown woman. Even though I'm taller than my mother, as Ruth is taller than hers, and both of us are living on our own to the repeated misery of our parents and grandmother, who approach us like a chanting chorus, creating suitable background music, they imagine, to our travails.

"Why don't you come home?" they drone.

Sometimes I wish they were covered by face masks, like the players in Greek theatre. I wish their voices had the tireless anonymity of Gregorian chants, because certainly their messages are repetitive enough.

"How can you do this to us?"

"What nice girl walks out from her parents and takes her own apartment in a tenement?"

"What will boys think of such a girl that lives on her own?"

"The neighbors are always asking, what has become of that daughter (granddaughter, niece) of yours, how is she making it without her family?"

"What are all the people thinking about us in this neighborhood, that their oldest (or only) daughter should walk out on us to live in a slum?"

"How can you bring such disgrace down upon your own family? What is the matter with you?"

"You have surprised us all. You have turned out bad."

Although no one has been surprised by Ruth. She was expected to turn out bad.

I have a snapshot of myself at this particular post-Yom Kippur dinner. I'm skinny from the Dex but my face is puffy—sleeplessness? Or the effects of the new pills I've started taking once in a while to help me get some rest? Miltown. Doriden. Nembutal. I'm wearing too much pancake makeup. My hair is pulled straight back from my forehead like a dancer's and there are thick doe eyes drawn over my eyelids, badly. In the photo I'm holding my head high on my fragile neck—which looks dirty in black and white—and staring out into the middle distance, as if regarding someone who awaits me there. Zalman, undoubtedly—I'm imagining him watching this family dinner, which, by now, I myself am finding very dull. I'm wondering what his camera would make of this group of aunts and uncles and cousins, all chomping and chewing and guzzling away, led in their passionate fastbreaking by my grandmother, a tall woman with a permanently sallow face and a collection of double chins.

Or of Ruth's mother Mildred, for that matter—who manless, twice abandoned, has become quite huge in middle age, and to make it all worse, has grown a little mustache. You can see from the way Ruth has turned away from her that she despises her mother. Their life together has been a battlefield from the beginning, and it's a wonder to me that Ruth returns home for family dinners even once or twice a year, although it's far less often than I do myself.

And yet, to do her justice, Mildred has managed to maintain a decent job for many years; has managed, all alone, to provide herself, her daughter and her parents with a stuffy three-room apartment, adequate food and clothes, all necessary medical and dental care and even, which Ruth despises most of all but which everyone else honors, the thin, cracking veneer of respectability.

"Yes, dolly, so where is the Jonathan Logan I bought you, the day it was on sale at Ohrbach's?" my mother demands, in a nagging tone I hate almost as much as the dress in question. "Morton," she addresses my father, who, sulking under his skullcap, would prefer to address himself solely to turkey. "Morton, why is she dressing only in black? Is it some sort of style now?"

Naturally, Morton would have no idea of what the style is, and blinks in boredom and annoyance. The question is really meant for me, with my dramatically pulled-back hair and painted doe-eyes. This is my sole idea of glamour. I wear it home to impress them—or perhaps myself—with my sophistication. How to make my mother understand?

"And a little lipstick? Can't you wear?" Sylvia persists.

"I look horrible in lipstick, Mother. My mouth's too small."

"This is nonsense that you're talking. A small mouth. What is the matter with you? You've got a perfect face." She looks for support to the others at the table, who nod their heads. "A beautiful girl and she doesn't know it."

Then she passes around the Waldorf salad. Salad after the meal, she always says, like they do in Europe. In Europe, however, I now know, they don't chop apples and canned pineapple into the mayonnaise.

"Beautiful and smart," she says, "even if she *did* get into trouble with the college this year." She proffers salad tongs.

"Hah. Neither of them two're up to any good," spits Mildred, violently, through food. "So what happened?" Mildred spits. "How did she get in trouble?"

Ruth and I exchange a glance, too quickly to make any genuine eye contact or touch any feelings, either of hilarity or sorrow. In fact, the incident that my mother brought up occurred four months ago, in the Spring semester, and I can't understand why she would mention it now, in front of all the relatives—unless it's just that she wants to make it up to Mildred in some way, at my expense, for being the lucky, or at least the luckier parent. My temper begins to rise.

"It's nothing much, Mother," I begin, feigning patience. "I was just temporarily suspended. I cleared it all up this semester."

"And 'suspended' means?" Mildred smiles at the air in satisfaction, whether because of my plight or the crunch of the turkey bone she's chewing, I can't be sure.

"Means I couldn't register for Fall classes until I'd been cleared by the dean."

"So you're sure it won't make a bad mark on your record? Something like that could haunt you for the rest of your life."

I shake my head. "Can't we just drop this?" I mutter.

"So what did you do?" My grandmother turns on me, fork

poised in air, a harpy if I ever saw one. "What did you do to get this 'suspended' by the dean?'"

"Well." I put down my own fork. Where to begin? I take a deep breath. "I wore bifurcated clothing."

"You wore what?" Mildred blurts. Beaming with triumph.

"Bifurcated clothing, Aunt Mildred. You know. Cut in half? Anything bifurcated is against the college rules."

"You're walking around in clothing cut in half?"

Now my father, nervously chewing dark meat, has become engaged by this conversation. The idea that his elder daughter, who over his dead body lives alone in some horrible walk-up in a neighborhood he can't even see without wanting to throw up, now walks the streets of the city in inadequate or even suggestive clothing, makes him put down his fork, his face ashen with horror and grief.

"Not down the middle, daddy. Here. In the legs." Bravely, I allow myself a tiny giggle, but only because Ruth has turned away. I notice that Ruth's face, upon which the faintest vestige of her mother's mustache has already begun to sprout, is dark with unspoken anger.

"It isn't funny!" my father cries, and, as he again looks like he is about to erupt, I decide to explain myself more fully and end this discussion.

My college is run by a dean who has notions, first of all of what makes for the ultimate in feminine behavior, and second, of her own, absolute power. Both stem from her training at one of the Seven Sister colleges, many years ago, and neither bears any relation to my school, a gigantic, city-run institution of which at least three-quarters of the population is composed of young women from lower- or working-class families, trying to better themselves by becoming Education Majors or librarian trainees. The dean's name is Katherine Upson. She's a tall, pale woman of about sixty, who stalks the hallways wearing a nervous grin and an expression of vigilance. Although this is soon to change, my college is only for women, and certain standards are demanded of the young ladies. One important rule is that we may smoke nowhere but in the cafeteria and certain lounges, and another is that we may dress only in what Katherine Upson considers appropriate clothing.

One day, a terrible event takes place which possibly changes Katherine Upson's life, and which certainly changes her attitude toward her students.

Since the Education Majors have no interest in anything other than getting their degrees so they can husband-hunt in earnest, the school literary magazine has been taken over by a group of people who are the college's only intellectuals. The leading lights of this group are a black lesbian welfare mother of five who writes good poetry, a young man with a Greek accent (evening students can be male), and a dreamy, almost catatonic young woman from Brooklyn.

These three choose everything printed in the literary magazine, and one day they choose a poem which galvanizes Dean Upson and shocks the whole school, because it contains the single, ultimately unanswerable question:

Does Christ urinate?

The poem has been written by one of a pair of young woman poets who are rumored to be lovers. Both of them have round, staring brown eyes, hook noses, thin shapeless bodies and towering ziggurats of frizzy brown hair.

That they're both also Jews isn't particularly surprising, as there are more Jews in New York than in Tel Aviv, and a good half of them have sent their daughters to our college. Jews aren't usually raised to venerate Christ or to hold him in awe, which explains why they could so easily discuss his ability to urinate. It might also explain why they couldn't foresee Dean Upson's ability to go berserk when confronted by their question, accustomed as she is to the delicacies of weekly campus chapel, discreet sermons by the chaplain, and rooms full of quietly praying girls.

Horrified by the offending line, she rushes down the hallway snatching up copies of the magazine. "The moral fiber of this college has sadly deteriorated!" she cries, "and I must now do everything I can to restore it!"

She confiscates and then destroys every copy of the magazine she can lay her hands on.

"Henceforward," she announces to a college assembly in her most pear-shaped tones, "Henceforward, smoking is to be banned even in the cafeteria"—which ends my days of meeting Victoria and Ruth in its ugly depths—"and everyone is to adhere to dress codes. Absolutely *no* bifurcated clothing will be allowed."

Which means that pants, shorts, culottes and the like—all are to be banned.

We must wear skirts.

My problem with this is that I hate skirts. Skirts mean stockings, and stockings mean garter belts that, while possibly being sexually appealing to certain men with sadistic tastes, are also minor instruments of torture. Garter belts, no matter how humanely designed, all have little rabbity buckles and knobs designed to bite into the thighs, leaving raw indentations as deep as scars. Furthermore, stockings leave the inside of the legs quite bare, and certainly do nothing to ease the cold of New York winters.

"As a matter of comfort," I whine to the dean, hoping for sympathy, "bifurcated clothing is better than anything." It doesn't matter to me that it's unladylike. My daily outfit, now that I type letters in a watch-bezel factory after school instead of in the barren front office of a stationery firm, is a sweater worn over a pair of old black corduroy jeans and some ratty white sneakers, faded to grey.

But the dean doesn't care.

Since I may no longer bifurcate, I'm filled with resentment. I hang up my corduroy pants in the closet and plot revenge.

Which comes swiftly, first glimpsed in a Lerner's Shop

window near the Public Library in the form of a pair of cleverly-made culottes, tailored in herringbone tweed, which, when I'm sitting or standing carefully, look exactly like a skirt but which have at least some of the advantages of bifurcation.

Garbed in my new, warm culottes, with woolly knee socks and my usual greying sneakers, I feel almost comfortable as I leave for class. I've become friends with Chloris and Zoe, the two young women responsible for *Did Christ urinate?* and through them am getting to know the entire literary crew. I have little time for such recreation, but find them fascinating, in the same way in which I find Ruth and Zalman fascinating. They paint or write, they create, they pull new things out of themselves and let them breathe, even if they're only poetical speculations on the nature of Christ's pee. Often I wish that I could do the same thing myself, but I have no talent; or rather, my talent is to excavate and observe, and then to annotate, record. I'm an archeologist; what I want to do is to reconstruct the cities of the past.

"Why not write a poem about that?" Chloris (or Zoe—they always seem interchangeable to me) demands. "It's what you know and understand. It's what you have feeling for. That's what you should write."

"Everyone's a poet," Edie—or Zoe—adds. "Everyone has talent. There's really no such thing as talent. Talent is only the ability to develop music out of the ordinary, like picking up a theme that's already there. You can do it if you want."

They make it sound so easy.

How can I explain to them that someday I will see them, too, as excavations? That I'll be able to dig them up and dust them, carefully, with my sable brush, hold them to the light like pottery shards and try to figure out where they will fit, to which part of what vase or amphora they may belong?

How can I tell them that this New York, in which we're all living so vitally and frantically, will also be a city of the past in the not-too-distant someday, in a time when I am not even old, so that I can look back and record the lists of deeds and doers like the King Lists of the Hittites. These were the literary people: Audre and John, both of whom became well-known writers; Rose, who didn't; Michaela, Chloris, Zoe. This was Zalman Finster, and this was his history, and these were his exploits. This was my cousin Ruth, and the rest of my family—my mother's sister Mildred, my own younger sister Ellen, my mother, my father, my grandfather who's only the thinnest sliver of a memory for me, my grandmother who sat there stout and stalwart at every crowded family dinner, the uncles and the aunts.

"So how does this bifurcation get you thrown out of the school?"

"Suspended. Not thrown out. I'm walking down the hall one day and this dean, this Miss Upson, notices that my skirt doesn't quite close in the middle at the leg, not the way skirts should. So she makes me come into her office and she examines it and—"

Here my father's already light eyes lighten and flare with the look of an eagle about to devour prey.

"What do you mean, examine?" he bellows. "What did that old bitch do?"

"Morton," hisses my mother.

"Wait a minute," he shouts back at her, his face turning darker with mounting anger. "The poor kid wouldn't know anything about it. She's still innocent enough, thank God. How could she tell if the woman was being unnatural, or what?"

"Morton," hisses my mother.

Ruth's long black eyes slide across my face, like two black slugs crawling across a plate. They're full of illegible emotions; rage, humor, hysteria about to break like huge waves. Looking at her, I can hardly wait for us to huddle inside the shadows of the looming El on our way home and smoke our first joint of the evening together, shaking with laughter in the darkness.

"Jesus," I can imagine Ruth's muffled howling. "Being unnatural. The girl's too innocent to know. My God."

"Upson unnatural," I will howl in return. "What a thought! Can you imagine making it with Upson? 'Do it darling, just don't touch me.'"

"I bet she does hate men, though," Ruth will speculate. "Everything they wear is bifurcated."

But right now, in the glaring light of my parents' dining room, we have to force ourselves into control. I decide to stuff my laughter down by cramming myself with the ice cream melting on top of a glistening slab of warmed-up pie, which I don't even like, and at which my grandmother stares balefully, because ice cream is milk and we've just eaten meat and the combination, while riotously American, certainly isn't Kosher. (And on this, the Highest Holiday.)

"Anyway," I go on between mouthfuls of pie, "she discovered it was culottes and not a skirt and she told me I'd have to see her to be 'cleared' before I could register for Fall semester. I kept saying it was really a skirt but she didn't care. She kept saying, 'It's bifurcated and I made a rule. From now on, Miss Elphrick, you must put on a skirt!'"

After I finish this speech, swallowing my pie at the same time, even my sister is looking at me with so much sympathy that I begin to wonder whether I've deviated a little too much from the absolute truth.

"So? You get good grades, hah?" growls Mildred, scooping a second helping of pie à la mode into her dessert bowl, which isn't even empty of the first helping yet.

"Sure she gets good grades, Mil," says my mother, maybe to make up for her earlier betrayal of me. "She's a straight A-getter, this one." She looks at Ruth and flashes a sudden smile. "Like yours," she says. "They're both smart, Mildred. The two of them."

"You don't have to get straight A's," Mildred sputters,

through pie. "You could get C's, better, and meet some nice boy."

At which Ruth, trying unsuccessfully to suppress the urge for a cigarette, throws her spoon into her own bowl—her pie untouched—and lights up, with the desperate air of someone taking a fix.

"You know," her mother bellows, grabbing the lighter out of her hand, "I said no smoking at the table!"

A sharp edge of the lighter, catching Ruth's skin, leaves a long, radiant gash across the palm, through which a thin line of red begins slowly, very slowly, to well.

"Mil, maybe you're a little too rough with the girl," my mother whispers. As she always has. It's amazing that Ruth still seems to hate her so much, despite her sympathy, but she covers the whole family with contumely, as if her mother's actions and attitudes have contaminated all of them.

Except for me, I hope. Sitting very quietly now, averting my eyes.

She's got to learn," says Mildred.

And Ruth, getting to her feet, announces, "I'm going home."

Later, watching Ruth skid along the wet street in her spiky black shoes, I want, for one of the few times in my life, to take her arm. Maybe, I think, it's because she looks oddly vulnerable in a thick plush coat, too heavy for the weather—this tall, Amazonian young woman, so self-reliant and angry, with her inscrutable black eyes and her tough sexy clothes like armor. Over the gashed hand, which my mother inadequately patched with a Band-Aid, she wears a thin suede glove, soft and supple as a second skin.

"Does it hurt?" I ask after we've walked a few blocks, but the expression of Ruth's face as she expels cigarette smoke— she began to smoke the minute we hit the street—discourages idle conversation. I remember with regret how eagerly I anticipated going downtown with her, perhaps to connect with

Zalman in Stanley's or the Cedar, maybe to just hang out. I imagined that we'd stop and share a joint under the El station and laugh about my father's reaction to Katherine Upson. Fat chance, I think now.

"You wouldn't want to hit the Village later?" I ask tentatively anyway, even though Ruth still hasn't answered my first question.

She flicks the sparks of her cigarette into the wind. "I've got a date."

"Another time, then?"

"Sure."

Ruth's mouth is a thin scar of red. At moments like this, despite my disappointment, I feel I understand her; that I know her apparent hardness, the cold way she talks about men, even her devotion to her work, are all results of a vulnerability as deep and painful as an unhealed wound.

Maybe, I think, she even paints as well as she does because she can bleed on canvas without worrying about it.

"Listen," I blurt suddenly. "Ruth. Listen. Why don't you ever talk to me? I'm more than just your cousin, aren't I? And I've seen it all, the whole rotten family. Can't you believe they drive me just as crazy as they drive you? Grandma and your mother, my parents, what everybody thinks of us?"

"Look kid, it's not your problem, okay?" She mutters this quickly, barely turning, so that all I can see of her are her shoulders, teddy-bear fluffy in the shaggy coat.

The two of us plod along, side by side, in silence.

"Look what she gave me," Ruth says suddenly, stopping under a streetlamp at the corner.

"Who?" I ask naively. "Your mother?"

"No, dummy," Ruth brays with a proud, self-satisfied smirk, holding out her left hand and fingering a lump under the glove. "Not *my* mother. Yours."

She draws off her thin soft glove, to reveal the gash, looking almost trivial now, the useless Band-Aid already peeling off her palm.

"No, not that, stupid. Anybody could have a Band-Aid." And she turns her hand over, revealing—as my heart stops— a garish but beautiful ring, made of rows of pearls linked with gold and layered like the tiers of a Siamese temple.

"My mother gave it to you?" I breathe.

Ruth nods.

I've wanted that ring, I've lusted for it, for ten years or so. Ever since I became old enough to try it on my short chubby finger, to polish my nails, to imagine myself going out in a black evening dress with that single ornament gleaming on my hand. I've asked my mother for it, not once but a dozen times, even just to borrow it for a special date, for an occasion. And I've always been refused.

Ruth draws on the glove after turning her finger this way and that in the light, and the ring makes a little pyramid under the material. My sympathy for her is eclipsed by greed and jealousy. Ruth lowers her face a little; there's almost no expression in her eyes, but I imagine that I see in them anyway a gleam of pleasure as she looks at me. A kind of triumph.

How could she have known about the ring? But maybe all her eyes show is an anticipation of the oncoming night, her "date," the festivities that will begin as soon as we hit the city, where she'll leave me with a casual pat on the back, a nod so brief it will be as if we hardly know each other.

And only a moment before, I had wanted to put my arms around her, to invite her to cry on my shoulder, to tell her how deeply and personally I understood the rage and repulsion she feels against her mother, against the entire family—a rage and repulsion which, for my own reasons, I always thought I shared.

"Well, Helene," Ruth says, drawing the glove over the taut golden skin of her arm. "Another family dinner, what do you say?"

And together, we go up the stairs to the elevated train.

PART TWO

NINE

The drifts of the first November snowfall wisp and gather on the streets outside. In my apartment, Zalman and I lie snugly in the living room and contemplate the steatopygous Bushmen dancing across my wall mural by flickering candlelight.

"I'm glad I got these candles," I whisper, looking at the tracing of rose light through my fingers. I feel bathed in warmth.

"So, Helene," he whispers back. "What do you think?"

"I don't think anything." I turn and lift my eyes to him. He's staring down into my face.

"You're thinking nothing? Nothing at all?"

"How can you expect me to think right now?" I smile blankly. "What do you want from me?"

We've just been making love, and what I want is not to be roused from my physical torpor, like that of a cat in a warm lap. From my record player in the corner, Coltrane's sax makes a noise like a squeal of human pain.

"Well, *I*," he says, "know something."

I sigh. "I can't possibly guess."

"I'm going to open a gallery," he announces. His voice doesn't change, but I sense a new urgency behind it. A real involvement, under the lazy subterfuge. "All I have to do is find a space," he goes on, gaining energy as he speaks. "That's the hardest thing, finding the perfect space."

"What do you mean, a gallery?" I struggle against his shoulder and sit up.

"An art gallery, of course. To show my work."

"But how?" I wonder. "It must be fabulously expensive to run a gallery. What have you got, a sponsor or what?"

He stares at me with his usual smile, but what I see in his eyes suddenly is raw hunger.

"I've got lots of sponsors, as a matter of fact. Do you want to be my sponsor?" He asks this softly; so softly that we can both pretend I haven't heard him. I sit very still for what seems like a long time, thinking of how I'm going to answer if he asks again. Instead he begins to snap his fingers to the music, grinning at me as if it were all a joke.

"Things are happening, baby," he jives, laughing, as the record comes to an end. I realize with relief that I'm expected to get up and put on a new one. But now I feel restless and strange. An artist can go a whole lifetime without a gallery to show his paintings, even a good artist, I think, remembering Ruth; remembering the small but glowing collection of her etchings and prints and oils, a collection which grows slowly, year after year. I think of Ruth's canvas called "Blue," tiny but as perfectly formed as a rare old enamel in a museum. Will a gallery ever hang that? When I ask her about the possibilities she sounds discouraged, as if she doesn't even want to try.

"It's a scene," she shrugs, her mouth turning down. *"You got to know people or it doesn't happen."*

Does Zalman know people, I wonder? And then the thought occurs to me, gently but like the whisper of a demon, *Does it count to hang your work in your own gallery so no one else can possibly reject it? Isn't that really a kind of fraud?*

I feel my stomach knot with a new feeling. Shame. Not for myself. For him.

His art isn't good enough, the thought comes. *He hasn't spent enough time with it. He doesn't really care, not the way you have to if you want to be good. Not the way Ruth cares, say. But he'll show it anyway. And people will probably praise it.*

A kind of fraud.

"Things are finally happening," he carols from across the room. He's still on the sofa. "Things are really happening now."

I push back my curtains—I've recently replaced dull green with glowing purple—and look down at the raw brick airshaft, growing softer under falling snow.

Zalman has been changing. He has bought himself new clothing, like a new skin; he dresses these days in tight green pants with a belt in the back, a black leather storm coat, thick turtleneck sweaters of the finest wool, all of which give off hints of new wealth, a smell of power. He has become more important to himself, a man at the top of his stride. A success. He never did get to meet William Burroughs, but it no longer matters. Other things have happened, and now he will open the gallery and show his art. His name will be printed in the gallery section of *The New York Times* and *The Village Voice.* Jonas Mekas and Andre Pincus will write about his films, vying for the most obscure interpretations. Perhaps one day Burroughs will walk in off the street and discover him anyway.

"I'm very happy for you, Zalman," I say softly. I don't understand why I feel so calm as he brushes my thick hair from my shoulders. Is it so very easy to kill love? I wonder. But then I myself brush the thought away and again in his face I see the smouldering of night's fires and the answers to all the secrets I have ever wanted to know.

After all, every head turns when he walks into a room, and

his eyes are a blue lake in which all my anxieties can drown. And he's brilliant, he has taught me about literature and jazz and modern art; he has studied Kabbalah and Joyce, he has found a way to help me escape ordinary life. Just tonight he sold me another plastic vial of Dex, and gave me a tiny slab of rare Moroccan hash as a lover's gift. And something new as well: a spansule of amyl nitrate, a heart medication that comes in plastic cylinders which we break under each other's nostrils, pinwheeling onto my mattress in a wild ride.

It all gives him the right to at least a little fraud.

"Let's go downstairs and walk in the snow," I beckon, sounding like a child, even to myself. "I've always wanted to see the park in a blizzard but I'm too scared to go alone."

"It's a cliché," he says. "We've got better things to do."

And he laughs and reopens my robe, kneeling before me in a lover's attitude of prayer and rolling a new joint with his other hand.

The gallery, a storefront on Lexington in the 20's, opens in February, when the snow has frozen, grey and hard, making a treacherous rink of the city streets.

It opens *finally*, he says. *Finally*, after much fuss, after many excursions to various sites throughout the city, and after many complicated negotiations, all of which take a great deal of time and endless discussion. Which is why he can come to see me only infrequently now, and why it's all he talks about when he does come.

He invites me to the opening, and although I could have brought a friend, neither Victoria nor Ruth wants to come with me and I can't think of anyone else who'd be interested. So I come alone, more than an hour late—when everyone else is already half drunk—and, as usual when I have to penetrate unknown territory by myself, clutching a book under my arm like a life preserver.

The gallery has been lined with chairs, and at one side a

130

movie projector has been set up. Zalman's newest pieces—
huge slabs of cardboard, heavy and bending with layers of
collage, and smeary formless prints which have been framed
and matted professionally—are mounted on the gallery-white
walls. The place is jammed with as many of Zalman's influen-
tial friends as he can manage to phone or find in bars, people
vaguely famous, minor celebrities, whose names bump up
against me from time to time like rudderless boats, somehow
comforting in their familiarity.

When I edge into the room it seems to me that everybody's
talking at the same time, meeting each other and circulating at
top speed while knocking down vast quantities of rotgut
chablis and cold cuts which have already turned oily brown at
the edges under the glaring lights.

"And what are *you* doing here?" the man says, sliding up to
me as I stop blankly before this scene. He has bright black eyes
that look like glass buttons, and he speaks with a German
accent.

"Being ignored, I guess." I peer down into my book, which
happens to be *The Brothers Karamazov.*

"You're too attractive for that." Not discouraged for a
minute, he grabs my hand and beams at me. He pronounces
'attractive' *ettrektif.* It isn't.

"Um," I say.

"And are you a friend of Zalman's? Zalman has so many
interesting friends."

"Yes."

"Do you know Flower? Do you know Zelda? They're both
here."

"I'm glad," I say, blushing and dropping my book. He
stoops to retrieve it for me.

"What are you reading? Dostoevsky! My God! Not very
talkative, are you?"

"No."

He gives up too quickly, nervously scouting the room for

another interesting person to talk to, and I drift away, holding the book open and turning a page, wondering whether he was somebody important.

Most of the people seem either to know one another or to be bent on picking one another up. They circle and eye each other like shoppers at one of my mother's bargain sales, most of them paying more attention to the food and drink and the other people than to the paintings on the walls, with a few exceptions.

"Such extraordinary plasticity," one man is saying loudly, as he peers at one of Zalman's pieces with professional acumen. "But little else."

I figure he's a critic because he carries a small black notebook and several other people are arguing with him while he writes things down.

"The influence of Pollock," says another man to the supposed art critic, who is now stubbing out a cigarette under his foot, "is obvious."

"Masterful painterliness," adds a third. But I notice that he can hardly stand up and looks as if he's really too drunk to care.

Not far from this trio, two beardless males, both with miraculously tiny hips and perfectly groomed hair, are engaged in a slow, discreet, almost silent dance. They take turns approaching one another, then backing off, smiling, passing each other wineglasses and cigarettes before turning and glancing feverishly around the room. I can't watch them for too long without attracting their attention or seeming rude, so I pick up a glass of bitter rosé at the littered table which serves as a bar and make believe I'm ignoring them.

"Darling, are you holding?" I hear one of them murmur to the other without missing a beat.

"Of course. What extraordinary *pic*tures," his friend answers in exactly the same tone. "I had no idea that Zalman was so influenced by Dubuf*fet!*"

"Dubuffet? Isn't it more like Pollock? I mean, look at the manual dexterity, the sweep of the line!"

"But the composite *material*—I mean, look at the texture of that impasto, will you? What do you think that is anyway, on the collage. *Sand?*"

And then he bends and whispers in the other's ear, and a tiny plasticine packet exchanges hands so suddenly that it seems to whir through the air like a hummingbird's wing, and I remember the sad ghost men in Zalman's apartment on the first day we spent together, and look calmly at another wall, pretending disinterest.

"What disturbs me," a grave though well-dressed woman comments to her friends, who pay such close attention to her that I begin to wonder what kind of power she has over them, "is the complete nihilism of all this kind of work. Its deathliness. Art that seems to have given up on art. Writing that is only about style. Music that destroys the very sense and notion of the musical."

"It reminds me of a concert I went to in Rome, where one of those young composers took apart a piano," one of her admirers agrees. "He apparently felt that to dismantle the piano was the ultimate musical statement. In reality it was hideous cacophony and destruction. Nothing more. Nobody else could stand it, either; everybody in the audience ran out onto the street, leaving the composer and his music all alone."

"Exactly," the woman says. "Taking things apart and leaving them destroyed. Exactly."

But I notice that this woman and her entourage don't run out onto any streets. They stay until the last collage has been examined, the last film shown. The last scrap of French bread and salami and cheese and the last drop of wine consumed.

"It's just that you're still such a kid." Zelda swoops down on me from the other side of the room, jamming a joint into my fingers, which coupled with the wine makes my knees buckle and my head swim. "That's why you're so shy and uptight. Hiding your light and all that. You goodlooking bubbies take longer to grow up than other people. You're always involved in trying to make an impression on people so they'll think you've got a mind along with the body. Or maybe you're so used to being looked at all the time it warps you. I mean, dig the book. *The Brothers K.* for God's sakes. Don't worry about it. You'll come around when you get a few lines or a stomach bulge or two."

Goodlooking bubbies? I think, wobbly. *Does she mean me?*

Zelda, Zalman's other mistress, is a raw-faced blonde. Ruth says that Zalman likes her just for her brain, which is supposed to be brilliant.

"I'm not such a kid." I ignore the issue of my looks, for which I have no answer. "I'm older than I look."

To which Zelda sneers, "Hah! How old *do* you goddamn look, for God's sakes? Sixteen?"

Zelda is one of the only three people I know in this room, and I'm not quite sure why she has approached. She has, though, pushing her jay into my hand with a thin smile, making me an offhand welcome with the grim line, "So kiddo, you got yourself invited, huh? It doesn't look like you're having such a good time, though. What's the problem?"

I search around for Zalman, and spot him talking to another man, younger than he, with a short haircut and a bright, alert face.

"The first time I ever turned on to grass, man," the young man is saying, "I was 80,000 feet up, flying a jet. I mean, I was in the Air Force, of all things, and one of my buddies lays this joint on me and says, 'Look, man, try it and you'll keep on flying even after the plane comes down.'"

"I can understand that," Zalman comments.

The pilot says, "It saved my life. No, hey, man. I mean, *changed.* It *changed* my life."

The two of them make eye contact and breathe deeply into one another's faces.

"It *saved* your life," says Zalman. "Fantastic."

The young pilot nods devoutly.

Zelda, having lost interest in me, is busily talking to some-body else. I watch the two men for a minute, then move away.

Then I sit down uncomfortably on one of the rickety folding chairs to watch Zalman's films, a series of images shot with a hand-held camera in black and white. They're jumpy and zigzagging and hard to follow. Men in makeup and feathers; garbage cans at a corner. The city, grey under rain.

"But what's it about?" a man near me demands, his voice thin and petulant above the crowd.

The woman he's with answers, "It's not what it's about that's important, honey. It just *is* something, all by itself."

If so, I think skeptically, then what it *is* is something grainy and dark and boring. But people are laughing and nodding, as if some profound statement about art has just been made.

"Fantastic. Fantastic," they say. I get the feeling that they're pleased with their own approbation more than anything, pleased with the inside wisdom that lets them understand, like the cheering crowds in the fable about the naked emperor.

But then, what do I know, anyway? I know more about ancient Sumerian cylinder seals and the monumental statues of the Egyptians that were made the same way for five thousand years than about modern American art. To me Zalman's work seems odd and raw—*a kind of fraud*—but I could be wrong. Still, I wonder, why doesn't he pull out his Bell & Howell and start shooting the scene in this gallery, right now? He could shoot the long table covered with stale hors d'oeuvres and overturned bottles of wine. Or the crowd of interesting faces, bent over plastic cups and cigarettes. The people milling around, stamping their feet, running out into the street or into the bathroom for a quick smoke or a hit of something else, whatever it is that cheers them, that makes them feel as though they're living "real life."

He could even hold the camera up to his own face, which is as changeable as some landscape over which clouds pass, as he moves from person to person among his guests. Never too eager or hurrying, never taking his eyes off the face of the person before him until some new face comes into focus. I can't hear what he's saying but I can easily imagine as I watch him: "It is fantastic; *you're* fantastic," as he acknowledges each story, smiles at each joke.

He stops before the two beardless males, still engaged in their dance of seduction, and, putting an arm over the shoulder of each of them, he weaves between them, touching their bodies with his own so that the three of them sway together as if dancing to inaudible music. To my amazement, one of the men, the blond, places his cheek all too gently against Zalman's and looks up into his eyes. Both of them smile, dancing to their music. The third man, irritated suddenly, turns away and crosses the room.

But he doesn't leave and neither do I. Although I consider it, crossing the room in his wake. Trying not let anyone see my distress, I go out and stand on the street for a while.

It's suddenly turned warm for a February night. The ice is thawing, melting into slush. People pour out of the gallery onto the sidewalk. I look around for a familiar face. Someone to talk to. Even Zelda would be welcome, but she and Flower are pressed into the crowd and surrounded by friends. I think of Zalman traveling from each person to the next, pausing attentively, dancing with the young blond man as the other man rushed across the room, his face twisted and dark. I think about the night we spent with the boy, Darryl, the power Zalman had over him, the power he had over the woman with the red skirt, as the others stirred it in a pot to make skirt soup. I think about the power he has over me. How could I have understood about Flower and Zelda without realizing there must have been others as well? How many others? *"It doesn't mean this isn't love,"* he'd said to me, but that didn't mean it was, either. And here I was. One of many. More in love than loved. Out of control.

Which is what I'd wanted, wasn't it?

Lost. Lost.

"You're taking this scene too seriously," says the man, coming up behind me. "I've had my eye on you."

It's Andre Pincus, the film critic, whose work I've read and admired. He reminds me a little bit of Zalman, with his penetrating blue eyes and his Lithuanian accent. But his skin is sallow and his nose is bent, and no one has ever called him a Prince of the Jews, or of anything else, for that matter. He wears a tweed overcoat so heavy and long it seems to be sweeping the floor.

"I read your reviews every week," I begin to tell him, very shyly, once I've recovered what's left of my poise. "I like what you wrote about Antonioni. Judith Crist was just scathing about 'L'Avventura,' but I felt that your opinion. . ."

"Thank you," he cuts me off drily. Maybe he's been told it all too often before, or maybe my opinion doesn't matter. Stung, I turn away.

"Do you keep a diary?" he springs on me suddenly.

"What?"

"I've been watching you, and you look like the kind of girl who keeps a diary."

"What kind of girl is that?" I bumble. Taken aback.

"Sensitive. A sensitive girl. All Zalman's girls are sensitive. Soulful. He seems to like the type."

"Who?"

"From Brooklyn, aren't you?" he goes on. "Brooklyn or the Bronx. Or Queens. A baby novelist. Or a poet. The kind of girl who writes about her feelings because it's so hard to communicate. With anybody but him, that is. That must be at least half of the appeal, I'm sure. Attentiveness is his greatest charm; he listens to you all so well."

There's envy in his bitterness. I recognize it. I stammer, "Yes?" curling my hand around my book. My heart begins to pound. I don't keep a diary, but I could start one tonight, just to show Andre Pincus, the semi-famous critic. Would he publish it in one of his columns? Would I become semi-famous myself?

"I'd like to read it." He peers sharply into my face with his narrow eyes. It occurs to me that he, too, is more than a little drunk.

"You would? Why?"

"I'm doing a film now about a young girl who keeps a diary. She's about eighteen. You are about eighteen, aren't you?"

I'm more like about twenty-two, having recently had a birthday, but I nod obediently anyway.

"Well, I'd like to read your diary. I could use it for the film." He holds out his hand and offers me something. It's a pencil. "Here," he dictates. A man used to giving orders, he pulls a stained leaf out of a scruffy black notebook in his pocket. "Take down my number."

I scrawl it on the paper, leaning against the wall, and he snatches the pencil back out of my hand.

"Don't take it all so seriously." He waves his arm around, indicating the gallery, the scene, the people. Zalman's paintings on the walls. "It's just a game," he says.

"A game?"

"The art scene. Buying, selling. What does it have to do with talent? The dealers find somebody, they make him, they break him. They come into a painter's studio, and what do they like? His best work? Usually his worst. You're looking like it's all a matter of life and death, but what will happen, this fellow Finster will make out all right just by selling his own pictures, he'll have a little vogue for a while and then he'll settle back into being a happy has-been, living off his memories. And so what? You'll go home finally to Brooklyn or the Bronx and find a nice boy and get married. That's what you all do in the end, you young girls in the Village."

"I don't think so." I surprise myself with my own anger. "And I do take things seriously. It's the way I am."

In response to which he tilts the cover of my book and looks

down at the title with the usual amusement. Why does everyone find Dostoevsky so funny, I wonder? Or is it just the fact
that I'm reading him?

"You keep a diary, all right," he insists, darting back into the
crowd. "Don't forget to call."

"What did Andre Pincus want?" Zalman asks, looking after
the critic.

"Just to talk."

He nuzzles my cheek. "What about?"

"No, don't do that," I whisper, shrugging away.

"Why not?"

"Because of Flower. It will hurt her feelings."

"Flower doesn't mind. Why should she mind?"

Nonetheless, he steps back a little, still touching me casually on the shoulder. He isn't a man to kiss in public, but he
needs to make it clear that he possesses me anyway; that I am
his.

After a few minutes he leaves my side, and as I watch him
move sinuously into a circle of people, I realize that I've
managed not to really answer his question about Pincus, the
critic. I've managed to maintain some privacy for myself, and
I have a sudden new sense of my own freedom. *I can leave him
if I want to,* I think, but then my heart begins to pound again,
in pain this time.

It doesn't mean this isn't love.

At three o'clock in the morning the room has begun to
empty. The sky is calm and dark. I stand alone for a few more
minutes, looking around, not knowing quite what to do next.
Shall I telephone Pincus the next day and present him with a
made-up diary? But how would I have it written in time? If I
actually did keep a diary, would I really give it to this man to
read? Letting him know about my love affairs, my studies, my
loneliness, my embarrassments? My passion for Zalman, our
nights together, the crazy times spent laughing with my friends,
all the things I've done?

I fold the paper in half and slip it into my pocket, from which I retrieve it the following morning, when I awaken alone in my apartment. And pin it conspicuously over my desk, where Zalman sees it plainly the next time he comes to spend the night, eyeing it plainly with a gratifying mixture of jealousy and pride.

TEN

"Should I get married? Should I be good?
Astound the girl next door with my velvet
suit and faustus hood?"
— *Gregory Corso, ca. 1955*

March is the worst month in New York.

Not April, when the forsythia in Central Park begin to bud, and then suddenly spring up, yellow, out of what a day before was hard and barren earth. Not April, when the green shoots push out of the branches on the trees, oblivious of exhaust fumes in the dark, laden air, and prepare to leaf just like ordinary green shoots anywhere. No. As far as this city is concerned, T.S. Eliot was wrong; in New York, the cruellest month is March.

It's in March that New York shows its teeth. The entire city smells of sea. When you least want it, when the air is just humid enough and beginning to warm up a little, the bitter river fog descends, making you feel cheated, robbed. In March you wear your first spring dresses and the wrong shoes and get caught in a freak blizzard and catch the last flu of the season, which leaves you weak and drained. When New York summer comes with its torrid blasts, you can't believe it. The heat is almost a relief from the winter chill, but where was spring? It was promised in March for April, but it never really comes. It is a cheating New York lover, it makes you hate the city more than anything, and by May I'm always ready to go away. Always.

During the March of our senior year in college, Victoria takes up with Richard Loess.

She agrees with me about March.

"And to make it all worse," she confides to me later, "March is when everybody else is cramming for midterms and you and Ruth always desert me. I saw Ruth once, but I never saw you at all. What'd you do, stay home and huddle over your books all month? Some friend you are."

I find it hard to convince her that I'm too poor and desperate not to take exams seriously just because she herself doesn't need to. On her own, Victoria always has a sort of breakdown. She goes out drinking with her rich friends and ends up hungover; catches flu; fights with her mother.

This year has been particularly bad. Her mother has gone on a long-anticipated vacation. Victoria has now left NYU and is studying acting at a private school, which she finds ridiculously easy; her rich friends have all gotten married or been sent to Europe. She doesn't know what to do with herself.

She hangs around Stanley's more often than usual, but without us to hang around with her and make her laugh, it begins to be dull.

So she goes to parties. At one of them she meets him.

That takes care of March.

It's not until April that I find out what's happened to her. Not until we're well out of March. Of course I wonder what's wrong when I stop hearing from her for a while, but I've hardly heard from Ruth either, and overwhelmed by my own problems and by the demands of school, I have to admit that I haven't tried as hard as usual to see either of them. When she finally calls me I'm not exactly surprised; just sorry.

Sorry, for one thing, that I'm not at the party at which she meets him. To which I've been invited, too, by Wallace Wigmore the bartender, whom I turn down as usual without a second thought.

Victoria, on the other hand, is all too eager to accept the invitation, which in her case comes from Ruth.

"I'm not sure I'm going to show," Ruth tells her, uncharacteristically vague, when Victoria manages to contact her by telephone. "But hey, dig. Go anyway, man. I'm hitting the books but maybe I'll fall by. Who knows? It could be a gas, the party of the year. Like, make the scene with me or without me. What difference does it make?"

"So I went alone," Victoria tells me later. First bedecking herself in her most lavish second-hand finery: an old fox coat bought for twenty dollars in a huge warehouse filled with antique furs on Great Jones Street, one of her mother's preserved black chiffon dresses from the 30s, long black stockings, pointy shoes. Only at the last minute rejecting a velvet cloche hat purchased impulsively in the newly fashionable Chelsea district, which hugs her temples like Marlene Dietrich's hats did in "Blonde Venus." It's too much, she decides, hurrying out of the house.

"Still," she confides, "I have to admit I looked pretty good that night;" and I can imagine what "pretty good" looked like; her lips lined in coral, too much blue shadow around her eyes to make them look even larger, expensive pale powder from Elizabeth Arden which gives her face a luminous pallor so that she looks like one of those orphan children on the posters in cheap art shops. "Of course, Richard Loess doesn't like women who wear makeup." She sighs. "But then, he never notices what I wear anyway."

"I first saw him coming up the stairs behind me," she lets me know, on the night when she tells me the whole story. "I asked him, 'Are we both going to the same place?' as he passed me on the stairs. The party was on the top floor of a tenement near Paradise Alley—it was thrown by some artist who had made a loft for himself by knocking down the walls of two perfectly decent apartments, and it took an awfully long time to get up the stairs."

I can understand how the sense of her own beauty has relaxed her; it's like an elixir, a knowledge of certain power. Which he dispels in about three seconds, by pretending to ignore her completely.

What she doesn't yet realize is that while both of them are going to the same place, at least one of them is also wondering why. His friends have invited him, but he has always hated parties. And what can he say in response to her blasé cheerfulness? *I hate parties? I don't know why I'm here?*

So he says nothing. He likes being rude, anyway. Rudeness gives him a sense of importance.

At first sight Richard is just a young man of medium height with a large head, heavylidded eyes, a shaggy haircut and a trimmed beard. A long shabby overcoat, extremely dark above flat feet, completes the picture.

"José Ferrer playing Toulouse-Lautrec in 'The Moulin Rouge!'" she laughs hysterically—but only in April.

She might have whispered this intelligence to Ruth or me that very night, had either of us been there at the time. Which would have reduced us all to laughter, our most potent weapon as well as our most effective escape. If Ruth or I had been able to be with Victoria at the party, her whole life might have been different.

But we aren't there. Ruth does put in an appearance later on, but for some reason she avoids Victoria. So Victoria has no one with whom to laugh about him, and therefore she's condemned to take him seriously.

As for Richard himself, mounting the stairs behind her, he amazes himself by staring at her trim calves, her tiny ankles.

"He kept gaping at my legs," she observes. "He may have enjoyed being rude to me, but he wasn't blind.

"On the other hand, I couldn't have cared less about him at that point. What *I* was worrying about was ruining my new gloves on the absolutely filthy bannisters. Don't people ever *clean* those buildings? And I was afraid I'd get a nosebleed from the altitude—of course there wasn't any elevator." She hangs onto her coat when they finally reach the party. So, probably for reasons of vanity—he stoops, and has a narrow chest and a little pot belly—does he.

"What a nice apartment," she chatters as they pass through the open door. "Big, isn't it?"

She turns to him as if she knows him. After all, he has intrigued her by his silence. And he was her sole companion mounting six long flights of stairs.

Not a very good companion, however. Because in response to her all he does is bat his lashes, suck his teeth, and keep still.

They both sit down in a corner. There's nothing else for them to do. Neither of them dance, Victoria because her heels are too high, the man—who still hasn't taken off his almost-floor-length overcoat—because he can't. He never learned.

"I squirmed," she tells me. "I simply *squirmed* in my chair."

I can imagine her squirming, shifting her feet in their uncomfortable shoes. Where's Ruth? Where am I? She knows no one at the party, and the man beside her stares out into the middle distance for a long time. She might think he was profound were not his beard so short and his coat so long. However, he does not appear to be dirty and she doesn't think he smells.

"Do you have a name?" he asks, after a while.

His eyes, over which the lids curve with an expression of

disdain, stare politely into the crowd, in which they see no one they recognize, and do not meet hers.

Offended, she doesn't answer. But after a while she counters his question by saying flatly, "So what do you do?"

Which he takes as a joke. She, figuring him for the type who doesn't like women who smoke, lights a cigarette and inhales deeply.

"You?" I interrupt her. "But you can't *stand* to inhale."

"I can now." To prove it she removes a half-empty box of Du Mauriers from her purse and lights one up. "I started then."

She may be only five feet tall, but she's totally convinced that in her own blonde beauty is that touch of Marlene Dietrich. With or without the cloche hat, she can play Blonde Venus. And often has. After all, she does have the apartment on Central Park West. The view of the park. The very excellent responses to her acting from teachers and students alike at her new drama school, about which (if she were to be perfectly honest), she doesn't really care very much. At least two discarded lovers, if you count Mr. Wo as a lover. The antique fur coat. She lets smoke funnel through her nostrils. She feels very cool. She meets Richard eye to eye.

"My name is Victoria Andersen," she remarks after a while. "I'm at Herbert Berghof's."

"The department store?"

She can't believe it. "The department store is Bergdorf *Goodman*," she stammers, breathless with incredulity. "Herbert *Berghof* has his own School of the Theatre. . ."

"Oh."

"It's about the best in the city, as a matter of fact. And of course, he directs when the right vehicle comes along."

"You're an actress," he deduces.

"Clever." She knows when she's being patronized.

In a few minutes she decides to make up. It's too much trouble to try to navigate the party before she's warmed up, anyway. "What about you?" she persists, taking up the theme.

"Are you a painter? Do you write?"

"Somewhat."

"I see."

It's a contest. Neither is winning. But even a child, she says, could note the signs of more intense involvement. The flaring nostrils. The arching calf. The removed overcoat, which allows her to see his various defects.

"Were you invited by one of the people here?"

"Of course."

"Of course."

"She's not around right at the moment. Ruth Moskowitz. She lives in the building next door. She goes to the Cooper Union. She paints. Very gifted. Do you know her?"

"No."

"You will, I'm sure."

He licks his lips. A woman who is neither inarticulate nor intimidated by him, badly-dressed nor ugly, does not fall so often within his reach. If for no other reason than that his reach very rarely leaves the vicinity of East Third Street and Avenue B, where such women almost never go. His life, soon to be touted in mythic proportions to lure her, is actually a rather lonely and sorrowful affair. He's twenty-five and has a pose to keep up, which is an alienating proposition.

"And you?" she drawls. "Study anywhere?"

"I have studied. Ye-e-es."

"Oh? With whom?"

"Most recently with Baziotes, here in New York. Before that, with Hofmann in Provincetown. Of course, de Kooning lets me work in his studio occasionally."

He's waiting for her to be impressed. He doesn't realize that behind her Blonde Venus eyelids, drooping with the semblance of boredom, she *is* impressed. Her heart is beating wildly.

"No dilettante, this one!" she cries to me. No tattooed man, she means, whose appeal as a grotesque will wear off all too soon. "A painter! Real!"

She can hardly wait to see his work, to measure beneath half-closed lashes his primed canvasses, heavy with acrylic and varnish (judging from his masters), rich with color and the slashing, ripe line of spontaneous control. She's ready to trot out her own notes on Jackson Pollock, Rothko, and a little lecture about Kline all saved from her one year as an art student at the Cooper Union, where she and Ruth first became friends, otherwise all but forgotten.

"But that's all behind me now," he says, and yawns.

"It is?" For a moment she almost reacts. But fortunately they can scarcely hear one another, what with the music so loud in the room and the dancers beginning to gyrate before them, women in flapper dresses trembling with beads, men with top-hats, garish waistcoats, long cigarette holders, flowing scarves. A tall, handsome fellow whom Victoria knows slightly comes by and sizes up her black-stockinged legs, long for a woman of her size. He turns up one corner of his shapely mouth as he approaches her, seeming to make a decision.

"Hi! Oh, hi, Dick," he says, acknowledging Richard, who is now slipping his overcoat onto the nearest chair, as if to bar his way.

"My name is not Dick," Richard snaps, compressing his buck teeth with an emotion strongly resembling annoyance. Or even jealousy. "It's Richard."

"Oh yes, hello, Bruce," Victoria murmurs, barely moving her head toward him. Bruce is a graduate student in philosophy whom she met at NYU and to whom she is cautiously attracted. But now it feels as if the tables have been turned, and she notes this new man's—Richard's—reactions with some interest. *Annoyance?* she's busily thinking, watching both of them with poorly concealed joy. *Jealousy? How intriguing.* However, she has been demurely stalking tall and handsome Bruce for about a year, and she doesn't want either man to get the idea that she's easy prey. She smiles and again lowers her eyelids, subtly gazing in his direction, but Tall and Handsome isn't particularly responsive to subtlety. He moves away.

"A friend of yours?" Loess mutters, through his teeth.

"I know him. But, oh! There's my friend. Over there."

Reluctantly she waves to Ruth, who waves back, smiling lazily, and sizes up Victoria's companion. Not with pleasure. And then smiles lazily again—Ruth is smiling lazily with increasing frequency these days; her tensions seem to have been put out like a candle—and drifts away.

"She hardly even knew I was there," Victoria tells me, "but then I noticed that Ruth was lazily drifting next to Zalman Finster, that artist type you were seeing for a while. Are you still, by the way? The one with the cap, *you* know."

"Ruth was with *him* at the party?" I parry, not wanting to answer too directly. "But she always said she detested him."

"Well, I didn't say she was *with* him, just that she was next to him." Victoria responds to the panic in my voice, so she doesn't tell me then that on the other side of Ruth is the woman usually seen with Zalman, whom everyone calls Flower but whose real name is Flora. Nor does she tell me that the three of them seem to be floating along together, directionless and yet perhaps really going somewhere, and that this vision of them fleetingly fills Victoria with dread. Which remains with her only for an instant, and only as a trace; it drifts away very much as Ruth herself did, lazily, as soon as Richard Loess turns back to her and asks, "So what's your name again, anyway? I didn't catch it the first time."

Confronted by the reflection of herself in this new man's small grey eyes, set above his beard, kinky and stubbled as his hair, she can suddenly think of nothing else.

"Mine is Richard Loess," he says, as if making some major disclosure, revealing some terribly important particle of knowledge. "Richard, mind you. Don't call me Dick. Please. Ever."

And so, she tells me, he lets her know his name. Richard

Loess. Not Dick, ever. He has been launched into her life, like a light boat suddenly let loose upon a river. But his own river is composed only of language, and he sputters off into it, remorselessly rowing away.

"Actually, I'm not painting at all now. Haven't painted since my show at the Tibor de Nagy," he tosses off, dropping the name of the most prestigious art gallery in New York. She has to control herself to keep from blinking too much.

"It's my feeling now that art has become too static," he rows on. "Too frozen. I agree with Duchamp that what's had to be done has already been done. Mere 'beauty,'" and here he pauses, pronouncing the word with a drawl of contempt, "mere *beauty* has no more real value. I'm no longer interested in art which is concerned only with the purely decorative."

Having delivered himself of this wisdom he looks over at her to make sure she has been duly impressed. She sits passively, staring before herself, her eyes a little glassy; she tells me she was thinking about her own paintings, which were frankly decorative and far more 'trivial' than Ruth's, or even than Zalman's, which I had dragged her once to see after his gallery opened.

"Wow. They look like upchuck," she'd commented, out of Zalman's hearing. "At least some of mine might make good fabric designs. Do people *buy* these?"

But Richard Loess has just increased in size and stature. Despite his buck teeth and his silly drawl and his fuzzy hair, she feels suddenly that she has met her match. Beneath his phlegmatic air of utter boredom there is, she senses, an intense young man, bristling with sincerity, good manners, and the right values.

"At last," she says to me in April. *At last.*

Richard Loess leans forward a little. His face is animated for the first time. He looks into her eyes. She finds no trace of the usual hungry glare in his; only a kind of latent adoration. Which reassures her.

She keeps her mouth shut.

"Actually," he goes on, warming to his subject, "what I'm interested in now most of all is prosody. I've begun to write. I think that art has survived only in the Word. And, of course, in Film. The cinema is a synthesis of all forms of media brought forward into our own time. Except that I feel it's important to step back from our own time. That's why I'm so interested in anthropology."

"Oh? Anthropology?" Now she's worrying about me. Her friend Helene. She says vaguely, "I have a friend who studies that," but she has already begun to think hard about my good points, she confesses to me—vivid coloring, a nice face, intelligence—and to comfort herself with the bad. The fact that I'm both shy and opinionated. That my hair frizzes. That I talk too much, or not at all. That I'm too insecure and intense, not like Victoria herself, who has never really suffered from jealousy or loss.

Nonetheless, she determines not to tell him anything much about Ruth or me for a while.

"Anthropology," she repeats.

"Comparative myth, actually," he continues, nodding his head, excited. "Creation myth. Mother goddess myth. Have you ever read Robert Graves?"

Vaguely, she remembers *I, Claudius*, which was required reading in one of her high school English classes.

"I mean, of course, his great study of myth, *The White Goddess*. I've been doing a study on *The White Goddess* for a college paper."

"You go to college?"

"Only in absentia. I have one rather spectacular professor— the other courses are simply too ba-*nal*. I have no interest in getting any sort of diploma or degree."

"Oh, of course not," she says. "Quite right," she says. (Ba-*nal*, she thinks). "I don't want a degree either. I'm a college drop-out, as a matter of fact," she confides, and then realizes that this too might sound rather ba-*nal*. However, by now it wouldn't matter anyway. He isn't listening.

"What purpose would a college degree serve in my life?" he demands rhetorically, becoming more and more animated as he warms to his favorite subject: himself.

"I have no need to teach, to take some 9 to 5 job as do these unfortunate drones you see on the campuses of inferior schools. If it comes to that, I should rather work on the docks, be a longshoreman. Get my merchant seaman's papers."

"Could you do that?" She looks him in the eye. She remembers Patrick Parker, who really *is* a merchant seaman, and wonders how well this young man would get along with him.

But, "Of course!" Richard patters on, and continues, "I already have, in fact. Of course, right now I'm working in a gallery." He shrugs this off, self-deprecating. "And also, of course, I'm doing a film script in my spare time.

"But in the past I've done one thing and another. Jack of all trades, rolling stone and all that. Went cross country on flatcars when I was 20, did some logging out in Oregon. Drove out to California with my friend Jack."

"Kerouac?" she asks, openly gaping. (A lapse). He nods briefly, and goes on.

"Biked through England. That was when I was fourteen." As if in answer to her next question he says quickly, "I'm twenty-five now."

But she's thinking of something else. "Your parents let you do all that? Go biking all alone? When you were only fourteen?"

"My mother let me, yes. And I *was* alone. Dreadfully, I'm afraid. My parents are divorced. Sometimes I think they never really married, just that my father lets me bear his name out of the goodness of his heart. If he has any. I hardly know."

This story so reminds her of her own that she feels touched on an altogether different level, but then like a shadow his name begins to glimmer through to her, and it seems to her she remembers seeing it on an intricate logo in front of a huge plateglass window on Madison Avenue. LOESS GALLER-IES.

She wonders if his could be the same.

"L-O-E-S-S?" she questions absently.

"Yes. As on the gallery. Just so."

She looks up to see if he's being sarcastic, but he isn't.

"The gallery is my uncle's," he informs her gravely. He's looking full into her face now, leaning forward; she showers him with aquamarine fireworks from between her lids.

"You're quite lovely," he announces with gravity, as if making some momentous decision. His voice seems choked with emotion. "Fortunately, beauty still has some significance on the human face."

"Oh," she says. "Does it really?" Which startles her, she tells me, even more than did his declaration.

"You have a quality of sculpture," he murmurs. "Vaguely Grecian. Phidias's Athena Lemnia, perhaps, grave and perfect. Called 'the Beautiful.' Or a maiden of Chios, of an earlier period. Calm and elaborate. Beauty had significance then in art as well."

"My parents are divorced too," she stammers.

"Ah, so? On the other hand, my ex-wife Deirdre was like a Celtic noblewoman of the pre-Christian period. Tall, red-headed. It was probably she who inspired my interest in the comparative myth of the early Britons in the first place."

His ex-wife? she is thinking. *He's already been married?* "Do you really believe that?" she asks aloud. "That it's all been done, I mean."

"Yes. It has all been done."

"And there's no more reason for art?"

"Art simply has nothing left to say. Or if it does, I no longer have any real interest in saying it. Do you know who Marcel Duchamp is?"

She nods, too entranced with him to feel as insulted as she

might have if someone else had asked her the same question. Duchamp's painting "Nude Descending Staircase" is world famous; it is material for every art history class on earth, let alone New York.

"A friend of my father's," he mentions casually, turning away from her as he utters this triumph. "He's stopped painting. Become an art dealer. He had done it all, definitively, in his work entitled 'Nude Descending Staircase.' After he finished that painting, there was nothing left to do. He had solved all the problems left to western art."

She sits quietly, forgetting the party around her. She sees nothing but his face and her own two hands. She feels very empty, very sad, almost as if she has left some part of her childhood behind. She did not care so very much about western art—not like Ruth—but it was somehow important to her nonetheless. And now—if he is to be believed, which she feels he is—it is finished. On the other hand, she experiences something almost like jubilation. She wants to grab Ruth by the hands and pull her around the room. She wants to call me.

"I've met Mr. Right!" she's planning to shout. (When she's good and safe in the relationship and not too vulnerable to risk mentioning him to her two attractive girlfriends.) "I think we're going to get married!"

This last will be more subdued, but she'll be perfectly serious. She thinks with delight of Ruth's envious contempt and of my envious surprise.

Because, even at this crowded party, surrounded by people and having listened to him for only fifteen minutes, Victoria has no doubts. This is, simply and precisely, the life she wants to share. She's not yet even certain why, except for the fact that she can see them together in a loft painted white, entertaining Larry Rivers and Willem De Kooning at wild yet discreet dinner parties, carousing through the night with Kerouac and a few gallons of Italian red, attending gallery openings together, Richard in a velvet suit, his beard elegant just above the collar, herself in slinky black. . .

"There's no more space in our society for the building of cathedrals," he is telling her. "That's why, to be really creative, we have to step back from our time."

"I thought the bike trip to England would be magnificently liberating," he says. "I wanted it. In fact, I simply insisted upon it, if I remember correctly. And yet all I can recall of it, frankly, is how cold and wet it was in the Lake District, which I thought would be so romantic. Instead, it seemed like months of pedalling through mud with my head lowered against the rain. . ."

Rain now pelts the window of his apartment, where they sit together in candlelight over the remains of a tunafish casserole and cheap white wine. It's the day after the party. They've spent almost all of the past 24 hours with one another, parting only to go to their separate homes to sleep. Now they're curled up across the room from one another, talking, listening, trying to share everything. Except she keeps wishing that she didn't feel such enormous pressure building inside herself.

But of course, she says that only later, much later, when she's telling it all to me.

He has recited his poetry, shown her his thesis on *The White Goddess*, and read her one or two of his more trivial pieces on the history and development of art in our time.

As far as his personal life is concerned, he has stopped at opening scrapbooks and photograph albums, but she has gotten verbal portraits of everyone who ever passed through it, even for an hour. In a room full of people, she could probably now recognize his mother; his father; his first wife Deirdre; the bisexual female poet with whom he was in love for a while and with whom he still remains friends; the poet's famous ex-husband, the radical black activist; all the hoboes and vision-aries and saints and bards he ever spent time with; his uncle the gallery-owner whom he doesn't like very much; and two or three family pets. In return for which she has told him almost nothing about herself.

He hasn't heard about her mother, Elaine, who prizes her alimony-supported wardrobe, furs, and impeccable apartment above everything on earth, rejecting the idea of anything but the most advantageous second marriage, keeping herself lonely for profit but heartily resenting her own loneliness. He hasn't heard about her father, Hank, who has embarked upon his own second marriage to a much younger woman as if it were the simplest and most natural thing in the world to do, and who seems content to keep his old, first wife and daughter stunned into silence by his willingness to pay through the nose.

"Why does our parents' generation seem to be content to live only in a series of clichés?" he complains to her at one point, referring to the inadequacies of his own progenitors. Which might allow her the perfect opening to tell him about the clichés with which she herself has always been surrounded, if only he would give her the slightest chance.

But he doesn't. So he knows almost nothing of her parents, or her schools, or of the things she likes to do. Nor has she said anything about Ruth or myself after that first dim mention of us at the party, when she was still secure enough to tell him she *had* friends.

As far as Richard Loess is concerned, Victoria might be living in a bubble of light. She has become painfully aware that every comment, every reminiscence, every single phrase she utters in response to his ongoing stream of self-revelation must be syntactically excellent and grammatically correct. When it is not, he fixes her with that round-eyed stare which lets her know that she has said something ba-*nal*; but when it is, he praises her with such a pithy comment on her beauty and uniqueness that she feels she must live up to it, must blossom with his praise into exactly the perfect woman he imagines her to be.

Her head is beginning to ache.

With each revelation she has become more and more aware that this boy, hardly older than she is, has already been everywhere and done everything she might ever have wanted to be or do.

And what gave him that right, after all? What has allowed him to be so free and so resourceful in his life, while she's had to stay home and take art and acting lessons she didn't really want and shop for clothing and look her best all the time and think mostly about finding a man she wants to marry—which she thinks she now has done—so she can "settle down" before she's ever really started up? What gave him the right to go off by himself at the age of fourteen and pedal his way across an unknown nation? She could no more have done that than she could have flown to the moon, and not just because her mother wouldn't have let her, either. It would never have occurred to her to have walked, or biked, or hitch-hiked across some alien country, any more than it would have occurred to her to have done so across her own native city of New York.

"I'm amazed," says Victoria, the April night when she finally reveals all about Richard. We're alone together in my living room, curled up on the ugly sofa.

"I'm just amazed by the simplicity of it all. Not only did he just *do* these things, he was even *encouraged* to do them. Encouraged by his parents, by his friends, by society, by books, by history. I think men are *supposed* to travel to unknown territories and climb mountains and ride around the country on boxcars and drink whiskey out of pint bottles and make friends with bums; they're *supposed* to try to seduce as many of us as possible. And if they decide to settle down after all that and devote themselves to some demanding career and a lifetime of hard work, whether or not they get married and raise a family, all is not only forgiven—they get nothing but praise. Catch a woman trying to live like that! The only thing women have ever been expected to explore and climb on is *men*."

But in March, having made up her mind that she's really in

love for the first time in her life, Victoria listens to him by the hour, really wanting to take his experience into herself, to make it her own. And to seduce him. To make herself indispensable to him, because she isn't really sure of him yet.

Sitting with him in his dreary apartment, she smiles and nods, nods and smiles, looking completely interested.

But the ache in her head gets worse.

"When I first read Nietzsche I got sick," he confesses, sipping wine. "Sick from exultation, sick with frenzy. The way an epileptic becomes sick just before an attack, with an ecstatic burning light behind his eyes . . .

"My mother and I were living together in a studio apartment on Hudson Street, and I read a few pages of *Thus Spake Zarathustra* that she had lying around the house. Just a few pages. That was enough. I couldn't stay inside. I threw my coat on and ran out into the wind and stood under an awning at the corner, retching. . . I was sick for days. That was when I was fifteen."

She nods. She wants to ask, "Then did you ever read it again? Did you ever finish the book?" But she herself hasn't read it and she realizes her questions would be so ba-*nal*.

"How can I help being ba-*nal*, anyway?" she confides to me, finally beginning to laugh a little bit. "I come by it naturally— the only reading matter *my* mother ever had lying around the house was every copy of *Vogue* published since the beginning of time."

So instead, delicately rubbing the old jelly-jar from which she's been drinking wine against the palm of her hand, she begins to reply to him as if her answers should be a kind of counterpoint to his revelations. She decides to come up with a few revelations of her own—not too personal, perhaps, but suitably poetic and philosophical.

"I remember when I first discovered how life could be," she murmurs. (Which she realizes is also a pretty ba-*nal* statement, but she has to take a few chances or risk boring him with her silence.) "Do you know what I mean about discovering it? Really understanding it, seeing it for the first time? I was sitting on the bank of a small lake on our place in Connecticut. . . it was summer, it was beautiful there, my parents were still together. I was only twelve years old and I still believed in God. I prayed every night, the way my grandmother had taught me to pray, asking God to please bless everyone. . ."

"Curious," he interrupts, "that you should associate monotheism with childishness. As if as one matures one automatically becomes an atheist."

"I did."

"Ah. Well." He smirks. She knows she has committed an error, sprung a fault, like a boat springing a leak before it founders. She watches him, her eyes dilated.

"When my parents were divorcing I prayed all the time that they would make up and stay together. I suppose I lost my faith in prayer when they didn't."

"Yes, of course. Unanswered prayers are always an excuse for lapsed faith." He smirks again, and takes another sip of wine. "But do go on," he says indulgently.

"Well, this one afternoon, I was sitting in the rushes and there was a snake, with its mouth wide open. And as I watched I saw it was sucking in a frog, drawing it right into its mouth which had unhinged and opened so wide that there was more than enough room for the frog to go through into the snake's body. It was horrible. But the frog couldn't move, and neither could I. I watched it being drawn deeper and deeper into snake's mouth. Finally a friend of mine came and she just threw a rock at the snake and somehow that broke the spell. We were both able to get away, and the frog escaped. But I saw something important, I saw that frog being drawn in, slowly. . . How life is . . . not cruel, exactly, but—what's the word?"

"Remorseless," he murmurs, hating to have been quiet for so long. "Inexorable."

"Yes." She refuses to mind the interruption. "I guess, I

mean, how something can pull us in despite ourselves, and how we can't move out of its way, no matter what else we want to do. I saw that."

Her voice is trembling. She's been trying to recover lost ground.

"Ah," he whispers. "I like that you saw that. And I like the way you told me about it."

She breathes more easily.

They face each other across the room on two small separate couches. One of which is his bed. Between them is the littered table, covered with the refuse of the meal. She expects him to try to make a pass at her. Isn't it to this all their philosophy and anthropology and personal reminiscence have been leading? All talk of mythology, travel, worship of art and women? What else could be the dark cave of the myth if not the cozy space between her thighs? Prepared to give, she's impatient to get it over with.

Her head has begun to throb, very definitely.

Earlier, she hurried through the streets with him through the dark March rain. Buying tuna for his casserole, bell peppers, Camay soap, toilet paper.

Feeling domestic and exhausted, she accidentally steps into a pile of dogshit, deposited on the sidewalk before his house.

"My God!" he exclaims, as if some prized work of art has been desecrated.

One of her fancy black pumps is completely smeared. She feels like an utter dolt for having been so careless. But he falls on his knees before her, and out of his own pocket takes a huge oblong rag—his handkerchief—and carefully, reverently, begins to wipe her foot. On his knees before her on the sidewalk.

"Let me do it," he pleads, as she tries to move away. "I'm so sorry. Oh, dear. Let me take care of it."

He's in a state of apology for the entire city, because she got dogshit on her shoe.

So now, expecting him to begin to make love to her, she sees in his drooping eyes the kind of adoration only a poet or a maker of myths could create; a professional adoration, scrutinizing and exacting. She wants to have sex with him so she can be sure, as she was sure with Patrick Parker, that he's in love with her. She feels a tiny premonition of dread, but desire draws her on. She moves closer and closer to him. Inexorably.

She is Eurydice on the way out of the underworld. Psyche in the chamber of Eros. Victoria at twenty-one, frightened and made greedy by first love.

"Drink your wine."

She drinks. A wine-dark rain pelts the windows. He has stopped talking, and the silence terrifies her. What will we do next? she wants to ask. But to ask it would be so ba-*nal*. She keeps her mouth shut.

"The things we want the most always show us to ourselves with our pants down," she whispers to me in my room that night.

"I didn't know you were so smart," I say.

"I didn't know it either."

In Richard's room, on Richard's hard bed, she is no longer Marlene Dietrich. She's a skinny frightened kid from Central Park West. She's the daughter of divorced parents who do not love each other, and who possibly do not love her very much, either. She will soon begin to age; the yellow hair will dull, the face will square with years, the nose will get bigger. The hollows under the eyes will grow. She will start looking like her father, with her mother's nose. She will be ordinary. Richard will be bored with her soon. He already is.

She goes to his couch and makes him kiss her. And the kiss is not good.

I see them together, only once, by accident.

In a small coffeeshop, not far from the Cedar Street Tavern. It's not even a very nice coffeeshop, but one of those places executed in pink and lime green plastic that serve bad coffee. Chrome everywhere, to punish the eyes.

I go through the door of the coffeeshop and see them sitting in a tall green booth, side by side, not looking at each other. Not saying anything. He eats a sandwich. Later Victoria tells me it was a tuna sandwich. On rye. He's addicted to tuna, Victoria tells me later, as she tells me all of it later, even what I would prefer not to have known. Now, in the pink and lime green coffeeshop, Loess chews tuna and Victoria stirs coffee. Neither look up as I stop at the door; neither of them notices me or anything else.

Victoria's face is strained and ashen. Richard Loess's face is pale and dull. When he turns to her she seems to draw into herself, like someone who has just been scolded. It's very late at night, when I see them. I go in because I'm hungry; I've been at the Cedar to score some Dex—it's term paper time and I've been up all night and then working all day, no time to eat till now. I entered the place anticipating a late-night sandwich, tasting it just as I can taste the sleep that will follow it as soon as I can finish eating and catch the subway and get home, into bed. Food and sleep; my little stash of pills. Elemental comfort. A very windy night. Cruelly cold and damp, like the middle of winter.

As soon as I see them, my hunger vanishes. I want to leave, to get out of there at once, but I'm afraid they've already seen me. So I move toward them hesitantly, gesturing with my hands. Feeling like a maniac, as always when I meet someone who doesn't seem to see me. Are they ignoring me on purpose? Is it a deliberate snub? Should I push myself into their consciousness or just go away?

This time I go away.

Back out on the street, I watch them for a moment through the big plate glass window of the place. Loess finishes his sandwich and gets to his feet. Victoria rises to stand beside him.

"I'll take you home," he says to her, and Victoria nods.

From the far corner to which I've retreated, I can see them leave, weaving together down the long wind-tunnel of the street, followed only by the city's blowing dust.

ELEVEN

"I ripped into her like a maniac and she loved it."
—*Neal Cassady, 1950*

"I've met a boy who wants to marry me," Victoria announces to me on the telephone the next time we talk. A month has passed; it's April. Almost May. The rain is cold, but soft. The wind has quieted down. Victoria's voice is high-pitched and shaky.

"I guess that was him I saw you with the other night."

"The other night?"

"A few weeks ago, really. It was near the Cedar. In a luncheonette?"

"Oh," Victoria says. There's a pause. "That wasn't him." Neither of us knows exactly what to say.

"That was Dick Loess. I mean Richard. Richard Loess," Victoria says. Finally, after a long silence, as if she's too exhausted to explain herself, she continues, "I've been hanging out with him."

"Oh," I say.

"He's not the one." Victoria begins to cry. She covers it by putting her hand over the receiver, but not efficiently enough; I can hear moist sniffling over the line. "This other fellow is a law student. Burton. Burton Pogue. A really *nice* law student," she says, and her voice slides upwards; the three of us have always translated the word "nice" into "horrifyingly dull."

"Actually," Victoria goes on, "I've known Burton for a long time. We grew up together, as a matter of fact. His parents are friends of my parents. Of course, he doesn't know much about art or the theatre, but he's interested in learning more. Really interested, he says. He's always liked me a lot."

She's beginning to hiccough from the tears. We both try to pretend she isn't.

"We even made it together once." In imitation of her former self, she tries to laugh for a few seconds. "He really wanted to. So I let him. He's been kind of waiting around for me ever since.

"Actually," she says after another long silence, "I may *have* to get married. It's such a drag, trying to get an abortion. Of course, Mother's been looking. She says it's too expensive to fly to Puerto Rico unless we locate a definite name, and apparently they've arrested all the good people operating out of Jersey."

She explodes into a series of wet gales. This time, helpless, I join her.

"What kind of man are you going to marry?"

They sat in the lobby of a hotel on Eighth Avenue. An ugly hotel, across the street from the old New York Post Office. They had gone to this hotel from his apartment where they had spent the night before, first leaving her apartment and going to his apartment, then leaving his apartment and walking the streets. Back and forth, she tells me. Back and forth, looking for some place in which to feel relaxed together.

Victoria's eyes were like moons, with huge shadows around them. She no longer wore any makeup. He said he didn't like women who wore makeup.

"Of course, I was plastered with the stuff the night I met him and that didn't stop him from being attracted to me, but neither of us remembered that or talked about it later on," she lets me know.

They were sitting in the lobby because she didn't want to go home. Her hand was on his arm, a delicate triangle of white on the rough wool of his coat. She could feel nothing through the sleeve of that coat. No warmth. No skin. Nothing.

It's this scene she shares with me on the telephone, after she finishes crying; crying and then laughing, until there's nothing left. No tears, no hysteria; nothing but the facts, which she obviously needs to describe in alarming detail.

"A cowboy," Richard Loess said that night in the seedy hotel lobby. "You're going to marry a cowboy. A tall man with hair going grey at the temples. He'll be a self-made man with pots of money and a big cattle ranch. And leathery skin. He has to have leathery skin. He'll drive a Cadillac. . ."

"Why won't you come with me?" she asked him. Her mouth was tight and small. Her skin was sallow and her hair was limp. Tears would come only later, with the sense of solace. "The apartment is still empty. My mother's still in Bermuda. I don't feel like being alone."

"We could rent a room in this hotel," Richard said, evading her. Looking at the lobby, carpeted in red with a floral pattern. Green walls. Huge armchairs made of shiny red leather. Cigarette burns in the furniture. "We could lie down together on a worn out old bed, we could pretend we were. . . a whore and her customer."

She stared at him. His eyes were half closed with apparent boredom but there was strain on his face. He wanted to be away.

"Shall you be all right?"

"All right? What do you mean?"

He wanted to be away. "I mean, if I leave you here?" he said.

"Leave me? Here?"

"Shall you?"

"I don't know. I will . . . I. . ."

"You mean, you *shall.*"

What was he talking about? she wondered. Wanting to be sick. Feeling sickness take her, a rough hand at the back of her neck, feeling it lift her off the stubborn, ordinary ground of the hotel lobby, off Eighth Avenue, out of the city, into a place she had always known, a familiar place to which she had never wanted to return. Where within her body there were only claws; where she was always reeling from the pain.

"Why should he want to hurt me?" she asks me on the phone, her voice quavering.

And yet there was something familiar about real pain, she says. She had met herself there, closing her eyes.

They had screwed just once, she tells me, not in his apartment but on her mother's eiderdown comforter, kissing one another with eyes and mouths closed, squeezing their bodies together against a resistance both of them felt, cold with the business of sex. Two swimmers with their teeth chattering. She felt those teeth, closed to her, as she felt all the hard surfaces of his body, the bones of his skull, his temples, where she grazed him with her mouth. Their legs, too, were odd, grotesque; his spread wide when he pushed into her, then hers spread wide and his between them, and both of them glued together at the pelvis; always awkward, always uncomfortable. All the postures distorted and ugly, even in the dark. She could see the outline of his body in the light that came in the windows from the street, falling over the outline of her body like a shadow.

"The positions of love are all so funny, just looked at objectively, taking all the emotion away," she chattered, wanting to be witty, wanting to be wry and wise and still impressive to him.

"This isn't love."

She sat in the hotel lobby with him, her legs crossed neatly as she had been taught to cross them, and she experienced, with wonder, the barrenness of herself when all her vanity was gone.

When they got up and left the Eighth Avenue hotel and walked on through the city, it seemed to her that they were walking only in the most dangerous neighborhoods, on the worst blocks, where she never went alone and which she generally avoided. On 42nd Street, outside a place where the spicy whiff of hotdog steam floated into the street with the sound of men quarrelling and women laughing, a drunk slid up to them and screamed at Richard, "Hey! Beatnik! Write me a poem!"

Was he a beatnik, then? she wondered, trying to understand. Was that what it meant? To automatically not like her because she slept with him? To be cold during sex? To cover himself with a long overcoat, to bike through England at fourteen, to feel that art was finished, to write long papers for college courses "in absentia?" To court women with endless gusts of words and then to leave them flat in bed?

Was she herself a "beatnik," in her black dress and black stockings and old fur coat? Perhaps all three of us, Ruth and Victoria and myself, were "beatniks" because we smoked pot, hung out in the Cedar Street Tavern and Stanley's, and said we didn't want to get married (at least not right away), so we could study art and other difficult subjects and pursue careers and freedom. Was that what was wrong with her life? That she herself had become one, that she had surrounded herself with "beatniks?"

Never before has she longed so fervently to be ordinary. To dress in pastel colors. To tease her hair. To date nice boys with fraternity pins and slow manners and fast cars.

But she wanted him still; his sighs, his elegies, his artistic comparisons, his celebrity friends. She walked along beside him, so sad she could hardly even register the ugliness of her surroundings or remember how she had arrived at them; until suddenly and without warning she bumped against a hard little corner in herself, an edge that had always been there. Invisible, until this moment.

"Did he really say we could rent a room in that hotel; that I could pretend to be a whore; that he had never been in a hotel with a woman? Did he really say that?" she asks me later, baffled, as if somehow I might know more about it than she does herself. And even that night, sleepless and winded and feeling the claws as deeply as she did, she found herself turning to look him directly in the face, and realized, right for once, that she was never going to see him again.

And didn't care.

Until a few weeks later when she realized with a shock that she was also not going to see her period again for a while. And why. Even why she had become pregnant, as she explained it to herself. She had conceived a child with Richard Loess for the simple reason that, for the first time in her life, a man had failed to make her laugh.

TWELVE

"How nice it'd be to come home to her and sit by the fireplace and she in the kitchen"
                              —Gregory Corso, ca. 1955.

It's a dazzling wedding. I think of it as a society wedding, or as close to a society wedding as you can have if your mother is living on alimony payments and your father, deeply involved with his second family, can hardly even find the time to put in an appearance. But Victoria's father does show up finally, looking trim and youngish in a morning coat, to give away the bride who, as she puts it, "Isn't really his to give away in the first place."

I've attended a wide variety of Jewish weddings, ceremonies performed under the *chuppah*, the canopy, ceremonies in living rooms, ceremonies in fancy restaurants, even ceremonies in the rotunda of the City Hall. But I've never before seen a wedding in a small but elegant church on Madison Avenue, in which the grey stone carvings and marble hallways ring with venerable authority as if by an act of God. Nor have I ever been to a reception in a small but elegant hotel nearby, at which a string quartet plays foxtrots and waltzes and the bride dances the first dance with her almost absentee father and everyone discreetly applauds, even Elaine, ignoring the reality that the dancing bride and her father have seen one another perhaps five times in the last five years. Adding force to the belief, as venerable and delicate as the carvings of the church and the whorls and strains of outdated music, that appearances count more than anything else on earth.

And if this wedding is to be taken as an example, appearances are wonderful. Victoria looks like the heroine of a 19th century novel, tiny and wasp-waisted, her golden hair up around her crown in curls, entwined by a coronet of flowers and pearls and a long spill of lace, her grandmother's, very old and expensive, falling down behind. And this is it, folks—the 19th century novel's perfect, happy ending. The fadeout of the movies we cried at in high school, before we knew enough to be embarrassed by them. Jean Simmons in the arms of Michael Rennie. Elizabeth Taylor in the arms of Michael Wilding. Merle Oberon being carried to the open window by Laurence Olivier, not yet 'Sir' Laurence. THE END.

Victoria has had the abortion a week before the wedding. Her mother has already ordered everything at the caterers. They've hired the string quartet as well as a dance band in the banquet room of the excellent hotel. Her dress is fitted and paid for. Her grandmother's veil has been attached. So even after she finally finds a doctor willing to do it and the abortion goes off without a hitch, she decides to marry Burton Pogue anyway.

She's flushed and very happy. Their families come, and all her friends, and he puts an emerald ring on her finger that has been handed down to Pogues for generations. Everyone drinks champagne and eats cake, and she chatters to her guests about the dress and her grandmother's lace veil and about where she and Burton are going on their honeymoon—the south of France—and once, only to me and only vaguely, she mentions the abortion. Which is over.

But neither Victoria nor I as much as whisper about the last time we saw one another alone. That afternoon when I had come home to find her sitting in the hallway before my apartment door. Just sitting. On the dirty tiled floor on her balled-up coat.

"I have to find him," she had sobbed. "I just have to find him, no matter what."

"Hey." I had bent to her. "What you've got to do, Victoria, is to pull yourself together."

She just sat there, in the dust of my apartment building hallway, to which she hadn't deigned to touch the soles of her new suede shoes just a few short months before.

"Come on," I beckoned, sympathy clouding my better judgment as I unbolted my door. "My housekeeping is pretty disgusting these days; I've been doing research papers. And it's my senior term, you know? I need to keep up my grade point average."

But Victoria ignored it, as if none of it existed—the unwashed dishes, the papers scattered everywhere, the piles of books and dust kittens on the floor. She fell into a crumpled heap on what passed for my sofa, not even noticing her surroundings. Which wasn't like her.

"Most of the lights have blown," I apologized. "I've been up studying, most nights; I guess I just wore them out."

Victoria bent forward and cried for a while. After that she made me listen to the whole story all over again, even though I might not have wanted to listen to it. Even though I might have preferred to have gotten good and stoned, gone to the Satyajit Ray trilogy playing at the neighborhood art theatre, and tried not to think about why Zalman hadn't called for weeks or about midterm exams and research papers or about whether or not I was going to go to graduate school.

"So now, you want to find this guy?" I asked when Victoria had finished, simultaneously offering her the last thin piece of toilet paper in the house as she blew her nose for the hundredth time. "What's the matter with you? You haven't had enough insults? You want to go back for more?"

Victoria looked at me as if I were crazy.

"*You* should talk," she retorted, which convinced me that she wasn't going to die of a broken heart. "Aren't you the one who went with that guy Zalman for more than a year? You're still seeing him, for all I know. And anyway, I don't want to find *Dick*. I mean Richard." She pulled her hair away from her damp cheeks. "Who gives a damn about Richard? No, I'm not even crying about him any more," she lied, blowing her nose again. "It's *Patrick* I've got to find. Patrick Parker. Do you remember him?"

"Sure."

"I tried to call him last week. Well. . . " Meeting my eyes, she looked away. "You do remember, I guess, that he wanted to marry me. I keep thinking, actually, that that wasn't such a bad idea."

"What about the law student?"

"Who? Burton? What about him? Oh, well," she sighed. "You know. We're just about engaged. Anyway, I thought of Patrick. But when I called, his phone had been disconnected. So I went around to his apartment. And he wasn't there. The superintendent of his building was this horrible old man who kept looking at me and putting his hand in his trousers. I think he was feeling himself up. And . . ."

"Patrick?"

"He told me Patrick had just packed up and shipped out. Gone back to sea. But Patrick said he never wanted to go to sea again. And now he's gone. Just gone. So I asked the old man where Patrick had shipped out to, and he said he didn't know. Maybe if I called the Seaman's Union I could find him. Or maybe the old man was lying. Maybe that's what Patrick told him to say, and with a little money he might change his mind. . ."

She was sniffing again, and reached around wildly for another piece of toilet paper. It was all gone. I went to my dresser and got out a kerchief.

"I can't blow my nose on one of your silk scarves. It'll be ruined."

"Pretend you're a Renaissance princess."

"A maiden of Chios." Victoria laughed damply.

"Listen, Victoria," I continued. "I honestly don't think Patrick would want to marry you any more."

"It doesn't matter. I need to find him."

"Why? What for?"

She glanced up through her dirty hair and sighed. "I don't know," she said. Then she put her hand down and I saw her face, exposed. "I do know," she whimpered. "I'm just ashamed to say."

She put her head down, talking into her hands.

"It couldn't have been easy for him to come to my apartment that time. To meet my mother like that. It couldn't have been easy. And I laughed at him."

"But we always laugh at people," I soothed her. "That's what we do together."

"I've got to tell him," Victoria said. "He was . . . he was stunned when he went away that day. When I sent him away. Laughed in his face and sent him . . . For the first time now, I know how he felt. Why can't we ever say the right things to people at the right time? Why do we have to hurt some people and be hurt by others? I don't understand it."

"Even if you find out that he did go to sea, even if you track him down in Okinawa or Manila or wherever his ship might have docked, he probably won't be back for a long time. If at all. And what would you do, say you're sorry over transatlantic radio? Ship to shore? Probably with the whole crew listening?

Think about it. What good could it possibly do?"

I had always figured that Victoria could take care of herself. Or get taken care of, which amounted to the same thing. It had been Ruth and myself that I'd been worrying about recently. It shocked me that I'd been so wrong.

As for Ruth, I hadn't seen or heard from her in months. I'd called her a few times and gotten either no answer or a busy signal—I suspected that she took the phone off the hook when she didn't want to be bothered. And there was no talk of her at home. Even Mildred was silent on the subject. Which was ominous. Why hadn't Ruth called me to talk about some recent boyfriend or an interesting art show, to share some weed or a good party or another go at the bazoukia music, which she knew I loved? Why hadn't she called Victoria since that party? When I'd journeyed down to Paradise Alley to look for her, I'd found only her empty apartment, the door padlocked, not a trace of her in Stanley's or the Cedar Tavern.

But even her absence was eclipsed, because I had other problems. For one thing, I was seeing Zalman less often. I knew he was busy with the gallery, but it scared me that he might stop calling me altogether. How was I going to get by without him? Not only did I miss him, my supplies were low. I'd scored a couple of times on my own, but it wasn't easy. Some dealers thought I was too young to be trusted. Others expected sex and were angry when I didn't put out. Once I'd even gotten burned, by a young guy who had split with my money to score for me, he said, and never returned.

"Well, I wish you weren't seeing that guy Zalman at all, but at least you're seeing less of him," Victoria offered, after I told her some of this. (I noticed that she referred to him as 'That guy Zalman' every time she said his name, but it didn't occur to me to question why.) "And I don't agree that everything's going wrong for you. What about your education, your career?" She had cried herself out and was considerably calmer, probably already wishing she could get home and wash her hair. "You're ambitious and smart. Like, I always envied the kind of courage you and Ruth have: living alone, going all over the place by yourselves at night, being so turned on by your work. What I do is pretty nothing by comparison. And I'm scared to go anywhere at night except by taxi."

"My studies aren't going very well either," I said. "In fact, they're a complete mess. Okay, so I've been accepted to the University of Chicago . . ."

"Hey! Good deal!" Victoria exclaimed.

"Yeah, you're right, it's a good deal. I should be happy. Except there isn't any money to go with it. Not a dime towards the tuition. No scholarships or assistantships. No grants. And how am I going to go if I don't get any money?"

"By going to school and working part-time like you're doing now. Why can't you make it in graduate school the same way?"

"Because my undergraduate college is free if you live in New York. Even the books are free. Why do you think I go there? I could never have raised the funds for my tuition—I can just about make my own living. And how am I going to do that, without any financial assistance, in a strange city where I haven't got a job or an apartment and don't know my way around?"

"So go to school in New York. Why do you have to go to Chicago, anyway?"

"All my teachers told me it was the best school in the country for funding digs and field trips. After a few years in Chicago I could end up in Machu Picchu or the Tigris Euphrates Valley. Someplace I've always wanted to go. But how am I going to live until then? No way." I was having trouble fighting back my own tears.

"Hey. Now *you're* scared," Victoria said, her eyes widening.

"What are you talking about?"

"My mother always says that New Yorkers are more scared of moving to some other city than anything. Like they think they're going to be surrounded by savage tribes or something if they cross the Hudson. She's from Chicago herself, you know? The climate there's a little weird, but it's okay. It's fine. You ought to get over it and just go."

I watched her patting her hair back into place. Already she was regaining her old smug aura of wealth and privilege. What did Victoria know about trying to support herself? How could she possibly understand how I felt? The issues that confronted me were real. Tuition. Living expenses. Where was I going to find the money? I'd been told to get a low-interest education loan, and to look into the possibility of government grants. There were apparently ways in which graduate archaeologists could make themselves useful, and therefore loans could be underwritten, grants could be funded. And so on.

But there was something about going to the government that worried me.

"I had this friend," I told her, as we sat there together. I had actually made a pot of coffee, something I rarely did. I was out of Dexamil, but I didn't want to sleep anyway. "He was on his way to Ankhara; he said it was to teach at Roberts, this American college in Turkey. But one of the other anthropology majors told me that he was lying. That he was really going there to be a spy."

"A spy! You're kidding, right?" This was too much like one of our former evenings together, sharing jokes about men; Victoria couldn't resist the habit of laughing. I even took out my cigar box of grass and rolled a joint for the two of us out of the last of it; I was getting jumpy, sitting there without one.

"I'm *not* kidding. Lots of those government grants, especially the ones for studying culture and language in foreign countries, are really sponsored by the Overseas Secret Service. They let you get the initial training at some good American school and then they ship you out and teach you how to pick up information. That's why it's called 'intelligence.' They want to know things. They must have thousands of little agents out there, disguised as archaeologists or teachers, picking up tidbits for them, most of them useless, but some of them about the Kurdish insurrectionists or the Central American underground. Who knows what they're interested in anyway? And they can make use of anybody. My friend told me, and I'm sure it's true. The most unlikely types. As long as they know the language and something about the culture. Anybody."

So now I was faced with the decision of whether to risk getting involved with spying for the government, going deeply into debt, or to giving up archaeology altogether. If I took out loans in order to go to graduate school, how would I ever pay them back? What kind of work would I be able to do? Could I gather "intelligence?" Or write useless studies about the effect of ancient burial mounds or modern urban mores, as had one of my friends who had graduated two years ago, had gotten a Master's degree, and now couldn't find a job?

I hated to admit that my parents were right when they talked about "practicality" and jobs that were "useful" for women, but somehow my own faith in the work I had chosen had been undermined. Wasn't I just going to end up getting married someday anyway, meeting the proverbial "nice boy" that Andre Pincus had referred to and settling for an ordinary life, the way everybody said I was? Everybody but Zalman, Ruth and Victoria, that is. Only now, Zalman was disappearing, Ruth was incommunicado, and Victoria was sitting in my apartment, pregnant, rejected, and mourning a relationship that had been over for a year. About which we had only laughed together uproariously, if I remembered, at the time.

"We always laugh," I said to her. "That's what we *do* together."

And she cried, "Why can't we ever say the right things to people at the right time?"

It made me wonder just how deeply we felt about one another, Ruth, Victoria and I; just how much we'd ever be able to help one another, to take care of one another. To give each other anything real.

But now Victoria is herself again, bright and desirable and confident, sipping champagne at her own delightful wedding.

"Mummy worked so hard to find the proper doctor," she informs me cheerfully. We're huddled together in an anteroom filled with coats and ashtrays. For a minute I think Victoria's going to roll a joint and ask me to share it, but instead she pulls off her emerald engagement ring and pushes it back on her finger, staring at it without seeing. I guess that despite her animation, she's tired. And I don't recall her ever calling Elaine "Mummy" before.

"*Mumm*y:" what the Ivy League crowd—Burton's crowd— call their mothers. Before this she has always called Elaine "mother," or "Elaine."

"And isn't it ironic, anyway?" Victoria sighs. "Because the perfect doctor was right here in New York. Right in Manhattan. I can't really tell you his name but if you ever have a need, call me. He's wonderful. Incredibly expensive, but wonderful.

"But what a search! It went on and on; we even contemplated flying to the West Indies, but Mummy kept saying that most of the people who did things there were butchers. Not that she would know. Still. Burton was such a brick through it all. I mean, so stable. So reliable. Really there for me. Of course, he didn't really know about *everything* that was going on. I guess—I imagine—he thought the baby was his, you know? and that I just wasn't ready to be a mother. I was almost about to give up, but then finally we did find this wonderful doctor."

She breathes out in relief. "Ironically, when he examined me he said that I would probably have miscarried within a few weeks anyway. He says I simply don't have an appropriate pelvic structure to bring a child to term."

She has leaned forward to whisper all this to me. Her eyes are merry. "Please do let me know if you ever need anything like that, Helene. Of course, just for yourself, you know. I mean, I don't want to be called by any strangers."

Something in the way she speaks tells me that we won't be seeing very much of one another in the future. My clothes are shabby and I'm not even going with anyone who'd make a suitable fourth on a double date with her and Burton. Nor would I dream of calling my own mother anything but "mother" or maybe, "mom." It's pretty clear that I'm part of a former life which Victoria is all too gladly giving up.

Burton Pogue looks into the room and frowns slightly when he sees the two of us whispering together. He's a tall young man, slightly sallow, his hair already thinning. His ring seems much too large for her finger but I feel suddenly that she'll grow into it. It flashed on her hand as they danced together, first a traditional waltz and then a chacha, and last of all a twist, which has just been invented.

The only one of Victoria's friends who doesn't show up to dance and drink champagne is Ruth. She has been sent an invitation, and as I stand around the banquet room, uncomfortable in my old black party outfit and admiring Victoria's beauty and the charm and lavishness of the decor and food, I wish Ruth would put in an appearance. But she doesn't. There has been no card from her, not even a call. The afternoon wears on, and dark yellow light falls across the hotel carpets. Victoria and Burton thank everyone for the unopened wedding presents which are piled like a miniature Alp of silver-wrapped boxes in a small reception room, and then, after dancing the last dance of the afternoon together, prepare to leave.

Burton rushes to get his coat, somebody calls for the car to be brought around, and Victoria floats over to me one last time, starry-eyed from staring at the mountain of gifts.

"She never came," she whispers.

"Maybe she was ashamed that she had nothing to give you,"

I offer diplomatically. Thinking of all the things Ruth might have given her friend. Laughter. Advice. The touch of a hand. Even a painting, wrapped in brown wrapping paper. Anything.

"That's shit," Victoria says. "She would have come anyway, if I know Ruth."

"Maybe she forgot."

We're alone together in the soft light. Me in the old black silk skirt and top I've worn for the fiftieth time, Victoria in her white wedding gown. Ruth absent. I wonder what she's doing.

Victoria strokes the peau de soie of her dress.

"And to think I tried to reach her," she says.

"You did?"

"Dozens of times."

"Me too," I admit. "Maybe something's wrong."

"There's nothing wrong," she says. "She just doesn't feel like seeing us any more. Fuck her," she snaps. "The bitch."

Why do I have the feeling that this is the last real thing she'll say for years?

She turns swiftly and runs through the door and down the steps of the hotel to her brand new husband waiting beside a limousine in the center of a richly dressed crowd discreetly tossing rice. She pulls in her enormous skirt, and, gracefully lifting her hand, throws her bouquet into the crowd, at the back of which I wait, as hopeful as all the rest.

It's a magnificent bouquet of white roses and baby's breath and calla lilies and lace. I run after it with inheld breath and a panic I would have never expected from myself—and do not catch it.

Victoria sweeps into the car, Burton beside her. The chauffeur squints into the sun and the oncoming traffic and heads the car toward Park, and then they're gone.

"Fuck her," she had said bitterly in a low voice. "The bitch."

And I know that she is gone for good.

THIRTEEN

". . . learning to be mad, in a dream—what is this life?"
— Allen Ginsberg, ca. 1959

I have no time to think about her, however, or even about Ruth, because a day or two later my father dies.

His death comes only a few weeks before my college graduation. It comes without warning, although according to my mother he's been having pains in his chest for years. Pains in the chest are a standard item in the 1960s Jewish-parent repertoire; they're the groundwork for all punishment and blame, for all fear of loss and all anger at the absence of real love. But for his own reasons my father hides the fact of his chest pains from me during our last conversation, on the phone the day before it happens.

I've called to make sure that he and my mother will be coming to my commencement exercises. For years I've been looking forward to my graduation day: to putting on a cap and

gown, to receiving honors (which I do win) while my grandmother, her horrible prophecies of my doom silenced for a few
hours, watches me walk down the aisle, not for marriage but for
academic honor, which I myself have chosen. In my fantasy my
parents, proud despite themselves, are wondering where they
went right, and my father forgets just for a moment all he has
so recently condemned me to, despite my early promise:
kindergarten-teaching, long summer vacations to tend the
suitable husband and the inevitable kids. And the housework,
which I've never wanted to do and for which I have no aptitude.
But during that last conversation he seems unimpressed by any
of my achievements, and keeps repeating, "Be realistic, Helly"
as he talks to me on the phone. "You've got to think about what
you're going to do later on, about how to meet the right kinds
of people. You. You're dreaming. You think you can always
live just the way you want to, no matter what anybody thinks?
What do you know about real life, anyways?"

What, indeed? Even as I'm going through the first days of
loss and grieving, I bitterly reflect that not only had my father
lost his faith in his own dreams as well as mine, he couldn't
even live to see me graduate. Now he'll never hear my name
called with the magical suffix, "Cum Laude," attached to it.
Because of my own indecision I haven't yet told my parents
about it, so he'll never even know that I've at least been
accepted to do graduate work at the University of Chicago. Not
that he would have cared anyway, I tell myself angrily. He'll
never give me the satisfaction of saying "I told you I could do
it," when I finally get my doctorate, my outstretched hands still
dusty from the sweepings of some dig.

For which reason I refuse to go to my commencement
altogether. As he isn't even there to see me commence, it seems
not to matter.

I speak to my father on a Monday night, and his voice is
strained and tired. Only in retrospect does it occur to me that the
word "love" has been used more often than usual, and that the

idea of recrimination is a constant motif winding in and out through the holes in the conversation, creating a background music, a theme song which I will probably never live to forget.

"I love you, Helly," he keeps saying, in his bland, nasal voice. "I wish you'd be like you used to be, like all the other girls in the neighborhood, come back home to live with your parents, make a decent life for yourself for a change, and the reason I wish this is that I love you. In a million years I'll never understand what a young girl has to do she can't do home with her parents."

"But wasn't it you who made me into a rebel?" I demand during that last talk. Taking more chances than usual; making a last, doomed effort to explain. (How do I know that it's the last, and doomed? What are we saying to one another, under all the words?) "Isn't it true that I'm not like everybody else you know in the Bronx because mom constantly told me about her own Bohemian youth and all the interesting people that she was friends with? I mean, how many mothers in our neighborhood whistled on the radio for a living, for heaven's sakes? And," I go on, taking a quick breath so he won't interrupt me, "and because you went on about your lack of education, saying all the time that I had to get a Ph.D. and be the first person in the family to be called Doctor?"

He hangs up finally, refusing to answer, and I'm left to puzzle alone over the questions of why my mother still weeps with shame every time I make my own decisions: to let my hair grow long, to choose my own clothes, to study what interests me, to live away from home, and why my father still gets so frustrated with me that he slams me into the wall every time I do something he doesn't like.

How can they have trained me to be special and then lost their tempers because I was? What expectations did they have of me that I didn't try to meet? Is it because I'm ordinary or because I'm extraordinary that they've been angry at me all this time?

I only know that there are no words with which to comfort my mother when I come home to the Bronx, following her summons.

Which comes at seven on a Wednesday morning, just when I'm getting up to go to work.

"Helene? Is that you?" she whines at me when I pick up the phone on the second ring. She does this every time she calls. Who, I wonder, does she think is answering my phone? Some unknown woman? A man, disguising his voice?

"Yes, Mother, of course it's me," I mutter, annoyed at having my last three minutes of sleep disturbed. Already pulling the tangles out of my hair, thinking about brushing my teeth; yawning. "Who else would it be, Mother?"

"I wouldn't know," she says in her stiff voice, which means something is wrong. What's she calling for at seven in the morning anyway? Too innocent to suspect anything, I turn over and moan a little bit, indicating sleepiness and disturbance.

"Listen, Helene, I've got something to say."

"It's a little early, Mom."

"Your father got sick last night."

I sit up finally, feeling the first pangs of anxiety start up.

"But I talked to him on Monday," I stutter. "He was fine."

"Monday he was fine. He was still fine yesterday. He was perfect until last night. Then he got sick."

I'm young; I've just turned twenty-two. I know how love of any kind can hurt, but I haven't yet learned how quickly the hand grabs out for us, how quickly civilizations can fall and turn into rubble. In a minute or two. Overnight.

"What happened? What did they say is wrong?"

"It was his heart, Helene. Just like he always said. His heart was bad, like he told us."

My own heart stops. More than anything I have a desperate need to go to the bathroom. "And he's in the hospital?"

"Yes. They took him there."

"Can I go to see him? Look, I'll call in sick to the factory right now and I'll just skip school. I can get there by ten, just tell me where . . ."

"It's too late, Helene. He's gone."

"Gone where? What are you talking about?"

"He died in the hospital at three. Last night, Helene. He's gone."

Her voice is flat. I can imagine her holding herself on the other end of the wire, her black bird eyes staring out into nothingness, a loose blue sweater wrapped around her arms.

"Why didn't you call me?" I shout, hearing my own words echo back at me from the phone like a hallucination. When I get to the Bronx, I find my sister Ellen sitting blank-faced and empty, a wind-up toy wound down. She's only twelve years old. Our mother washes the floor a dozen times, muttering to herself and gnashing her teeth like the heroine of her favorite movie about life in a mental institution, "The Snake Pit."

"Are you going to have a nervous breakdown like Olivia de Havilland in that movie, Mom? Because if you're planning on that, I'd like you to please remember Ellen. There's really nobody to take care of her. Grandma is getting too old now, Mildred isn't interested, and you certainly wouldn't want her moving in with me and the rats."

My mother slaps my face and refuses to talk to me for an hour, but gradually she comes out of it, stops washing floors, and puts on a respectable dark dress with a torn black mourning-ribbon on the collar, just as she's supposed to.

The whole family gets there, sooner or later. Mildred shows up. And my grandmother, whose face is as bloated and white as the underbelly of a flounder, and whom I hate with an apathetic coldness when she adds her little rank two cents.

"It was having an ungrateful daughter killed him. That was what."

Later in my life I laugh when I hear someone joke that every

Jewish orphan is considered the murderer of his/her parents. And even later I realize, with the breathless letting-go of self-forgiveness, that my father ate his way into the grave with his mouth wide open, inhaling killer smoke from his cigars, gorging on butter and sour cream and cream cheese, greasy whitefish every Sunday morning, fancy sirloins three times a week to measure up to his own standards of affluence, heavy kreplach swimming in chicken fat. Pies, cakes, cookies, dumplings, Coke, ice cream, endless streams of treats and goodies with which to placate himself, like an intractable child who had to be constantly bribed with food.

"It was having an ungrateful daughter killed him," my grandmother says now, accusingly, and even the doctor, whom I ask plaintively, "Why did it happen so quickly, doctor?" answers,

"You should know."

But my mother later tells me that an hour or so before the fatal heart attack my father had devoured half a watermelon, ice-cold, to fend off the humid summery heat, and it was with indigestion that the chest pains came, irremediable this time, infinite, and bearing death.

The greatest surprise of the funeral and the seven-day mourning period afterwards is Ruth.

"Where've you been?" I cry when she shows up at my mother's apartment. "I called you a dozen times but you're never home."

She shrugs. "If I wanted to tell you, then I would," she replies coolly.

To everyone's amazement, Ruth has let her hair go natural; it is once again plain black and limp, like her mother's hair. Which has the odd effect of making her seem even more attractive than before, as if some hardness has been taken out of her with her hard blonde coiffure. Or as if now, suddenly, she has begun to acquiesce to things instead of fighting them, as she always did before.

And her behavior seems strange, at least to me.

She comes into the house, she speaks to no one, she sits on a box in the middle of the floor with her shoes off like you're supposed to do in the Jewish tradition of sitting *shiva*, spending a week mourning and tearing your hair and eating all kinds of traditional Jewish foods and talking about the deceased, how ungrateful his children were and whether or not he left life insurance. The mirrors in the house are all covered or turned to the wall. Like the rest of the family, Ruth wears a torn black ribbon on her collar. (You tear the ribbon instead of tearing your clothes in grief and sorrow—it's economical as well as respectful of tradition.)

"For God's sakes, Ruth," I say, getting her alone behind the locked door of my sister's bedroom for a smoke. It used to be my room too, before I left; I still know all the secret places where I hid cigarettes, my diary (not that there was anything in it to hide), erotic novels I couldn't have been caught reading. I know how to jam the door so it can't be opened from outside (a trick which my sister never learned—she's also pretty ignorant of most of the hiding places), and I do it now, cramming myself in with Ruth, behind it.

"You don't have to go through all this stuff, really," I say, meaning to sound sympathetic. "Sitting on boxes, for God's sake. Wearing a torn ribbon. After all, he was only your uncle, not your father."

For a moment Ruth doesn't answer. Then she looks into my eyes with so much anger that I think for a minute she's going to put her cigarette out on my neck. I've never seen her face so white or bony.

"Ruth?" I question, my voice trembling. "Ruth. Say something. Please."

Her tight clothes frame an unprecedented slenderness; her cheekbones are shadowed, her eyes deep and mysterious. In the new thinness of her face her mouth seems fuller, its corners curling as she turns away from me and breathes smoke out through an open window so our mothers won't smell it and come running.

"Why should I?" she sneers. "Morton was only my uncle, not my father."

"I didn't even know you cared about him."

"I don't." Her voice is as cold as before. "Shit. Why should I care about him?"

"Then why are you here?" I might ask her, continuing the logic, but I suddenly decide not to pursue it further. I look out the window and I remember Ruth's stepfather, Louie, the unsuccessful lawyer.

"You sure didn't sit *shiva* for Louie," I remark, and to my relief, Ruth bursts out laughing.

Into her fatherlessness he came, bumbling and ineffectual as a balloon. And as round, I think.

What a salvation, from fatherlessness.

Mildred had met him through her work.

"Because of food," my mother added, when I was old enough to listen. She knew that she was being snide, as she could only be snide about her family. "They met because of food."

I believed her. Neither of them seemed to care about much else. I couldn't imagine Louie ravishing Mildred and leaving her filled with a baby, as Gutterman, Ruth's father, had. I couldn't even imagine him touching her, and long after they married and moved in together I would go into their bedroom and stare down at the massive queensized bed with awe, trying to visualize those two bodies sprawling out together under the comforters and touching, even cuddling, on the sheets. I was fourteen years old and such matters interested me more than I was allowed to say.

"But it wasn't like that," said my mother. "They started going out to Chinese dinners. They both loved Chinese food. Then they found they had a lot in common. They were both considered loners because they didn't like resort hotels in the Catskills and the usual places where Jewish people go. Louie all his life wanted to go out to Arizona and New Mexico and see the Hopi and Navajo Indians, how they lived. He wanted to do that more than anything—you think you're the only one in the family with unusual interests? Young people are such judges. We'd all be on the trash heap if it was up to you. And politically Mildred and Louie were the same way too, a little to the left of everybody else they knew, even though they were respectable people, hardworking people.

"So they were loners, two loners who liked to eat and who found each other. The only fly in the ointment was Ruth. They probably would have sent her away somewhere if they'd had the money."

I remember my mother talking about this, always siding with the awkward adolescent Ruth, worrying about her. There had been nowhere to send Ruth, nothing to be done with her. My parents couldn't take her in; we had no room, for one thing, and couldn't afford to move. And our grandparents were too old. She had to stay in the apartment; to put up with Louie's carping ways, as well as her mother's; his squeamish behavior (he had never been around a teenaged girl before), even, my mother told me later, with his desperate attempts to discipline her, to belt her, whenever she did something that he didn't like. Which was often.

Very often.

Now I hear Ruth's dark, insinuating laughter winding around me like a snake winding around a treetrunk. She's so sure of herself; sure in ways in which I'll never be. It takes a special kind of courage, a special kind of distance to say what you really think no matter what the cost, and I'm afraid that as long as I live, I'll never have it.

"What made you think of Louie, of all people?" Coolly, she blows smoke through the window.

"I don't know. Nothing." I stand next to her and we exhale

together. "Only that his was the last funeral, I guess."

"Yeah." Ruth smiles bitterly and looks away.

Louie had died when she was seventeen. "Too late," she had whispered at the time, amazing me with her cynicism. "Too late to do me any good."

He had died, not of pains in the chest nor of any natural causes, but of a car accident when he and Mildred had finally saved the money to visit Arizona, where the Hopi lived.

As they drove at high speed down an Interstate, one of the front wheels had come off their car and Louie had been hurled directly into the windshield when they crashed into a roadside ditch. He was taken to a hospital, but quickly succumbed to head injuries and internal bleeding. Only the fact that she had been napping on the rear passenger seat, and was thrown by the impact onto the floor rather than through the window, saved Mildred's life. She came home with a valise full of silver bracelets, and with Louie's body in a coffin.

After the funeral, when Mildred had gone back to work and their apartment, now a widow with a mess of broken ribs that had to be strapped with bandages for months, Ruth had packed her bags and taken off. At seventeen, she had already been accepted into the Cooper Union, which offered free tuition. Her mother refused to give her any money, but she had a scholarship from the state at first and then later she began to show up in the flashy dresses which I knew she had gotten men to buy her. It was only a matter of time before she had met Victoria, found her way to Paradise Alley, and once again made friends with her runaway cousin, me.

"I'm a little surprised you even came to this funeral, you hated Louie's funeral so much. And Grandpa's, if I can remember back that far."

I squash myself down next to Ruth on the edge of Ellen's bed, which used to be mine when we shared the room. And which, before that, before they were forced to settle into twin beds by sciatica and resolute middle age, was my parents'; it was the marriage bed they had bought just after their honey-moon. Now a pair of run nylons has been washed and draped over its elaborate headboard, where a copy of an eighteenth-century version of a Grecian vase is rather shabbily veneered.

To change the subject from Uncle Louie, I say, "I like your hair."

"What about it?"

"It's different."

"Different. Yeah." She looks out the window. Despite her laughter, she seems more depressed and silent than I've ever seen her. My father had obviously meant more to her than I'd thought. I knew he had been better to her, anyway, than Louie, who had nothing for her but resentment and violence. Better than the mean rich guy on the Grand Concourse who had deserted her even before her birth.

At least her Uncle Morton had given her checks for Chanukah every year, had gone to her high school graduation. Had been there for her as much as he possibly could—which perhaps explained her presence at even a few of those terrible family dinners—until now, when she is being asked, politely, by one of her best friends, not even to come and mourn.

"It was bringing me down," she says, in her quick cold way. "I was getting turned on by the idea of going to graduate school or having my work shown in some gallery. My hair just didn't make it any more. That's all."

"Oh, great. That's great," I say, happy to be pulled out of myself. To think about something else.

"It's kind of weird to go natural, though," she says, coldly glancing at my frizzy auburn mop, held in place by gigantic pins. "It's almost the same color as yours."

"Yours is darker. And straighter."

"Sure," she says. "You got the curls. It goes with the territory."

"What territory? What are you talking about? Hey, Ruth, I hate my hair. Didn't you know that? It breaks combs."

Her eyes glitter as she looks me up and down. I wonder how we've managed to get our wires crossed so thoroughly. She's wanted my hair; I've wanted hers. She loved my father and all I ever wanted was to escape him, since I couldn't please him anyway. "You can have him too," I feel like saying. Except he's dead, and the choice was never mine to make in the first place.

"So what happened?"

"What happened with what?"

"Graduate school. Galleries."

"Nothing."

We're sitting very close together. I see the lines along her lips in the white summer light from the window. My own face is shadowed above a wrinkled black dress which my mother bought me on the Avenue just for the funeral, as if I needed any more black dresses. I haven't been able to sleep for two nights and I'm dying for a roach, but I wouldn't dare, not in the house and not even in the neighborhood, with all the relatives and mourners creeping around on their way to pay respects.

"What do you mean, nothing?"

"Nothing." She raises her eyebrows and lets her lashes fall very slowly over her cheeks. I realize as she does this just how long they are. "Just like I said."

"Haven't you been accepted anywhere? You're so good. . ."

"Not sure I even want to make that scene, any more." Abruptly she turns and rummages through her purse. "I'm out of cigarettes."

"Not want to? But what else . . ."

I'm about to ask, "What else is there?" but I stop mid-sentence.

"Like, wow." She has found a crumpled half-pack at the bottom of her purse. Her expression changes. She half grins at me. "So I made it into a few good graduate schools for art. Far out. But, like, so what? There's no bread for scholarships anywhere. Nothing. Especially for chicks, know what I mean?

193

Maybe if I really knocked myself out I could find some ratty teaching assistantship somewhere, in some second-rate hole. But that's it. The art scene's shit, you know what I mean? Unless you're somebody already. Or somebody's old lady or kid."

"You're somebody," I say, but I doubt myself even as I say it. And what about me? I, too, am being threatened by the world's law of inertia. That that which is already in motion toward success becomes successful, and that which is not, stands still or maybe goes backwards.

Especially for chicks. I know what she means.

Her black eyes watch me, full of mockery.

"You've always managed to come up with enough money," I blunder. "You can make it. I know you can." I sound like Victoria when she talked to me.

"Yeah, I guess." Ruth lights up, fire very near her nose. She waves out the match. Her movements seem languid, weary. She's not convinced any more than I was. "Who cares how," she says after a while.

Then she stops and pauses, looking at me. Does she owe me anything? A few words? An explanation?

"So, like I met this one cat. This gallery owner," she begins, flicking her ashes. "One of my teachers knew him—the gallery handled his own work—and he liked what I was doing so he said I should bring the gallery owner my slides. So I did. I suppose he thought they were okay. Dig it." She laughs. "The dude invited me out to lunch."

"Did you go?"

"Why not? And pass up a lunch at some fancy restaurant uptown? Sure I went. Ever eat green spaghetti?"

"Green spaghetti?"

"Yah. Sitting in a puddle of red sauce like some Christmas decoration."

We're both silent for a minute. I'm about to repeat, "What happened?" when she starts again.

"So what did he expect, that cat? The gallery owner, I mean. He gives me this funny look, like he's thinking, 'So you're the one from the Cooper Union who the teachers think is so fucking gifted? Who are you kidding?'

"That's when I decided to let my hair go natural. But then I thought about it, really checked it out. Who cares, anyway? Who gives a shit what I look like? I don't even know if I'm going to go on painting. Besides, Louise Nevelson has eyelashes out to here and so much stuff on her face it looks like she put it on with a palette knife."

"Are they real?"

"Are what real?"

"Louise Nevelson's eyelashes."

"Are you putting me on?"

Louise Nevelson's "Moon Wedding" has just been shown at the Museum of Modern Art, and for the first time Ruth has become very interested in a woman artist. There might be a few others, she believes, who are not mediocre either in their lives or their art, but she particularly likes Nevelson, not only because of her talent, but because Nevelson's not afraid to dress as she pleases, wearing turbans and huge jewelry and pounds of cosmetics on her emaciated face.

"So what did he say?"

"The gallery owner? That it was a shame I wasn't a guy."

I can't think of any response to this, so I keep quiet and wait for her to go on.

"He actually said that. 'It's a shame you're not a guy.' He said he had a bunch of friends he could've introduced me to if I'd been some cat with the right hormones. Meaning, I dig, the wrong hormones. But since I was just some chick, just old me, bleached hair and all, nobody would be interested. And he thought my work was okay, but the best advice he could give me was to marry some rich cat and get supported. That way I could go on doing my art if I felt like it. I guess he was pretty sure I wouldn't have any problem finding a husband. A rich one, that is. But if I didn't, he figured I'd fall out from starvation before I made it on my own."

I can barely see her eyes in the white glare from the street outside. She hasn't moved. Neither have I.

But something has happened. I can feel the hollow of disaster within her as easily as I might be able to see a cliff, looming before me on a road.

She has been betrayed. Something has betrayed her.

She is trying not to recognize it. She is trying not to feel.

And I imagine the two of them there. Seated stiffly across from one another in a fancy restaurant on Madison Avenue. Facing plates of green spaghetti garnished with bright red sauce. Like Christmas decorations, out of place and unappetizing on a soggy spring afternoon.

The gallery owner shooting impeccable cuffs worn under a perfect suit and regarding her with mute grey eyes. Ruth has always thought that she could survive such eyes. She meets them head on with her own: cold black.

Except, within herself, the wall of coldness isn't enough.

"What do you think of my work?" she's dying to ask.

But the man is saying, with a brisk movement of the cuffs, not for a single instant realizing what he is doing to this self-possessed, bleached-blonde, rather vulgarly dressed young woman, *"My dear, your best bet as an artist is to marry a rich man . . ."*

"So, Helene? What do you think?"

"About what?" I ask, roused from my fantasy.

"About me getting married. For money, say."

"I think he insulted you."

She begins to laugh. "I think it's a gas."

"Really?"

"A fantastic gas." Her eyes change, and she stubs out her cigarette on the windowsill, a forbidden action which I may be called upon to explain.

"Middle-aged asshole," she says, and her voice is choked,

but at least she looks like Ruth again, shaking her head back and forth, sullen with anger. "Middle-aged asshole, telling me the only important thing in his life is his kids. 'Oh my God, if it wasn't for my kids I'd be dead,' he goes, because his own goddamn marriage turned out to be such a disaster, and then in the next breath he's telling me to marry some guy for his bread. It's like he's saying, 'You got the equipment, girl, use the damned thing. Whaddya think God gave it to you for? That's your only real possible talent, anyway. Didn't you know?'"

She laughs again, louder now, so that footsteps come toward us in the hall and I can imagine my mother's white and worried face, only recently redeemed from "The Snake Pit," appearing suddenly in the crack in the door to see what we are up to. Or even worse, my God, my sister Ellen. Who would undoubtedly run away as fast as she could go, screaming to my mother, "Mommee, guess what they're doing in my own room!" before I could stop her, the little brat.

"Shut up, Ruth," I say, and she doubles suddenly.

"Ruth. Have you got a pain?" I bumble.

"Shut up yourself." She's crying.

I never knew she even liked my father, and now here she is, crying at his funeral, although probably more for herself than for him, which is usually the case, I suspect. For this is the afternoon of the day he has been buried, and all the others are sitting around my mother's table stuffing themselves so they won't have to think about their own deaths, and all I can see in my mind beside Ruth's ashen, streaming face is the line of black cars, snaking to the cemetery, ready to put into the ground not only the body of my father but the life of my entire contradictory childhood, which I know, as they lower his box, is finally behind me and will never rise again.

And I myself don't know whether to laugh or cry.

"Ruth," I whisper, bending to her. "Ruth. I'm sorry about what I said before. About your not needing to do all this for my father. I didn't know how much he meant to you, and I was stupid about it."

"He didn't mean anything," she says again, shaking her head against my shoulder. She pushes me away with a strength greater than I would have imagined possible in her lanky fingers, her skinny arms. "Get off me, Helene. Get off me."

"But he did," I insist, letting her go. I have to give her this, this moment, even if she doesn't want it. "He did, and you know what? I think he loved you."

She looks up at me, her whole face puffed with tears.

Because I've never seen her cry like this before, the sight of her tears is even more shocking, even more desolate.

Except she shakes her head defiantly, staring blankly into my eyes.

"He didn't even know me," she says then. "He never gave a shit."

I think if someone had told me then what I find out later— if she or someone else had told me what she was doing, everything, I wouldn't have been so surprised. And maybe I would even have been able to do something, to help in some way, although I've never figured out just how. But of course, when Victoria finally tells me—as Ruth has told her, just once, and then pretending it's a kind of joke—there's nothing I can do. I'm helpless. I can only think of her as a strong young woman with an expression of self-confidence in her black mirror-eyes, Asiatic eyes which reflect my own face when I try to peer beneath their surface to see what's hiding there.

"But she was doing it anyway, even if she tried to laugh about it," Victoria confides to me later. And I'm breathless with amazement, remembering how Ruth and I sat together in my sister's bedroom and she stubbed out cigarette after cigarette on the window sill, and I worried about how my mother was going to yell at me when she saw the ruined paint.

"She was going to the Grand Concourse and standing in front of Gutterman's shop. Just standing there, sometimes for hours at a time, sometimes all day, until he came out. Of course," Victoria comments later, when she and I are able to discuss it at length, "someone weaker or smarter might have actually gone up to him and asked for help, or even just for recognition. But not Ruth—she just went and stood there, and sometimes he would come out and get into one of his big cars. She told me she used to watch him start it up and drive away. By then I guess he had a family, another family, and didn't give a damn about her, but if he had looked carefully, don't you think he would have been able to see the resemblance? And don't you think he would have sooner or later figured out who she was? I mean this girl, tall and pretty goodlooking, just standing there in front of his shop, following him to his car, looking at him, day after day?"

"He might have thought she was trying to steal something."

"It's not that easy to steal a fur coat," Victoria tells me, and she should know, since her mother has managed to acquire several. "Not that way, anyway. So the employees in the shop wouldn't have been worried—annoyed maybe, but not worried. Nobody ever said anything, at least not that she told me about, and she acted like she thought it was all very funny, just a big joke. That she could stand there. That she could wait for him every night after she figured out who he was, and even follow him around to where he left his car. I think she told me it was a white car that year, a Lincoln or a Cadillac, the kind a man like that would drive, and she would just stand and watch him drive away. She said something else, too—that he smoked cigars, big cigars, and that it reminded her of her uncle, who died that year. I realized that must have been your father, but she didn't say so and I didn't ask."

"My father, yes," I say. "He smoked cigars too."

"Right. They both smoked cigars, and they both did things with the bodies of dead animals, and wasn't that a coincidence, she said? She thought it was all very funny. And she laughed."

She would have laughed, I imagine. She would have laughed

as she told Victoria about standing on the street in front of her father's shop, for reasons which she couldn't have explained even to herself, just as she manages to laugh with me that day in the bedroom, not even bothering to dry the tears still on her face, but managing, by the power of her will, to ignore them.

Outside the door to my sister's bedroom there is now a line of people wanting to get in, because their wraps and bags have been hurled in an untidy pile all over my sister's bed. My mother has filled all the relatives and neighbors and other sympathetic mourners with pastrami sandwiches and lox and pickled herrings and various other culinary delights: honey-cake, cookies, and fragrant coffee loaded with cholesterol-rich cream, perhaps after all to remind them of darling Morton, who died after stuffing himself, although not one of these people is ever going to admit it. And now the time has come to void themselves, to flush it all downriver and into the sea, to make polite apologies, to leave. I have to get my cousin out of the bedroom. I have to risk letting my mother see the ruined paintwork. I have to say goodbye.

But when Victoria tells me later about Ruth's journeys, I try to see Ruth in this new way. Try to see her more clearly, with less judgment and less envy. Her height and new slenderness. Her sallow cheeks. Her hair, so recently turned black again.

Standing in the shadows before the luxurious shop. GUTTERMAN'S FURS, the sign reads. His name above the door in neon letters. Does she think, standing there, *But it should be my name, too? And I'm his, whether he wants me or not?*

When she sees him, does she immediately recognize in him her own black eyes, her swaggering walk, her hooked nose? Does she silently ask him as he walks towards her, "Can you really deny that I'm yours? Looking at me, can you actually deny it?"

But she isn't standing there working up courage to go in, to ask him for money, to ask him for his name, to ask him, even for a moment, to be her father. Of that I'm certain. If she wanted to, she would ask him. Ruth has never had to work up courage for anything in her life. Courage is in her veins, as it must have been in his as well. He had once told Mildred that he came to this country an immigrant orphan, penniless. And hadn't he impregnated Mildred and then left her, ruthlessly? Even this might have excited Ruth's admiration, because we're raised to admire killers, we Bronx women. We're raised to admire men who reject us, and who are seamlessly, guiltlessly cruel.

So then what is she doing, standing before that smug little shop in the Bronx, rich in its carpets and its mirrors and its gilt? Is it only to find out where she has come from, to look at everything in this life that has made her what she is now?

Is it to look, for at least a few minutes, tenderly, yearningly, at all the things and people that were in at the beginning of her journey, because she has finally lost her way and no longer knows how to seek its end?

"Hey!" she whispers, one minute after we finally open the bedroom door to let in the other people. "Look who's out there!"

I peer out through the doorway, and there, looking resplendent and very large in a navy serge dress with a white Peter Pan collar, is my old friend from high school, Edie Scheinblatt. She has obviously come to show off as well as to pay her respects, because she's decked out in a wild display of lucre, entirely out of keeping with her funereal garb. There's a gigantic yellowish rock in a shiny setting on her engagement ring finger, and around her neck, already crêpey and beginning to droop, hangs a garish locket set with small but obviously real gemstones. There are little brilliant earrings in her ears, and from the way she's got her hair pulled back to show them off I know that they, too, must be real diamonds, and that someone—her new fiance or some member of his utterly desirable, rich family, must have given them to her.

"It's Edie!" I gasp. "Wow. Look at her!"

"Fatter than ever," Ruth chuckles, with even more malicious zest than usual. "It figures she'd come to see you now. Ed. Majors always love to see their buddies down and out."

"I suppose I've got to get out there and be polite to her," I mutter, waving the last of the cigarette smoke through the window. "What a time to socialize."

"It's the only time these people even *want* to socialize, stupid. Funerals and weddings, bar mitzvahs and brisses. They live for that stuff. Or at least, that's what they call living."

We look at one another, Ruth and I, and for the first time I realize the extent of my defection. Edie was my dearest friend for four years. With her, I shared the laughter of the last of my childhood; I shared innumerable chocolate shakes and sodas; I even shared my tears. But now I'm entirely prepared to betray her, to tear her apart over a riotous lunch at the Russian Tea Room, to call her fat and conventional and dead above the neck. And all because, for maybe the first time in my life, my cousin Ruth has put her hand under my elbow in a gesture of what might even be understood as love, and because, so joined, we step together out of the bedroom to face the crowd.

PART THREE

FOURTEEN

But during the days after my father dies, the only person I want to see is Zalman.

Instead I spend the entire seven-day mourning period with my family, sleeping badly on the living room sofa, staying up late to watch old movies on TV while I kill of cans of Barton's halvah that I find stashed in my mother's linen closet. Crying alone in the darkness. How is it possible to miss someone who was mean to you? Who never understood you? And yet I do. I miss my father. I realize that I never understood him, either.

My mother hasn't reverted to her "Snake Pit" mode, but she bubbles over with the kind of hysteria that comes out of despair. "You're not thinking of leaving?" she pleads with me when she sees me packing my bag on the seventh night. "Aren't you going to come back and live with us?"

I don't know how she can believe this, although I've been discovering all kinds of new things about her, like the fact that she's taken to splashing Southern Comfort into her teacup every night.

"That's not tea," I observe when she does it in front of me the first time. "It doesn't smell like tea."

My mother shoots a look at Ellen, who's up past her bedtime.

"I need a little something," she shushes me. "Just be quiet, you."

I sit down with her at the table after Ellen goes to bed and splash some into a teacup for myself. It helps a little, and we sit at the table over whiskey and cigarettes together for the first time in our lives.

"Maybe," my mother offers, luring me with promises, "maybe we could all live together in Manhattan. You'd like that, wouldn't you, Helene? There's a bundle of insurance money," she cajoles. "Not enough for Ellen and me to live unless I got a job, but we could have a little fun with it, anyway, the three of us, couldn't we? We deserve to have some fun."

"Is that what you want to do, mother? Have fun?"

"Don't be such a judge, young lady. Wait till you get to be my age. Then be a judge."

I put my hand on her arm. "I'm not judging you, mother. But how can you think I'll just move back in with you after a couple of days? I've been on my own for three years."

There are tears in her eyes. Her round warm face is seamed with grief.

"Is it my fault?" she cries softly. Her breath smells of Southern Comfort. From the other room we hear Ellen's snores. "Is it my fault what's become of you?"

"What's become of me? What are you talking about?"

"You're not happy."

"How can I be happy? My father just died."

"Even before that. We were always worried about you, Helene, your father and me. All the time."

"Now you're going to tell me it was my fault he had the heart attack."

"I'm going to ask you if it's my fault you're so sad."

She turns off the overhead fixture and leaves only the nightlight on, so there's a soft orange glow in the kitchen. We both sip more "tea," and her eyes droop.

"Maybe sadness is catching, in a way."

"What are you talking? Make sense," she says.

"I only mean that you and Daddy were never happy either, and maybe you passed it on to me. Sadness, I mean."

"So you do blame me?"

"Only answering your question. You wanted to know if it was your fault."

"And you think it was."

I sigh. "Are we ever going to just plain talk to each other?" I finish my own cup of the strong-smelling liquor and start into the living room to finish packing. "Daddy could never talk to me either. He either scolded or yelled."

"How do you know we weren't happy?" She stops me at the kitchen door. "We were happy enough together, Helly. We were happy some of the time and not so happy some of the time. Like most people."

"So what happened to your music? Why didn't you ever work on the radio again after you got married? You spent your whole time shopping and cooking and looking after him and being bored out of your mind. You never did anything for yourself except going to sales and once in a while whistling the whole 'Third Man' theme in perfect pitch when you thought nobody was listening."

"So? That wasn't enough? Being a professional whistler on Sunday night radio shows is so important? Besides, by the time I met your father it was getting out of date to whistle. The bandleader kept nagging me to learn some other instrument, but I knew that all I had was my mouth, and it wasn't enough. And then, I had two children, too. And raised them and took care of them. *That* was pretty important, you should maybe remember."

"Mama." I haven't called her that since I was twelve years old. "Mama, is that what you wanted? What you really wanted?" I grip her by the shoulders and we look into each other's eyes. An unusual moment for us. "Did it make you happy?"

"It came close, Helene." Her voice is soft. "Closer than making birdsounds with a bad swing band."

"But close *enough*?"

"I don't know what *enough* means. And who says I had such a big choice?"

I shut my eyes.

"What I mean is," she goes on, "I really *wanted* to get married by the time I met Morton. I couldn't see much for myself if I didn't get married. Look at Mildred, she had to wait so long. I don't think she had such a wonderful life. And there weren't that many men that wanted to marry me. Nice men, I mean. In those days, even living with your parents at home like I did, you had to act a certain way to attract a man. And I was like you. I was a rebel. I didn't want to do the things that were supposed to matter, like dressing very prim and proper, not acting too smart or talking with big words, only dating Jewish boys, observing all the holidays. Instead, there I was with my job in Manhattan, whistling away on 'Lights Out' and 'The Third Man' Sunday nights, and it didn't look so proper. Your father was the first nice man who ever came along who didn't care about that. He liked me for who I was. He didn't even care when Mildred went out and got herself pregnant and had Ruthie. Somebody else might have felt disgraced and maybe left the family. But he stuck with us all. He believed in family more than almost anything except maybe education. That's the kind of man he was."

"And that was enough for a marriage?" I've never questioned this before. Maybe I do now because the apartment seems very cold and very empty without my father in it, without the smell of his cigars, the litter of his newspapers. The sound of his voice, booming from room to room with anger, irritability, grief. I realize for the first time how much his dissatisfaction has always surrounded me, like a kind of atmosphere, that of a dry, unhappy planet on which I've somehow learned to breathe.

"There've been marriages based on much less, Helene."

"That's not an answer."

"He was better than *my* father, Helene. And what you had was better than what *I* had, growing up. So maybe you'll do better than me, someday."

She's angry at me for disparaging my father, who's so recently dead. But I don't mean to disparage him. What I see as I leave her, sitting alone over her teacup full of Southern Comfort, is a long line of us connected to each other as if by heavy chains. Mothers and fathers and daughters and sons, all of us connected, all of us making do with sorrow. Passing it on. Calling it normal.

Calling it "ordinary life."

The following night I leave. I carry my bags to the El station and sit for a long time looking down at the lights of the city, glittering like a huge constellation of stars that has somehow gotten tangled in the wires of Earth. I'm so lost in my contemplation of this that I don't even see the figures approaching me until one of them calls out, "Helenie!" moving forward out of the shadows. "Helenie Elphrick!" she calls again. "What are you doing on the subway station all by yourself? Don't you know that something terrible could happen?"

It's Edie Scheinblatt again, my old friend Edie, and this time she's resplendent in dark blue crêpe de chine, her garish diamond still gleaming on the fourth finger of her left hand. The huge locket is bouncing up and down over her equally huge breasts, at the very tip of one of which, balanced over where the nipple must be, a tiny golden "frat" pin has been fastened, encrusted with rubies and pearls.

She's become a kind of Renaissance figure, Edie—she needs only a lacy wimple to complete the picture—and I'm about to warn her that she too is at this subway station all alone, and probably in infinitely greater peril than I am because of her jewels and finery, when another figure disengages itself from behind a girder and scampers toward us, pigeon-toed.

This must be the fiance, I figure. Edie had told me he was twenty-two, but, thick-bellied, dark-browed, balanced on unusually tiny feet, he looks much older than his years. In fact, he looks (I think) the way he's probably going to look for the rest of his life. Dull. Old. Tired. Overweight. And rich.

"Helenie!" Edie chides again. "Where are you going all by yourself this time of night?"

"Home, I guess," I answer.

"Home?" she cries. "But isn't your home *here*?"

"How are you, Edie?" I smile at her, wanting to be polite.

"The question is really how are *you*? Helenie's father passed away," she explains to the fiance, who offers absolutely no acknowledgement of this sad fact, not even a blink. "I'm so sorry, Helenie. And how is your poor mother doing? She looked so miserable when I came by to pay my respects."

"She's fine."

"But why aren't you sitting *shiva*?"

"No more *shiva*, Edie. The seven-day mourning period was over yesterday. And I'm on my way home right now."

"Oh. You mean to your *apartment*?" She pronounces it in a whisper, "apotment," and shoots an anxious look at the pigeon-toed boyfriend as though there were some shame attached to the very word. "I kind of thought you were going to be giving that up, now."

"What for? It's where I live."

"Oh. But your mother . . ."

"My mother has her own apartment. So when are you getting married, Edie?"

"September, Helenie. We hope you're coming to the wedding." She peers hopefully at the fiance, to whom she hasn't introduced me, but he's busy gazing at the tracks in the direction from which the train will come. I think of Victoria's wedding and nod my head.

"That's nice. I'd love to."

"I really shouldn't say this, Helenie, in after all, your bereaved condition, but you should be so lucky. I mean, Howie's ideal husband material. He gives me everything." She shakes her head back and forth so the light plays on her earrings and her locket, and the tiny frat pin trembles precariously at the edge of her tit. I watch it, fascinated, afraid it's going to tumble off and roll onto the tracks. Meanwhile the ideal husband material snaps a thick gold lighter and sucks in on a cigarette. He still hasn't spoken to either of us.

"You shouldn't smoke so much, Howie," Edie giggles. Howie inhales heavily and stamps his feet, still looking at the tracks. "That's his only vice," she confides to me in a low voice. "We're going to Grossinger's next weekend, our parents will be with us of course, and we're going to check out their Honeymoon Suite for the honeymoon. Isn't that sweet?"

I'm about to comment on her alliteration when the train comes roaring into the station, causing Howie to step away from the edge slightly, but without any change of expression. I pick up my suitcase, eager to get away, but Edie can't quite let go.

"And you should see his *car*, Helenie. He's got the biggest *car*. It's a . . ."

But I never find out what kind of car he has because at this point Howie himself steps up and grasps her by the shoulders, steering her through the subway car's door, still not having looked her in the face or acknowledged me. "And what about you, Helenie?" she gabbles, as I beat a hasty retreat to another car. "When are *you* going to get married? Have you met at least a decent boy?"

The doors close behind me and I put my suitcase down with a gasp of relief, but then the IRT rips me back into an underground so familiar and so threatening that I decide that if

I don't find Zalman right away, I won't be able to stand being in my apartment any more. I won't be able to sleep, or read, or wake up in the morning and go to work. So I don't even drop my suitcase at home but take the IRT straight down to the Fourth Street station, from which I walk crosstown to the Cedar Tavern.

A kind of radar guides me to the table in the back room where's he sitting with some friends. As I approach them, it sounds as if they're having an argument, but it turns out to be only the usual discussion about art. Zalman's eyes are rounder than ever with amusement, with the excitement of half-meaning what he says. He leans forward over the litter of glasses and cigarette butts that crowd his arms, stretched in the direction of the door. Although he smiles slightly as I sit down beside him, he doesn't speak to me and for a minute I worry about being welcome. But soon he reaches for my hand under the table, and I feel my pulse slow down.

"So come on, what about it? How do you define talent?" one of the others at the table is barking at him, eyeing me with obvious resentment. "Are you going to tell me that some people are not just more talented than others, that they have a talent for oratory or music or art or whatever, and what they do just naturally turns out better, no matter how much training they do or do not have?"

The speaker is a babyfaced, round-eyed playwright, whose plays are produced in tiny, fashionable theatres that used to be soup kitchens, artist's lofts or movie houses, Off Off-Broadway, so he has the authority of a man with acknowledged gifts. But most of all he reminds me of Zalman's friend Darryl, whom I haven't seen since the night he came to my apartment and nodded out in my living room.

"I mean," he goes on, "the whole new ethic is to be involved with any art form at all just for the sense of self-expression, but the problem is, you can't go out and do something you don't have any innate ability to do."

Zalman only smiles, squinting his eyes toward his cigarette smoke, which he blows away. "The concept of having or not having talent is simply an elaborate excuse for remaining stagnant," he responds finally. "Because listen—almost everyone is potentially talented. Almost everyone can be taught to do just about anything, if only he wants to enough."

"If he wants to enough," says the playwright. "That's the catch, isn't it?"

Zalman nods and goes on smiling. "That's the catch," he agrees. Then his smile seems to turn a little sad. I think of my college friends Chloris and Zoe, who once told me almost the same thing.

"Except you're wrong in this one, man. It's a nice thought but it doesn't make any sense," the playwright wrangles. "Talent is inborn. Like, the capacity for art or music; for doing math, for writing. We're born with it. It's in the blood. Look at yourself, Zalman. You're this writer and thinker and it comes right out of your background, doesn't it? Wasn't your father some kind of rabbi?"

"Not just my father. My brothers. My uncles. Even me. I was some kind of rabbi." Zalman goes on smiling. "But then where does the painting come from, if your theory holds? Why don't you tell me that, genius?"

"Like, how should I know?" The playwright is stymied. A point for Zalman, who tries not to look triumphant. "Maybe you're a throwback? Maybe there was some great grandfather or somebody that the rest of them never talked about?"

"Chasidic Jews don't paint," says Zalman, driving the point home. "It's considered sacrilege to reproduce the human form. Or even animal forms." He looks thoughtful. "Traditional Jewish art is restricted to calligraphy."

"Well. Maybe there was some calligrapher, then, in the ancient past of your family and you inherited his genes. But could you excel at playing an instrument—an oboe, say, or even a piano, if you had absolutely no ear for music? No matter how much you wanted to?"

"Perhaps not," says Zalman, "but. . ."

"But?" says the playwright. "You're going to tell me your grandfather was a cantor and you've been musical all your life?"

"But I was going to tell you that if I wanted to excel at playing the oboe then I would be driven to learn it," Zalman says.

"And could you be any good at it if you were just naturally born tone deaf? You see, I don't think so."

"If I wanted it enough, I would learn it and love it and bring it to excellence. And there's the mystery, for me. That there are so many ways of expressing what is. So many ways that we have to have the courage to keep finding them. What I call lack of talent is having nothing new to say. Remaining in one's own condition and simply repeating it again and again the way the old-fashioned figurative painters did in the European academies even after the Impressionists came along and exploded the vision of their age. That's talentlessness, as far as I'm concerned."

His eyes glitter as he says this, but I wonder suddenly whether he himself has ever wanted anything that much. Anything. Enough to bring it to excellence. I wonder.

The walls of his gallery are now completely filled with the work he has recently done to explode his own vision. Gigantic assemblages composed solely of materials found in the various trashbins of the city, some in the form of huge rectangles that buckle under the weight of everything that's been glued and pinned and pasted onto them, some shaped like towers with doll's heads and clock hands and various objects and pieces of things rising up out of what appears to me to be a dense primeval gunk.

Maybe that's why he's so emphatic about definitions of talent. How can anyone talk about the lack of talent in his huge messy pictures if an inability to understand them means an inability to understand new art?

The emperor's clothes, I think again. Still, somebody must have once also thought that about Van Gogh.

"There are mediocre artists galore exploding vision, for Chrissakes," the playwright goes on. "Fracturing it, as a matter of fact. Just walk into any museum. What do you see in there? Louise Nevelson's so-called sculpture. All those damned slats, painted black. It looks like stage design gone wrong. Talk about mediocrity."

"It's hard for a female artist to surpass mediocrity," one of the other men chimes in at last, looking up sleepily from his beer like the Dormouse in *Alice in Wonderland*. He's a well-known poet who has written about art, insanity, homosexuality and spiritual awakening. "The problem is, there's no way a woman can be a realized artist until she's had a child. The biological imperative is just too strong. And once she's actually had children, what woman has the time or desire to devote her life to anything as involved or difficult as art?"

I choke a little, hearing all this about Ruth's current heroine, Louise Nevelson. Just what, I want to ask the poet, does making art have to do with having children?

"I think that women do art for the same reasons that men do. They just aren't taken as seriously most of the time. That's all." I blurt this out suddenly, surprising myself, and in my anxiety to be heard my voice comes out high and squeaking. "But some people have a talent for making their whole lives into works of art. Women *and* men. And maybe that's even more important than anything else, even more than the other kind of talent, the kind only in the work itself, like painting or writing or making films."

Zalman turns to me, his blue eyes glowing. "Attentiveness is his greatest charm," Andre Pincus had said about him, and I know it's true. There's an expression of pride in his eyes now; he actually nods his head as if I've said something profound, something very important. "Turn their whole lives into art?" he repeats, tasting the words. "That's very good. I like that."

But not one of the other men at that table is listening to me, and if they were, they would probably just laugh and turn away. For all of them but Zalman, I should be seen and not heard, like a child. And even he would never defend me to them, never interrupt their conversation or go out on a limb to let them know I'm anything for him except a particularly intelligent "old lady." And I think suddenly—maybe I'm not. Isn't his approbation a kind of secret between us, something he usually saves for me when we're alone, like making love?

"Talking about the frontiers of perception," says Eli Bamram, grinning down at me. Eli Bamram is a composer who wrote the music for a movie that's just become a great commercial as well as artistic success, and he therefore commands the attention of all the others. "What work of art comes even close to the miracle of the human body? Look at this creature here, for instance," he goes on, favoring me with a wide leer. "What about the beauty inherent in *this* form? How can we mere men create anything that even comes close to what has already been created by nature, in this world?" And he picks up my hand and looks into my eyes, glaring down at me as if I were both Botticelli's Venus and a mouse about to be devoured by a cat. "By the way, I'm Eli Bamram, baby," he croons to me, opening his mouth so I can admire the sharpness of his teeth.

"No, but I think—" I begin. Except the composer has already dropped my hand in order to signal the waiter for another round of beers, and the young playwright has gone off on another tangent, turning away from me and stubbing out his cigarette in the ashtray so I can hardly reach it to put down the match with which I have just lit my own. And Zalman pats my thigh under the table and turns back to his friends, as though he's given me enough public attention for one night.

Sometimes I've wanted so desperately to be taken seriously in a conversation like this one that I've even thought of disguising myself as a boy to see if I'd be allowed to participate—because I've noticed that even the youngest, silliest boys get more respect from a group like this than I do. I might try it, too, if my voice were a little lower, or if I were just a little taller, or there were just the hint of a mustache on my upper lip, as there is on Ruth's. Ruth, with her long legs and her broad cheekbones, might bind her chest to flatten it and exchange one of her thigh-crunching, skintight skirts for a pair of pleated men's trousers, and actually "pass." Go back and visit her gallery owner. See what he has to say about her paintings then.

After an hour or so the others drift away, and Zalman and I are left alone.

"I'm glad I found you tonight," I say softly—my voice, having been unused all this time, sounds peculiarly thin.

"Me too," he says, rubbing my shoulders. "I'm always happy to see you."

"Your friends don't think much of women, do they?"

He looks at me, startled. "They like to argue with each other, that's all. That's what they enjoy the most, arguing. And *I* think much of women, baby. I think a lot of *you*."

"It's just. . ." How do I explain this to him? "I guess I just want to be treated like an equal."

"I thought I did." His voice is very soft, as though he's hurt. "I thought that's how I treated you."

We go out into the night and I take his hand, my pleasure in being with him eclipsing the pain of the past week. We walk the few blocks toward Washington Square Park and I'm about to tell him about my father when he turns to me decisively.

"Baby, I need a hundred dollars," he says, stepping into the street. Despite the heat, he's wearing his natty little cap with the belt in the back. He doesn't even bother to look away as he says this, smiling directly into my eyes as if it's the easiest thing in the world to ask your girlfriends for money.

"Zalman. You know I have hardly anything." I spread my hands, looking down at myself. I'm still wearing the rumpled black dress I wore most of this past week, and I carry my small green canvas suitcase. I shift it to the other hand and he takes it from me. "I've got barely enough money to pay rent on my apartment and buy my own food. I can give you something, but a hundred dollars is too much."

"That's not what I mean." We've reached the Square and he sits down on a bench, drawing me down beside him and lighting a cigarette with his other hand. "Look," he says. He fumbles in his pocket and pulls out a scrap of paper. Again, I think of Andre Pincus. "This is the address of a guy. He's got a package for me. What I need is for you to go up there for me and pick it up. It would be easier for you than for me because there's some people around who know me, and . . ."

I take the paper out of his hand and look at it. The address is of a building on a street way uptown, probably in Harlem. I have a sudden vision of myself walking into the building, watched by hidden eyes. I can see the back of my neck as I climb an unlit staircase. It makes me feel sick. "I know what it is," I say dully. "I know what's in the package."

He shrugs. "It doesn't matter, baby. It doesn't matter what it is."

"I don't want to make any pickups of drugs," I say. "It's too risky."

"Think of it as a kind of adventure." He grins at me, his eyes twinkling. "I thought you liked adventure, studying all that archaeology. I thought you wanted me to treat you like an equal." Then, without even changing expression, he takes a different tack. "I tell you what, baby. It's money. Just a package of money. This fellow has it for me."

"Then why doesn't he just come down and give it to you?"

"There are complications."

"What kind of complications?"

"Please?" He puts both arms around me, first throwing his cigarette to the ground. "Please?" he says again. Then he smiles even more deeply, and buries his head in my arms.

"Listen," he says. "Once you get more involved in this, your fears are going to look pretty silly to you."

I shake my head, suddenly ashamed of the fears he's talking about. "I don't know if I'm going to get more involved."

"Are you sure?" He looks up and holds me away from him a little, his arms still around my shoulders, his lips still smiling. "Are you sure you aren't going to, Helene?"

He gets to his feet and we continue walking west, too fast to say anything more. I almost run beside him, confused. The night is dense and steamy around us, the streets west of Washington Square still teeming with tourists and with city people like ourselves, too hot to go inside, to bed. I'm afraid he's going to march me to the subway stop and leave me, but suddenly he sees a huge trashcan brimming with papers on the corner.

"Wow. Fantastic," he says, leaping forward. Within minutes the pavement is littered and both of us are burdened by a mountain of assorted glittering trash, piled high in our arms.

"Zalman?"

"Yes?"

"Are you angry?"

He walks for a while before answering. "No. No baby. I'm not angry."

"I mean, I do want to be involved with you. I just don't. . ."

"Never mind, baby," he soothes, his voice calming. "Somebody else can get the package for me."

"It was you I meant when I was talking in the bar."

"Meant when? Meant how?"

"Nobody but you was listening. I said that some people use their whole lives as a canvas. That's their creation. Everything they do."

We sit down on a streetcorner, under a lamp. My hair has come down around my shoulders and my lap is filled with tin cans and assorted refuse. Which at least, I think, looking down at it, is dry.

"I know people like that," he says. "They're fantastic. Everything they do has to be unusual and perfect. Where they live, how they eat. . . "

"I don't mean like that. I don't mean that you're self-conscious. I mean that your whole life is a kind of creation, like a book or a piece of theatre. It's totally natural, the way you live. Totally absorbing. That's why I like being with you."

"Baby," he says, finally grasping that I'm paying him some kind of compliment. His face lights up with pleasure.

But within a few minutes he looks disappointed again.

"I thought you were in love with me," he says sadly.

And I realize that the true anomaly of art is that it's never perfect. Its creator is never satisfied. There would be no point in telling Zalman that I *am* in love with him. It would never, ever, be enough.

"My father died last week." It comes out abruptly, and for the first time since I've known him he's speechless. He reaches for my hand.

"It happened suddenly. No one expected it. It was just a few weeks before commencement and I wanted him to come and see me graduate. To have some pride in me, for once. But the worst thing is that I feel like there's nowhere to go back to, now. That I've burned my bridges."

We're at the corner of West and Christopher Streets, sitting together on the curb and holding hands. The streetlights are so bright and so close together that it seems like day. This is the portion of the city they call the Meat Rack. We're surrounded by a dozen cruising young men, none of whom pays even the slightest attention to us. From the Hudson River, only a few blocks away, the wind blows sea air into the city.

For the first time I realize what I've said. That the high, swaying El platform near my parents' home is like a bridge into the city and that I've burned it, by returning again and again to my apartment, my studies, my job, my random nights with Zalman. By making sure again and again that I'll go away.

These are my choices, though I'm not sure why I've made them.

"Baby, that's so hard for you. And you've been so cool." He speaks softly and again, his praise is a balm. "If it's any consolation, my father's still alive, but I've burned my bridges too."

And I understand just how much I do love him. That it may not be the kind of love around which you spin fantasies or to which you remain faithful, but that it's a true love nonetheless, a love that's going to hold me, although for how long or to what lengths, I still have not allowed myself to know.

FIFTEEN

" . . . the only people for me are the mad ones . . ."
— *Jack Kerouac, 1951*

Bud has blood on his hands. One of the glass panes of the French doors in his living room has been smashed. There are pieces of glass on the floor.

"My hand just went right through it," he tells us. "Almost all by itself. Just went right through."

He seems to be smiling. But he can't really be smiling, can he? How could he be? He holds a tissue to the wound. Ineffectual. The blood rolls to the floor in drops. I try not to look.

"Were you wasted?" I query, trying to sound wise.

Bud stares at me with a baffled grin, but Ruth gives me a glance that tells me to shut up.

I do.

"Yeah, too bad, Bud. Better take care of that," she says,

eclipsing me. Her mouth flares into a smile of complicity and warmth. Bud seems flattered.

Without even watching Ruth I can feel the tension in her body. I can hear it in her voice and see it in the way she rolls her eyes, focusing on the wall when she talks. Very rarely meeting anybody's glance.

"So," Bud says, mopping himself up for what seems like a long moment. "Got anything special around for me, these days?"

She nods briskly. He goes on mopping. When he turns to her again, his expression is prim and smug.

"Come into my parlor." Then he stares at me nervously. "You don't mind staying behind?"

"She's fine," snaps Ruth.

They leave me on my own in the front room, closing the broken glass doors behind them.

"Don't bother about her," I hear her tell him. "She just tagged along."

Bud is a short pale man with a moon face and glasses over narrow colorless eyes. He wears a serious expression but when he looks at Ruth it changes. I think of her fancy dresses, the long stiletto daggers of her shoes. To how many Buds is she indebted? With how many like him has she made laborious trades, smiling when she does not feel like it? Liking them just a little when they ask her to?

Ruth wishes I weren't here today, that much I know. She greeted me sullenly when I showed up unexpectedly at her apartment, and scowled when Bud looked me over with pallid interest when I came through the door with her.

"Just a quick trip I gotta make," she'd said, stopping in front of his building. She'd wanted to leave me in the street but I wouldn't stay.

In his mirror, also broken, I catch a glimpse of myself. I'm rumpled and hot in a pair of faded jeans, my wild hair in a ponytail. My face has paled and lengthened. There are shadows beneath my eyes and a curve of dissatisfaction to my mouth. How strange the world seems to me now, at the end of this prolonged period of going to school and working. How odd it is, during this gloomy summer, almost as dark in daylight as it is at night, when the neon casts a red glow over the low skies of New York.

Now that I've finally finished college, I feel that I have no more purpose or direction. I go to Katherine Upson's office to pick up my diploma, and, carrying it out into the street, I realize that there's no decision to make about graduate school, at least for the coming fall semester. If I can't get a scholarship, I just can't go. Not this year, anyway, and probably not ever. There are no private agencies that want to fund me and after what I've learned about them, government grants are out of the question. I probably wouldn't get one anyway; the government would probably know all about me, even about things I never thought were problems. The fact that my mother was a Leftist in the 30s, the somewhat shady political affiliations of Mildred and Louie. Maybe even my escapades with Zalman, my night with the Armenian, my experiments with drugs. So there's nothing for me to decide, at least not yet. I write a formal letter to the University of Chicago asking them to please put my application and acceptance on hold; I plan to start my studies with them, I write, in exactly one year, after I've saved enough money for tuition and moving expenses, which I'm sure they'll understand.

And I imagine that they do, because they don't even bother to answer my letter.

What I do decide is to get another job. A real one, this time. I need more money; I'm saving for graduate school, aren't I? So, squeezing myself into one of my tight little black dresses and a pair of high heeled pumps, I journey down to Wall Street on the subway in search of a higher salary, and end up typing invoices for a brokerage firm. It feels like the right place for me now, Wall Street. Between the caverns of buildings I feel appropriately anonymous: shrunken, lost.

Ruth and Bud emerge from the room. His scant hair is dishevelled but his face is bright. They look like they've been kissing. He smiles at me behind her back.

We go down the stairs into the street.

"Is he your lover?" I ask.

"He's just a friend. For Christ's sake."

She's been more nervous and jumpy each time I've seen her since the funeral. "Can't I just have a friend? Just an ordinary friend, just because he's male? What's the matter with you anyway? For God's sakes. Jesus Christ."

"Ruth," I say. "Are you okay? It's like, I hardly ever see you, and when I do, I can't tell if you're okay or not. Victoria was worried about you, too. Why don't you ever let us know how you are?"

She stops dead. In the middle of the crowded sidewalk. Tenth Street and Second Avenue. Crowds of people mill in front of the fruit store, or push us aside to buy cannoli and good espresso in the Italian bakery.

"Victoria!" she shouts at me. "That fucking bitch!"

Two or three people turn around, among them a dark-haired, Spanish-looking woman with worried eyes and three kids, whom she herds away from us.

"She cared about you. She was sorry you didn't go to the wedding. She said . . ."

"I don't give a shit what she said. Victoria! One measly abortion and she makes like she's cutting out for good! What a bring-down!"

We walk on a few steps. The crowds close around us.

"She's not the only person in the world who ever had an abortion, you know," she says, calming down a little. "I had to have one last year. Like, I couldn't afford some bigshot medic like Victoria's, of course. I had to go to some old witch doctor out in Jersey. She induced the damned thing with an insert, and I sat around screaming for a day and a half. Just lucky for me

I didn't get an infection. I had a friend who did and they actually arrested her while she was bleeding to death in the ambulance. Shit. What'd they expect her to do? Have the kid and go on welfare like everybody else so they could kick her around? Or die? Probably die," she mutters. "I almost did."

"I'm sorry," I say quietly. "I wish you'd asked me for help. It must have been hard."

"Not as hard as getting hung up with a kid I didn't want and no way to make a living. The hardest thing for me was raising the bread. Which couldn't have been a great big deal for Victoria, with her rich old man and 'Mummy.'" She grimaces, mocking Victoria's new prep school accent. "Except she was probably too scared to tell them."

"She did tell her mother."

"Yah. It figures." She grins in scorn, and I remember all too sharply that Ruth can't tell her mother anything.

She's jealous, I think meanly. Until I realize, so am I.

In the Italian bakery, her hand trembling over a glass brimming with caffe latte and whipped cream, she looks to the side of me with her black eyes narrowed and waves her spoon.

"I'm cool now, dig? I mean, it all cleared up real fast. So stop worrying, for Christ's sake. I'm just a little wiped out nowadays. Nothing to it. I'll be okay soon. Too many pressures. I just don't like to make the pressure scene. Like stress and all that shit. I'm probably going to split any day now."

"Does it get in the way of your painting?"

A pause. "There's too much bullshit on the art scene," she says finally, her voice low. "I'm not painting that much any more."

Back on the street, we stop in front of a store window. She looks in, examining the clothing. She is wearing, on a sultry Saturday afternoon, a green, sleeveless, A-line dress and backless shoes with such high heels it seems a miracle to me that she can walk.

For a minute she looks at me head on and I have a rare

opportunity to stare into her eyes. Even in full daylight they are what we called in the 50s "bedroom eyes." I can imagine her lovers saying, "Ah, Ruth, baby, you got bedroom eyes." But now it seems to me that meeting mine they're automatically lowered; exotic, full of lies.

We continue across the city. Heading east, toward Paradise Alley. I find myself wishing for a breeze. The smell of the ocean. Anything.

Later, a vivid New York sunset lights up the western half of the sky. My job on Wall Street is in an office on the 40th floor. My boss, a woman, stood next to the window with me one day and watched the sunset, streaked with brown and gold from the pollution and the clouds.

"It looks like the end of the world, doesn't it?" she asked me, crisply.

The end of the world.

I find myself wondering what it takes to be a woman on Wall Street. A crisp successful woman like my boss, wearing gray suits and having sleek blonde hair pinned away from her face in a French twist and cool eyes. Being able to dictate letters. Figuring out financial reports. Staying calm on the phone with clients. Striking her bargains, making her deals, going on home to Connecticut.

No matter what I do with this life that stretches before me like a carpet without a pattern, I know it will not be that.

"Dig it," Ruth says to me now. "I want to find out about getting a gig like yours on Wall Street."

"On Wall Street?" I am startled. "You?"

I have always been the "straight" one among the three of us. The one with boring office jobs, a tight but steady income, the kind of independence small skills bring. In touch with a world both larger and narrower than Victoria's or Ruth's, the world of high finance and commerce. The world that ignores artists and anthropologists and struggling young actresses. Ignores them and derides them and pays for them. That world.

Ruth wanting to enter that world spells disaster for me. It can't be reconciled with the painting, "Blue." It can't be reconciled with wild nights in Stanley's and the Cedar Tavern. Or with her snide intelligence, her brash self-confidence, her contempt for the phony and the dull, her gifts.

With everything she means to me.

And despite my own early determination to support myself through typing, I find myself wanting to keep her away from there, to keep her "free."

"Doing what?" I ask her, after a startled pause.

"You know," she says. "Some gig like you've got. Typing. Filing. That kind of stuff. At least to start with. Who knows? Maybe I could end up like a stockbroker or something."

"I didn't even know you could type."

"My mother made me learn, in high school. I guess she was afraid I would never be able to earn a living any other way." She laughs aloud, a wild, uncharacteristic bray. "And that no cat would ever want to marry me. She was afraid I'd starve, dig?"

"But Wall Street. It doesn't feel like you."

"Yeah. Sure. Remember that art gallery owner? The one who said I ought to marry a rich dude? Well, he ought to meet my mother, that's what he ought to do. They could really blab about me, the two of them. I wonder if they'd even know they were talking about the same chick."

"But why Wall Street?"

"Got to earn some bread."

"For what?"

"Need bread."

"But why?"

"Gotta live, kid."

"But you always have. . ."

"I'm sick of hustling."

With this burst of honesty her lids draw down again. Hustling in the 60s means one thing only. I think of Bud with the blood on his hands. I think of her new clothes. The gold chain around her ankle. The backless shoes.

And yet I still refuse to understand. "You could get that assistantship. You could teach art. You could even work in a dress shop somewhere, or in an art store. You could model. You're tall enough."

"You're working on Wall Street, aren't you? *You* could go to grad school or get some other job. You've always been a hypocrite." She turns away from me and lights a cigarette. "You always act so *nice*, you know? So damned *concerned*. But you never listen to anybody either, you just do exactly what you want and screw the rest of us. You've got everybody fooled but me," she comments. "How about a beer?"

We have stopped outside Stanley's.

"I don't know. It's too early." Stung by her words, I look through my tears into the bar's windows. Inside is no one I recognize.

"Ruth." I turn to face her. Her eyes are still and secretive, slanting slightly at the corners. "I *am* concerned. Only, except for the day of my father's funeral, you've never given me one sign of what's going on with you. All I see is exactly what you want me to see. Nothing else."

"There isn't anything else," she lies.

It's only later, only from Victoria, that I find out about her visits to her father's store. And it's only from Victoria that I learn about the other things, things Ruth has told her with the usual dose of laughter, her face contorted with her own self-derision, having as little mercy for herself as she has for anybody else.

And much less mercy for herself than anybody else will have.

"Everything's cool with you too, isn't it?" she asks me now, the corners of her mouth curling slightly.

"Sure." I lie just as easily as she does. "I'm fine."

"Me too." But her eyes say something different, and I find myself wondering why we've never opened to one another, even as much as we've opened to our other friend, the one to whom we're not related.

Maybe only because of that. We have no history with Victoria. There's no family between us.

"I still think there's something going on with you."

"Oh yeah?" Ruth starts to laugh.

I laugh with her. "Come on. What is it? Are you seeing somebody new? Is there anything. . ." I think of Zalman and how Victoria saw them together. I think of what Ruth might have to tell me and I feel afraid.

"Zero, kid," she says blankly. "Zip." But her voice is too soft, and she looks away.

Later we sprawl together on her cot, on the rumpled Indian bedspread under the bare lamp. There's nothing to eat in her apartment, just as there almost never is in mine. I'm hungry, and she wants me to go.

"So it's a deal? You'll help me get a gig?"

I have no idea of how to help her, and can't imagine what to say. Can I possibly just bring her into my office and ask my boss if she can work there? With no references, no experience?

"Let's get wasted and go out," I evade. "Maybe there are people in Stanley's by now."

I'm calling up the past. My own form of magic. It doesn't work.

"Okay," I appease her. "What do you want to do?"

"Get that gig."

"I mean now," I say. "Right this minute."

"I could stand to get high."

"That's what I said."

"Not what you said."

"What's the difference?"

She pauses for a moment, looking me over. Then, her eyes blank, she seems to make a decision. "I do schmeck," she says.

From her pillow she blinks at me, malicious. Suddenly I feel just as I did when I saw Victoria leave the fashionable hotel in a welter of white lace and flowers. That she is gone, and not coming back.

But I don't want Ruth to leave me.

For a moment I feel like a swimmer about to face the open sea. Knowing that too little holds me back. Or maybe nothing. I poise there, on Ruth's ugly bedspread, waiting to make the move which will define the nebulous remainder of my life.

"Oh yeah?" I say, trying not to sound surprised. I take a deep breath. *Go on*, I tell myself. "Well," I quaver. "I'm game."

"I don't have enough for both of us," Ruth says, after a pause. "I didn't score enough for two."

As if moving under water, I reach for my purse. "Let me have a taste. I'll pay you for it."

We look at one another in the darkness of her room. Her mouth turns down in scorn.

"You could just snort it," she says, "or would you want to shoot? You did it with Zalman the Cap already, right?"

"Other things," I answer. "Not smack."

She looks at me for a minute. There's a kind of new assessment in her eyes, something between derision and respect. Then she snaps her fingers and sits up.

"Okay," she says. "Sure. Why not? If you pay." She laughs. "What's worrying you, kid? Think you'll like it too much?"

She opens her purse and takes out a cellophane bag which holds about a quarter of a spoonful of white powder.

"Dig it. I hope you know what I'm doing for you. I hope you appreciate it."

"I do, Ruth. Sure."

She puts a pinch of powder into a twist of paper and I lean forward to breathe it in.

"You know how to show gratitude? Get me that gig."

"Sure," I say. "Sure. I'll try. I promise." Leaning.

Breathing. Putting a finger over one nostril to press it closed.

There's a knock at the door.

"Uh oh," Ruth says to me, in a whisper. "Hang on."

Very, very carefully she spills the powder back into the bag, then folds it and hides it under the pillow at the head of her bed.

She gets up quietly and goes to the door. "Who's there?" she whispers.

It's Bud.

I hear his voice from the other room. He is desperate, I hear him say. He didn't score enough this afternoon, he says, and he can't locate his regular dealer. He has to have just one more hit, to tide him over. And he'll pay double. I hear him say.

She comes back into the bedroom and looks down at me.

"Sorry," she offers me, offhand, motioning me out. It's the closest she's ever come to apologizing to me for anything. I get up to leave.

After I've left her apartment, I run half a block away from Paradise Alley and then stop to look again into the front window of Stanley's, which is dark and almost empty. Again, I have given away my life, I think, only to have to take it back. And I don't know whether I'm relieved or disappointed. I wish I could see Zalman.

Suddenly I decide to find him, right away. I have a little money. Enough. I'll go to the door of his apartment and knock, and if he's not home, I'll simply wait in the hallway until he comes back. Wait to score from him, like one of the ghostly men I saw the first time he ever brought me here, who are always sitting in or near his building, sad and pale in long overcoats. Eternally waiting, waiting.

But the door of his apartment is closed, and nobody answers when I knock. I don't know where to call him, or whether I should. He might want to be alone with Flower. He might want to be alone with Zelda. He might want to be alone with one of a dozen other people, men or women. As I stand in the hallway, thinking about what to do next, someone comes bounding up the stairs.

"Hey," the stranger shouts, going right past me. I have

already become a ghost, like one of the men in long overcoats. He knocks on Zalman's door, once, impatiently, and then calls, "It's me!" The door is flung open, and there, under the light of a single lamp, I see Flower, standing over the stove in a long stained nightgown, yawning, one hand thrust above her head. She's started to cook something but the pot has scorched; the smell of it pours out into the hallway along with a smell of rot and dankness, unwashed laundry, old dirt. And behind her in the shadowy disorder of books and clothes thrown everywhere I see Zalman spread out on a mattress on the floor, wearing a tattered green robe and a Jewish skullcap, a *yarmulke*, like the one my father used to wear to cover his bald spot when it was cold.

He, too, suddenly looks like a ghost to me. He seems shrunken and withered in his green robe and his skullcap as he rises and shambles across the room. His face is ashen and the rims of his eyes are red and filled with pus; he stops to rub them with the backs of his hands before he moves on.

"Flora?" I hear him call. "Did you make coffee?"

All his brightness, the intensity I love so much, vanished. Gone.

Then he comes up and slams the door. In the shadow of the flight of stairs, I am invisible. He hasn't seen me. And I myself have seen too much.

As I wait for the uptown bus on a deserted corner, a man hurries past me wearing a raincoat, too heavy for the weather, the collar turned up to hide a straggling beard. As he passes me he turns and stares down hungrily into my face, and his is clearly visible under the street lamp. He looks almost as wretched as I feel, and with a shock, I realize that I recognize him, even though I've seen him only once, and then from a distance, through a coffeeshop window. Still, when I see his face, his wretchedness, his hunger, I want to laugh. He stumbles away from me through the tunnel of streets, smaller and smaller under the lamps.

The man is Richard Loess.

SIXTEEN

I am marooned. I live in fog. I go through the motions of my life.

To Wall Street and back. The subway, the streets.

My apartment. Sleep. Or long nights awake.

College is over. All my student friends are gone. Victoria is married and living on Park Avenue. And Ruth? Ruth finally has the job she wanted on Wall Street. She's a clerk-typist trainee in an employment agency. Once or twice we meet for lunch. She's bought a grey suit and propels herself forward on stiletto-heeled black leather pumps. Her hair is honey-blonde again, expertly styled so that it curves up around her ears, and she carries a black lizardskin purse shaped like an envelope on a long gold chain. She looks as hard and guarded as an armored car.

I do not mention painting to her any more.

Sometimes I ask myself where "real life" has gone. Why I haven't found someone else to love, or even to marry—why I haven't gone to graduate school or at least found myself a better, more interesting job—in advertising, maybe—and bought myself a new grey suit, shiny black shoes, a modern cut for my long, unfashionable hair.

But the phone still rings late at night, and it's still him, and he always has something special for me, just a little something to tide me over. And that's a kind of answer, anyway.

One night, just at the end of September, the phone rings very late. This has always been my favorite season in New York. A cool wind rides up from the river and the streets seem liberated from the long summer dampness, but it's not yet really cold. Even on Columbus Avenue I believe that I can smell wood smoke. The sky is purple now, before night falls.

"Want to go downtown?" he asks me.

It's like always, I think at first. He comes over and we fall onto my cot, glued at the hips and mouths. He kisses me between the thighs, he turns me over and kisses my buttocks, he kisses my breasts until I melt into him, all my doubts about him, all the memories of him shrunken and sickly-looking in his Paradise Alley apartment, melted and scorched away. At three a.m., our habitual hour, we go together to drink coffee at a place in the Village, where we end up sitting until morning. Zalman in his leather spy's coat and corduroy trousers, talking and waving his hands, is indisputably "on," his huge eyes glittering. There's a wonderful pain between my legs.

We drink coffee. I recognize a woman whom Ruth, Victoria and I used to hang out with at Stanley's, and wave to her, recklessly, across the room.

He looks at her and then back at me, so quickly I almost don't notice.

"Helene?" he says softly. "Helene?"

"What is it?"

"I'll be back in a minute. There's something I want to talk to you about." He gets up and leaves the table.

When he enters the men's room, my friend from Stanley's

comes over and sits down tentatively, watching me with insinuating eyes.

"Haven't seen you in a while," she murmurs. "I didn't know
you were seeing Zalman Finster." She speaks casually, lighting a cigarette. "What are you, anyway? His old lady?"

"Are you my old lady?" he asked me once, what seems like
a very long time ago.

"I guess so," I answer her. "I guess I am."

"Yeah? Funny." She grins, and nods wisely. "I heard he dug
a ménage, but you never know till you find out, right?" Before
I can stop her she reaches for my purse across the table. "You
holding?"

"You heard what?" I mutter, baffled by the word "ménage,"
too uneasy to ask what it means. I do have some Dexamil, as
it happens, and she fishes the bottle out of my purse before I can
stop her and downs two spansules without benefit of water.

Retrieving the bottle I take one with a sip of coffee.

"Don't you know what a ménage is?" she asks, contemptu-
ously. Her voice is spitting and cold, and for an instant she
sounds like Ruth. Her eyes meet mine and I try not to wince
away from them.

I look around for Zalman. To my surprise, he's already at the
door. He's been standing there for a few minutes, watching us
talk but not approaching. He smiles at us now, still from a
distance. When he rubs two fingers underneath his lower lip to
stroke it dry, he looks exactly like a cat who has spilt the cream.

"Helene?" he calls softly. "Want to go?"

"What's with you?" I ask, as we slide through the doorway
and out onto the street. "You okay?"

"It's cool, baby." But I notice that he's watching me out of
the corner of his eye.

"So what do you want to talk about?"

"Oh, that. Yeah." He stops at the corner, as if reluctant to go
on.

We're on Macdougal Street, I realize. The street where the

girl with the red skirt lay in bed and laughed and cried, talking about her skirt cooking on the stove.

We cross at the green light. He takes my arm.

"I did something really stupid," he says. "I need to tell you about it." Again he scans my face from the corner of his eye.

Out in the daylight, leached of color, a grey-white Washington Square, grey-white treebark, grey-green leaves, we sit together on a bench and hold hands. Cars rush softly past on the streets around us, phantoms of the morning which will soon begin with a clashing of iron gates ringing as shops open; a percussion of cash registers.

"So tell me," I say. We pass a joint between us. Back and forth.

"I made a scene." He watches me, cautious.

"A scene? What kind of scene?"

"Dig it." He hesitates. Then he grins, as if relaxing suddenly. Letting out his breath. "I went to this wedding."

"A wedding? Really? You?"

"Yeah. An old friend's wedding. Like, I went with my ex-wife and my kid. I did it for their sakes. But very conventional, you know what I mean? Way out in Queens, at a banquet hall."

"My God. I can't imagine you there. What did you do?"

"I really screwed up. My kid was ashamed. . . she's twelve now, it's a hard age anyway. And I ruined it for my friend. She was the bride, and there was this whole family there, the chick's mother and father, the bridegroom's parents—the whole number, everybody taking it very seriously. And then all of a sudden there's this old bird, this soprano, up on a balcony somewhere and she's singing, and the bride and groom come wobbling down the aisle. They walk along with this old bird singing and everybody's looking very solemn and all of a sudden, I just couldn't help it, I began to laugh. And I laughed so much I became hysterical. They practically had to carry me out . . ."

"I don't understand," I say. "Why do you need to tell me

about this?"

"Because I'm ashamed," he says. "And because I think you know this person and I'm afraid somebody might have said something to you about me. Didn't anybody say anything to you about me? This kind of number worries me, that's all. I hate to hurt anybody's feelings."

"What's her name?"

He names somebody I've never even heard of, and I shake my head.

"Nobody's said anything to me about you."

He looks relieved.

"But what difference does it make, anyway?" I ask him. "The wedding sounds like a bringdown anyway."

He smiles, and puts his arm around me.

"Sure. That old bird singing on the balcony. That was the last straw. I shouldn't have gone."

I lean against his shoulder. "It wasn't so terrible," I say finally. "What you did."

"Yeah?" He holds me. "She was crying so hard I thought she must have had a nervous breakdown. The bride, I mean. I thought she'd never get over it."

Women cry, I think. Remembering some of the nights I thought I was going to have a nervous breakdown. We cry, and then we get over it.

"Did she get married anyway?" I ask him.

"Sure."

"Well, if she has a good honeymoon she'll forgive you within a month. And if she doesn't, it doesn't matter."

But I'm a little baffled. Why is he making so much of this?

By now we're up again, and on to the next place, and he's holding my hand very tightly.

"Are you my old lady?" he whispers to me, as we cross the street.

Up on the Fifth Avenue bus we go, up through the still white morning and into Central Park, where the trees seem to explode around us in the brilliant and dangerous colors of New York autumn, as they did on the first whole day I spent with him, long before. So long a time, I wonder suddenly, and I feel myself leaning against him with a deep warmth, and at one point as we walk along together it turns windy and he lets me wear his coat, and I enclose myself within it, its dark soft leather that smells of him and comes down almost to my ankles.

The lights of the city go out one by one and clouds come up against an azure sky. It's going to be a perfect day, but too bad, he says; too bad, because he can't possibly stay with me all day, the way he did that first time, long ago. He can't drop mescaline with me, or take me to the museum, bestowing glimpses of paintings upon me the way other men might bestow jewels or flowers. He can't even offer to do smack with me as I half-hope, half-fear he will. Today he has to "split," he says. He has business to do, he has people to see. He looks at me significantly, maybe to remind me about the pickup I never made for him, months before, but he still has something for me, "Something special," as he always says. I buy a couple of dollars' worth of Dex and some Nembutal to help me sleep, and before he says goodbye to me I put my arms around him, holding him close.

I go home and fall into bed in the middle of the morning, pulling the blinds against the flat city light. After an hour or two somebody wakes me up. It's my cousin Ruth; she's standing at the foot of my bed.

"*Oy veh*," she is saying, sounding just like her mother. "Look who's here."

I look up and there, framed by the window is Edie Scheinblatt, in her navy dress with the white collar, a virgin pin over one breast and Howie's "frat" pin glittering on the other like an artificial nipple, and dwarfing the finger of her left hand a gigantic diamond in a setting so huge and bright that it looks like a plumbing fixture.

"We're married now," Edie burbles, flailing her diamond,

"and I've never been so happy. He does everything for me. Weekends at Grossinger's. Breakfast in bed." Howie stands behind her like a somnambulant steer. There is absolutely no expression on his face, and beyond his shoulder I see a mass of Education Majors, all trooping into my bedroom on their way to weddings and funerals and brisses, from synagogues or from the resorts in the Catskills or from dinners or shopping trips with their parents or their fiancés who are Jewish fraternity boys and the sons of contractors and dentists. And the E.M.s are all wearing big diamond engagement rings and solid gold virgin pins, their bouffant hairdoes sprayed and lacquered into motionlessness like gigantic hats, and they're all dancing around (with dignity) and laughing at me and Ruth, and screaming into our faces, "Beatniks! Beatniks! Beatniks!"

Their screams turn into the ringing of my alarm clock and I lean over to turn it off. And waking, I finally know exactly what I really want, and what I'm going to do about it. What I want is not to be like them, like Edie and the Education Majors. What I want is to stay alive, like Zalman and Flower and Ruth. I want to refuse to end the nights, whatever the risks. I want to forget time, money, graduate school, my father's death, the demands of other people, what's expected of me, the questions of who will pay the bills, who will pay the landlord. I want to wake and sleep according to my own clock as Zalman does, and damn the landlord anyway.

And maybe now, I think, reaching for my alarm clock— maybe now, when my bridges all are burned, when there's really nothing else for me to do, I even can.

But when I lean over to turn off the ringing clock I realize that what I heard was really the ringing phone. It is five o'clock in the afternoon and I never set the clock. And the phone is ringing because my mother is calling to tell me that my cousin Ruth is dead.

SEVENTEEN

". . . burn, burn, burn like fabulous yellow candles."
— *Jack Kerouac, 1951*

"She died in a hallway. In the hallway of some building, all by herself like an animal!"

My mother's voice rises and peaks. I have a sudden impulse to make a wisecrack, to tell her that animals rarely die in the hallways of buildings in New York, but she's not in any state to be joked with and it occurs to me that it's a kind of insanity even to want to. Hysterical. I keep my mouth shut instead, huddling under my blankets and lighting a cigarette with shaking hands.

"Yesterday, they found her. Yesterday! She had been gone five days. Missing and nobody even bothered to look for her until the bosses at her fancy Wall Street office called the police. So where were you, her famous cousin? In five days, you didn't call her? You didn't notice she was missing? We should be grateful to the Wall Streets, they were smart enough to get worried when she didn't show up and nobody answered her phone. You can trust a gentile to call the police. They found her, all right. They found her in the morgue!"

There's a long, noisy pause, during which I can imagine my mother pulling another Kleenex out of the box which she keeps on a low shelf over the sink, bending over her cheerful kitchen table, stanching the tears which drip annoyingly down her cheeks, getting in her nose and mouth, making her speech muffled and slurred.

"I thought you said they found her in a *building*," I blurt, unclenching my teeth. Then I throw the cigarette into an ashtray and hang up the phone and run into the bathroom. There isn't very much in my stomach and it doesn't take very long. When I am finished my cigarette is still burning in the ashtray by the bed and my mother is calling back.

"What's the matter with you?" she yells at me. "Why did you hang up?"

"Couldn't help it." While she mulls this over I clear my throat and swallow. There's bile in the back of my mouth. "I thought you said they found her in the hallway of a building." My voice is flat but audible.

"What do you think, they left her there? They found her, they took her to the morgue!"

"What happened? Did she O.D.?" I'm thinking that I'm going to have to run to the bathroom again. My stomach heaves and again the bitter liquid comes up into my throat, but nothing else happens.

"Did she *what*?"

"Oh." I realize too late that I shouldn't have said it. "O.D. It means. . ." I hesitate. She is waiting for me to finish. "It means 'overdose,'" I say lamely.

"Overdose? Do you think your cousin committed suicide? In the *street*?"

"Drugs," I whisper. "I asked whether she overdosed on

drugs."

"What are you saying? How come you should ask such a question about your cousin, Helene? Was she using drugs? Are you? What kind of terrible lives were you girls leading together? What kind of horrible things were you doing?"

In the background I hear my grandmother's screechy voice. "She's a devil!" she's screaming. Cursing me the way she always cursed my cousin. "She's a no-good devil, that one. Listen to me! I know!"

"There are drugs around, mother. I didn't know if Ruth was using them," I lie, "but lots of people do. A lot of people die of that kind of thing in the city. It's not such an unusual question, mother."

"Not such an unusual question, did your cousin die of drugs. No, she didn't die of drugs. She was *killed*. She was beaten to death, your cousin. *Beaten to death.* Yes. It was so bad the police had to identify her through her dental records."

"What? What are you talking about?"

"Mildred had to come down to the morgue with Ruth's X-rays from the dentist so they could know who she was. They wouldn't let her look at the face. They'll have to bury Ruthie in a sealed coffin so nobody should see her. I don't even *want* to see her. Poor Mildred! How much tragedy in life can one person bear?"

"I don't understand," I keep saying. I light my next cigarette from the first one. It keeps down the taste of bile a little, but it makes me dizzy and I clutch the edge of the bedside table. "I don't understand."

But the awful thing is that I do understand; the awful thing is that memories of Ruth float through my mind like sharks through a murky ocean.

"You don't understand? Well listen, my dear, listen, I don't understand either. I don't understand why she should be in some neighborhood so terrible that she lay for two days before they found her, and when they did there was absolutely nothing on her, not a single scrap of clothes, not a single piece of identification, her face so bruised that they could only identify her from her dental records. The whole thing without reason. Senseless! What was she doing there, I ask you? You should know, you were so close to her. You know what she was doing? It was in the South Bronx, nowhere near where she lived. What was she doing on such a street?"

What was she doing on such a street? I should have known what she was doing.

I did know.

"Maybe she was brought there," I whisper. "Maybe somebody brought her there and dumped the body."

"But who could do such a thing, who would want to kill her? The police think she was killed where they found her, that it was a very bad mugging. But what was she doing there? What was she doing?"

She begins to cry again and I try to turn off the insidious whispers in my mind.

Ruth in high-heeled backless sandals, tapping her foot while she waited on a corner with a man.

Ruth saying, "I'm tired of hustling," but turning to me in the darkness of her apartment and saying "I do schmeck," defiant under the grim light of the bare bulb.

Ruth with Zalman. Drifting along with Zalman through the crowded rooms of parties. Doing schmeck with Zalman. Getting involved.

"Baby," he says to me. "I need a hundred dollars."

"Baby, I need a favor," he says. "I need you to pick up a package."

"But I don't want to make any pick-ups of drugs," I answer. "It's too risky." And I have a sudden vision of myself walking into some building, watched by hidden eyes. I can see the back of my neck as I climb an unlit staircase. It makes me feel sick.

But Ruth was never afraid of danger.

Not her. Not my cousin.

Who lay for two days before she was found. On a street where she had no business being.

Even as I dress, slowly, stopping before each new motion— even as I brush my hair, clean my teeth, drop water in the corners of my eyes—even as I clumsily button the cuffs of my shirt, I am thinking. I am thinking about Zalman. I am thinking about Ruth. I am thinking about the fact that Ruth was missing for days and I hadn't called her, and about the way Zalman had been the night before. That he had been strange, nervous, especially when he said, "I've done something wrong, I've got to tell you about it. Didn't anybody tell you anything about me?" I am thinking of how his story about the wedding sounded like a lie and of how Ruth was beaten to death in a hallway, on a street where she had no business being, even in the middle of the day.

As if she were asking for trouble. Looking for it, somehow. Finding it.

I am thinking when I take the subway uptown, up to the Bronx again to sit again with my mother and my sister and my aunt. And when I listen to the laments of my relatives and watch them eating too much in their grief and telling each other what a shame it is that this young woman whom they hardly knew and did not really like is dead. Yes. What a shame. I think this too, even though all of them confront me with shocked and angry looks as if they all knew—Mildred, my mother and especially my grandmother—that I had something to do with what happened to Ruth. That all along I knew something they didn't. That I should have told them. And maybe they're right. Maybe I should have. But even now, I don't.

I myself can no longer eat too much or even anything at all. I can't sleep any more, either. I can hardly even get out of my chair. I have no energy, just a constant tension that enervates me.

"It's a package," he says softly. "A package of money. I

thought you liked adventure."

I go into my mother's bathroom and try to bring the bile up out of my throat. But it doesn't stop. There's no relief for me. There are two fat orange plastic vials of pills in my bureau drawer at home. I remember them suddenly, remember that I left them. Why did I leave them? I sit there, longing for them, feeling their loss as palpably as I might feel the loss of a lover. Or a friend. Zalman. Ruth. My head feels thick, surrounded by cotton. I can hardly breathe.

Why did I leave them home? I cry to myself.

Finally, at the bottom of my purse I find a few odd medicinal crumbs of pills which I swallow without water. After a while color comes into my cheeks again and I can feel my pulse, but when the rush wears off I go back into the bathroom and take aspirin. There's a brand new bottle of Miltown prescribed to my mother in the medicine cabinet and I sneak a few of them and hide them in my purse, and for an hour or two that night I am able to sleep. When I wake at four a.m. I lie in the darkness of the living room and wait for the morning to come as if then, in the morning light, my exhaustion will be easier to bear.

But that next day they empty Ruth's apartment and bring back the few things she had there. Too few things. Her clothes and little else.

"And what a filthy mess her apartment was," keens Mildred, eyeing me in unspent fury. "How she could live in that filthy slum when she had a good home. . ."

Too few things. Some unsaleable art supplies, a few empty canvasses, a few that still have paintings on them, the one called "Blue" among them. "Blue." It has always been my favorite. When they bring it home I hold it for a little while as if it were a beloved child. And then relinquish it to Mildred, who is making a shrine of her daughter's room, hanging the few paintings everywhere she can although she never even looked at them when Ruth was alive and winning scholarships and grants with her talent.

Courageously, I say, "I really like this one, Aunt Mildred. I think Ruth might have wanted me to have it."

Mildred ignores me; my mother shakes my arm violently as if I were still ten years old and hisses in my ear after we leave, "How can you think of taking anything away from Aunt Mildred at a time like this? How can you be so abominably selfish?"

So I do not get the picture, "Blue," and I never see it again.

Returning to my dim apartment three days later, against the shrill objections of my relatives, I find myself again waiting for the time when the phone will begin to ring, late one night, when it can't possibly be anyone but Zalman.

Late fall now. Getting cold. Time for us to meander through the park together and drop small, ruby-colored spansules into our mouths and watch the clear New York autumn air crystallize and turn to smoke before our eyes. Time to spend the night under crumpled quilts on my small cot, traveling across the bedroom floor, out into the night, out over the chimneys, the houses, the airshafts, the people, across the densely packed New York backyards with their random trees, dark with the sense of danger and with living at the very edge of human space, "the very edge of the known," he used to say.

The very edge of the known.

It was at that edge that I've wanted to live, even when he wasn't there. I've wanted to look into the mirror and see in myself what I've admired so much in him; I've wanted to see the beauty of his eyes, gleaming back at me from my own face. I've wanted to perform daily acts of courage as I believe he has done. He and Ruth. Liberating themselves from the prison of their own limitations. Obliterating sadness, loneliness, the need for sleep.

There are no more medicinal crumbs at the bottom of my purse. The orange vials in my bureau drawer are almost empty. The light hurts my eyes.

I close them and get into bed and burrow under the covers, where I lie without moving for as long as I can; but sleep doesn't come and after a few hours my nightgown is soaked with sweat. I stumble out of bed and drop it into the bathtub and get back to bed. After a few more hours, the sheets are soaked. At nine o'clock the next morning I am jogged out of a pale dream by the phone.

"Trust a gentile to call the police," my mother said, so I pick it up. It is my crisp-voiced boss.

"Miss Elphrick, do you plan to return to this office?" she asks.

"No."

"You won't get a letter of recommendation from me," she snaps, abrupt as ever.

Then she hangs up and I cover my head with a pillow. My career as a secretary has ended. My future on Wall Street. I remember how at the beginning I wanted to give him my whole life, quitting my job, not going to school for days. He did not want it, he gave it back to me.

Now it's all gone anyway. So is my cousin Ruth. And school. And even my friendship with Victoria. How am I going to live, if everything is gone?

There's a pill for everything, maybe even for living. But I'm out of pills, and there won't be any more. Unless he calls, and I pick up the phone, and he brings them to me.

As he always has.

When finally the phone does ring one night, I can't pick it up. My hands won't move. It's eleven o'clock on a week night. It's him. Behind each ring I can feel him in a phone booth. I can see him, dropping a dime into the slot with fingers as grimy as charcoal. He will come to my door. He will want some food. He will desperately need a bath. He will want my warmth. Like a cat that's been rescued from the alleys for a little while before it rushes out again into the night, to prowl.

But when he comes to me, wanting all that, I won't be able

to give it to him. Not any more.

So I let the phone ring. After it stops I feel a little better; I get out of bed, open a can of soup, open a window. Then I wrap myself in my sweaty quilts and wait for it to ring again. He calls back almost an hour later. Maybe he'll come to my apartment, I think. Maybe he'll come to the door, and in my weakened state I'll have to let him in. My mouth is dry and I take a drink of water. I feel as if I've been here for a long time. If he comes he'll have "something special," something that will send me out into the streets again, blood racing in my veins, cheeks warm, eyes dancing. Something that will even make me laugh. The phone rings again.

The coffin of my cousin Ruth was not wood, as specified by the Jewish religion, but metal—grey, expensive, lined with blue satin which nobody saw but the undertaker and Mildred and my mother. The handles were real silver. Ruth lay inside it. They had restored her, my mother said. Put her broken bones back together again. Put pancake makeup over the bruises on her eyes. Dressed her in one of the last of her expensive dresses or maybe the new suit she had bought to look appropriate on Wall Street. And on one of her broken fingers or maybe curled in the palm of her hand my mother made sure to put the pearl pyramid ring she had given her, which she'd redeemed from the pawnshop where Ruth had turned it in for an extra hit or two, solace for a particularly dark day, perhaps—the pearl pyramid ring I had always wanted and which was never given to me, no matter how often I asked.

How ridiculous, I thought, watching them lower the coffin, to give her something she couldn't have wanted any more. How ridiculous, but how perfect for Ruth, because it's exactly the kind of thing she might have done if it were the other way around. If I had died. If she had survived me. Put something valuable on my corpse, let it be buried with me. Given me something she herself had wanted, but only after I couldn't possibly have wanted it any more.

She would do that, I think now, but what else would she do? What would she do about my death, if I had been the one who died, if she had gone on living? If I had made the pick-up on the dangerous street and been followed and mugged and left for dead, to be identified in the morgue later only by my teeth?

I don't know why I need the answer to this question. But I do.

It is very late at night, and a little pulse of energy comes back into my heart. Maybe I'll get straight again, I think. Maybe I'll even be happy. Maybe I'll even experience the feeling I call "real life." But not the same way. Never the same way again.

The phone keeps ringing. I listen to it. Then I lay my head down gently on the pillow.

And I know finally that even if he comes to the door of my apartment, I won't be weak enough to let him in.

EIGHTEEN

*"All the accumulations of life, that wear us out—clocks,
bodies, consciousness, shoes, breasts. . ."*
— *Allen Ginsberg, ca. 1959*

"From now on we can be like distant relatives." I look at her
across the cluttered table. "Meeting once a year or so at family
events. Weddings. Graduations."

"Sure," she grins. "Like cousins." But her pale eyes fly to
my face the minute she says it and she gapes at me as if at an
open wound. Does she think I'm going to explode? Accuse her
of deserting Ruth or of not coming to the funeral? I've gone
beyond explosions, and the fact that we're here together
cancels out her ever having to be sorry for anything, as far as
I'm concerned.

I feel as if I've returned from a long journey. It's hard for me
to experience my own emotions; even the surface of my skin
seems remote. Am I smiling now? A luxurious peace comes

over me in the cool, enveloping elegance of the restaurant. She orders champagne and I take a tiny, tentative sip, worried about what it's going to do to me.

"It's a special occasion," she says, pouring self-importantly, but I can think only that there have been too many special occasions in my life, and that I am through with them.

"What we *can* do," she relaxes now that the moment has passed, "is eat here together once in a while, for old time's sake."

I smile—I think I smile—reassuringly, and she goes on.

"I miss this place. I never come here any more—Burton hates the food."

"How can anybody hate the food in the Russian Tea Room?"

"He's a Tavern on the Green man," she says, taking out an enamelled compact and powdering her nose. "Strictly steak and potatoes, even when we were in France last summer." She sighs. "So what's the next big family event going to be, anyway?"

"That's easy. Your baby's christening."

"I'm not going to have any babies. Don't you remember what the doctor said about my pelvis?"

"There's always caesarians, Victoria. Or you and Burton could adopt."

"What for? I've decided to have a career instead of children. I'm going to finish NYU and go to graduate school. Get a Ph.D. I just haven't decided in what, that's all."

"But you don't need to work. Burton makes enough money for both of you, doesn't he?"

"Come on, Helene. Work's good for the spirit. And Burton can always stand the idea of more money. A house in the Hamptons, lots of trips to Europe, our own plane . . ."

I believe her. She sits across the table from me looking impossibly well groomed, the way women have begun to look in 1962. Her hair is cut in a sleek chin-length bubble like Jackie Kennedy's and she's wearing opaque white hose instead of the usual sheer nylons or black stockings, an Empire-waisted dress from one of the new fashionable boutiques on the Upper East Side and soft black patent leather pumps with small spool heels. She looks the way I want to look; she looks the way I've decided to look as soon as I can save enough money to buy new clothes. I even like her makeup, the heavy eyeliner, the pale pink lipstick. Her face is bland and doll-like and shows very little expression and I want my own face to be like hers, because it's extremely uncool to look like you've been sick and grieving, and I have.

What else I've been is an escapee. I've escaped my mother's scrutiny and my grandmother's rage and the memories of the dusty, grandiose funeral home off the Grand Concourse and the long procession of black cars out to Queens where they put Ruth in her sealed coffin into the ground. I've escaped the prison of my own room where I've passed the last weeks in a state of exhausted pain, caught between withdrawal headaches and bouts of dry retching as well as between sleep and waking, while the effects of pot and mescaline and amphetamines and downers, of Miltown and phenobarbital and Doriden and Dexamil, wore themselves out in a long slow dance of torture.

Now, on the safer ground of the Tea Room I can finally drown myself in Russian tea and blinis with roe and get the smell of dusty funeral parlor and fresh earth and senseless misery out of my nostrils. And be alone with her. I was amazed when she called me, when the phone rang in the middle of the day and I actually answered it, suspecting neither my mother nor my boss nor Zalman; suddenly like a remedy there was Victoria's voice on the line pleading querulously, "Helene? Helene? Why didn't you call me? Are you mad at me? Helene?"

I wanted only to get off somewhere alone with her. To talk to her about Ruth, whom I believe she knew better than I did, better than anybody, maybe. And to ask her a question, because there's a question that's beginning to torment me, and I don't think I can answer it all by myself. Not yet, anyway. Not yet.

If it had been one of us who died, I want to ask her, *do you think Ruth would have done anything about it? Do you think it would have changed her? What do you think she would have done?*

And sitting here with her now, I can even dare to ask it aloud.

Victoria's cigarette case is silver and her lighter is gold. The two of them clink together on the white linen table top. She looks at me for a minute as she takes her first puff. (Soon she'll get wise and quit smoking, without gaining a single pound. Her life in hand, she's already exhibiting a strength of character and purpose none of us expected of her.) Now she shakes her head, emphatically and with the authority only such a successful young matron can demonstrate.

"Couldn't happen," she exhales. "Neither you or I could do it."

"Do what?"

"Ruth died because she wanted to die. You and I don't." Her eyes meet mine. "You know it too, Helene. We're just not that desperate."

"I am," I say. I know that I tread dangerous ground, being so serious with Victoria. But you can't always laugh, and you can't always lie. "I've got a real problem with drugs."

The words, spoken aloud, are bald and ugly and don't even scratch the truth.

"Because of that jerk? That Zalman?" She shakes her head.

"Because of myself, I think."

"But he gave you the chance, didn't he? I'll bet he did. He's the one who got her started, too. On heroin, anyway. Oh well, who cares? If it hadn't been him it might have been somebody else. But he must have tried the same bullshit with you." She squints at my arm. "And I don't see any needle tracks."

"No," I say.

"That's what I mean. You've been unhappy sometimes, but you wouldn't try to destroy yourself because of it."

"Pretty close," I say.

"Pretty close doesn't count. Come on, Helene. Ruth smoked plenty of grass before she met him, but I can't help wondering if she would have done anything worse if he hadn't pitched it to her as a kind of artistic gesture. 'Think of it as a kind of adventure, exceed your limitations,' or some absolute bullshit like that. She laughed at him, but deep down I think she took him seriously. Of course, after she really started needing it he sold it to her. Not at a discount either, according to her. And when she couldn't pay she told me he used her as a courier."

She glares at me suddenly and I look into her eyes, light and raw. Her face is pale, under the doll mask. With what? I wonder. Rage? Remorse?

"I've stopped seeing him too," I whisper. "It was hard, but I've stopped." I shake my head. "I always thought Ruth was the strong one."

"You got it mixed up, kiddo." And she tells me about Ruth's trips to her father's furrier shop, about the desperation Ruth tried to disguise. By laughing, by acting tough. By being into danger.

By shooting up.

"I think she was terrific anyway," I say sadly. "So gorgeous and talented. And she could speak for herself. She could just speak right up, say what was on her mind. I always envied that."

"Right." Victoria looks at me for a minute, over her glass. "Didn't you know that you were the one she thought was really good-looking? She was always talking about you when we were alone together. How you had the kind of prettiness that men really liked while all they wanted to do was screw her."

I remember what she had said about me, to my face. *Cute enough, in an ordinary way.* I had agreed with her. But what had she said to Victoria, to Alex the playboy, even to Zalman? Something different.

"She thought your parents cared about you even though they were mad at you for moving out, not like *her* mother. And all she had, she used to say, was just a little talent. That's the way she'd say it. A *little* talent. She thought you were the lucky one."

We look at one another.

"It's like having a sister, all that rivalry," Victoria observes. "I'm glad I never had a sister."

I'm glad I have Ruth, I want to say. Except she's gone. And suddenly I know exactly what she would have done if it had been the other way around. If I had been the one who died.

I know exactly what and how and with what determination I will do it. Going to the phone, dialing the familiar number, waiting for the familiar ringing signal, putting aside anything that sounds like plea, apology, regret.

"Mother," I'll say when Sylvia picks up the receiver. "Mother, I want you to give me some of that insurance money you got when Father died. I really need it."

My mother will sit by the telephone with her hair in curlers and a little pink cap over all the steel pins, holding a cup of Southern Comfort disguised as tea. And if she asks me, "Why do you need it, Helene?" or "Why are you bothering me this time of night?" in an aggrieved tone of voice, I will answer without hesitation. I will speak for myself, speak right up, say what is on my mind.

"I need it to buy a plane ticket and get myself an apartment and tide myself over until I get a job."

"But you've *got* an apartment," she'll come back at me, whining. "*And* a job. And you can always move back here . . ."

Which I will counter with a single word. "Chicago," I will say, and that will sum up everything. "I'm going to Chicago."

I'm going to the University, I think now, sitting at the table with Victoria. I'm going to the Department of Anthropology. I'm walking right in in the middle of the term and demanding financial aid, a scholarship, anything, and if they've lost my application I will renew it, and I'll get the money somehow until I've earned my degree. My Ph.D. My work. All of which will come.

But right now I don't have to do anything. I don't have to move. I can finish my blinis and my tea and wipe my lips on the napkin and fold it. The decision is made. And maybe it will even be splendid.

Victoria waves for the bill and throws Burton's Diner's Club card at the waiter, and for the first time since we started going around together, I let her pay for me without even minding or hesitating. And after a while I collect myself and we go on talking as if I never even started crying, which Victoria has very discreetly managed to ignore.

"And Zalman?" I ask finally, trying to sound casual. "Was she just seeing him because I liked him? Or did she really fall in love with him?"

"Ruth never really fell in love with anybody," Victoria says. "Never in her life. Not that I know about, anyway."

"Me either," I agree, relieved that I know at least this much about my cousin.

"You're upset that I knew more, aren't you?"

I nod.

"You weren't supposed to know," Victoria shrugs. "I guess it was just because you liked him so much that she got interested in him in the first place. But after a while I think that changed. There was something about him, she said. She said it was all a gas. The way it happened, the things they did together. 'A gas,' she said."

"Because he turned her on, you mean?"

She looks at me. "You don't want to hear this."

"Yes I do."

"I don't want to tell you."

"I can't," I say, looking around the room, "stand any more secrets."

"Well, what it was," she says carefully, "is that they all did it together."

"I beg your pardon?"

"Him, her and Flower. The three of them."

"Oh." I remember the friend I had met in the coffeeshop my last night with Zalman. *"He likes a ménage,"* she had said. I realize now that I'm not really sure of what a ménage is, or at least what it involves. Victoria and I look at one another, wondering which of us is going to start talking first.

"So," I blurt finally, breaking the silence. "Tell me what they did."

"Well, I don't know everything," Victoria confesses. The corners of her mouth have begun to twitch. "I know just a little that she told me one night when were sitting around together in the Riviera, getting drunk."

"So?"

"It was pretty hilarious, if you ask me. At least the way she told it. *I'd* never do anything like that. One at a time is plenty, as far as I'm concerned. I mean, talk about being uncomfortable."

"Uncomfortable?"

"Well, for one thing they only had Ruth's little cot," says Victoria. "At least this one time. There really wasn't room for three. I mean, she said the poor bed was shaking like it was going to collapse and she kept thinking she was going to be dumped upside down on the floor in the middle of it all and maybe injure somebody. Or something. And then, the *embarrassment* of it all. It took a lot to embarrass Ruth, but she told me that the first time he took out his—you know—and kind of offered it to both of them she just about cracked up. Do you want me to go on?"

For the first time since Ruth's death I feel a tiny giggle rising to the surface, like a bubble of gas. Maybe it's partially due to my few sips of champagne—but isn't this really the Ruth Moskowitz Memorial Farewell Dinner? The two of us alone in the Russian Tea Room, sitting together over the impeccable linen and the tiny salty delicate pearls of roe, maybe even for the last time in our lives? And although my mother and my grandmother and Mildred would never understand it, wouldn't laughter be the only really fitting homage to my cousin Ruth?

"So after he took it out, what did he do then?"

"Come on, Helene. Are you sure you want to hear this?"

"Yes," I answer. "Yes, I do want to hear it. Let it rip."

"I wish we could get him arrested," she mutters. (And when he *is* arrested, a few months later, she sends me a copy of the local papers with his picture in it next to a snapshot of the gallery with a huge police padlock on the door.) "But won't it hurt, Helene? I don't want it to hurt."

"Not as much as I thought it would." I sip a little more champagne. "I think I knew most of it anyway. Even though I didn't want to know." I look at her. "Go on."

So she goes on. She goes on telling me. We go on talking, with one eye on all the other diners, who observe us with the usual adult cynicism—two young women, not quite old enough to be here unescorted in the evening, not quite respectable for 1962, out together on what looks like a binge. Two young women, on our way.